How to Charm a Nerd

HOW TO
CHARM
A NERD

KATHERINE GARBERA

HARLEQUIN®

 **BOOKS**

ISBN-13: 978-1-335-57481-7

How to Charm a Nerd

Copyright © 2024 by Katherine Garbera

Harlequin Enterprises ULC
22 Adelaide St. West, 41st Floor
Toronto, Ontario M5H 4E3, Canada
www.Harlequin.com

Printed in U.S.A.

For Courtney and Lucas.

Of all the good things that have happened in my life, being your mom is the best one. I love you.

One

Liberty lit her favorite autumn candle that she and her mom had made over the summer. It held all the scents that she associated with and loved about the season leading up to Samhain. Slowly the living room of her apartment filled with the earthy scent of the outdoors, of trees and leaves that had wilted with the first cold chill. All of the smells that reminded her of midnight and a big, full harvest moon.

She closed her eyes, listening to the sounds of the wind—which was in a playful mood tonight—pushing the branches of the trees around her apartment building against the walls and windows. She was tempted to get up and open the glass door that led to her balcony.

Liberty sat in that urge for a minute and felt as if she needed the wind spirits with her tonight.

As soon as she opened the door, she felt the lingering warmth from the September day and then the breeze came in, dancing around her shoulders and stirring her long hair with a crisp chill. Autumn was beckoning. Then winter. It was fitting that she was trying to deal with something that she'd always thought was dead to her.

John Jones.

Since she'd found out his name from Nan in March, she'd been trying to figure out what to do with the knowledge. It wasn't Nan's fault at all. But this news had changed her world. Alzheimer's hadn't exactly been a fucking treat, but they'd been managing. Liberty and her mom had been coming home after visits and laugh-crying at the caught glimpses of the old Nan, before her mind started to give in to the disease that was slowly taking her from them.

But damn.

She hadn't been prepared to hear the name of her biological father. Or to have Nan talk to her as if she were Lourdes— Liberty's mom—like a disapproving mother who wanted the best for her daughter.

John Jones had been a fucking cunt. Her mom didn't approve of the word, but it was the only one she could use when she thought of that man.

Liberty immediately shook her head. She cursed when she was mad and hurt.

Her mom had offered to tell her the name of her biological father when she'd been sixteen. They called him the sperm donor at home, but the reality was that her mom had been in a relationship with him when she'd gotten pregnant.

The asshole had offered her mom money for an abortion and then walked out of her life when she refused.

Fuck him.

After Nan dropped the name on her, Liberty immediately told her two closest friends, the sisters the universe had sent into her life. They'd been supportive. Whatever Liberty wanted to do; they had her back.

She wanted to tell her mom that she knew his name. To get her advice, because there was no one who she relied more on than her mother. But after saying she never wanted to know years ago...well, for the first time in her life, Liberty hadn't been sure what to do.

She'd drawn a tarot card from her Rider-Waite deck for clarity, but her mind had been a hot mess and the tarot hadn't really provided any guidance. It had instead been sensible Poppy who'd suggested she take one of those over-the-counter DNA tests and see if any relatives showed up on her paternal side.

She'd tried it and nothing came back. And fucking John Jones wasn't exactly a unique name so no amount of googling turned up any leads. Asshole.

Even now he was just...what? Was he dead? Or with a new family living his best life, never thinking about the daughter he hadn't wanted?

For most of her life, Liberty had been successful in completely ignoring the man's existence, probably because he'd always been nameless and faceless. But now he had a name, and a world of possibilities she'd never considered had opened up. She hated that and was so conflicted that she was making herself crazy.

So she decided to pull out her favorite Samhain oracle deck and pull six cards in a Witch's Tools Spread. Oracle decks were different from her Rider-Waite tarot deck in that they offered a more detailed and specific spiritual guidance. They also tended to have bigger energy. Since her magic felt like it was in flux, she needed everything the oracle deck could give her.

With the breeze moving through her apartment stirring the dark drapes and making the flame on the candle dance, she started to find her center again.

Liberty pushed out her curse words and that man's name and moved back to the small meditation pillow set in the middle of a circle of salt. She lit a candle before she sat down.

She closed her eyes and asked about the energy of her situation…pulling Grief from the oracle. *Interesting.* Was she grieving? The card probably meant that she had unresolved emotions about her father. Well duh, right?

"Come on, goddess, show me the good stuff," she said.

She pulled potions and spells…reversed.

Thank you, goddess. She needed to get clarity around the situation before trying to manifest him into her life.

She took a minute to sit in that information. There were consequences outside of herself to consider. Her mom was a big one.

When Liberty had been sixteen, a letter arrived from her sperm donor, and Lourdes asked her if she wanted to read it. And Liberty said no. She didn't need a man in her life who didn't want to be there. Neither did her mom. So they burned that letter under the full moon for cleansing and releasing and moving on. They danced around until his spirit had no power over them anymore.

Now Alzheimer's had brought him back. She had to admit she'd been disappointed when she opened the DNA results and saw no paternal connections. Maybe that should be it.

Except when had she ever let something go?

Never.

Like *never*, never. If she got a mosquito bite, she scratched and scratched it until it scabbed over even though she knew she shouldn't.

This felt the same.

She wanted to find out more about him. She needed to.

She closed her eyes, moving on to the third card. How could she feel supported moving through this?

Intuition.

Liberty always used her gut as her compass. It hadn't let her down. Her gut led her to the job at the coffee shop near campus where she met Poppy and Sera—her found sisters. They'd all had small businesses of their own, and the universe directed them to open their shop here in Birch Lake. WiCKed Sisters had been bumping along making a nice profit until Amber Rapp—yeah, the mega pop singer—stopped in and purchased a journal from Sera, handmade tea from Poppy and a tarot reading from Liberty herself.

Then everything changed.

She'd been manifesting change into her life, but she'd only wanted it for the store and *maybe* where that hot, nerdy cousin of Poppy's was concerned. But the universe answered with John Jones as well.

She opened her eyes and looked around her apartment.

The fact that Merle was on her mind too didn't surprise her. She'd seen him earlier when they'd both been closing the shop. He'd been reading books on adventure… By the goddess, that guy was so into Dungeons & Dragons. But he always perked up when she was around. Glancing at her when he thought she wasn't looking.

She did the same to him.

On paper they made no sense, but in her mind and body… well they would be electric together. Like heat lightning that lit up the sky all summer. Stirring up something frightening, exciting in her. Thinking about Merle took her out of her thought spiral. He was really good with computers—was some kind of programmer in his day job from what Poppy had said. Merle also helped out when Poppy was short-staffed at WiCKed Sisters.

But to be honest, whenever Merle came up, Liberty conjured images of him with his shirt off, leaning against the back of the delivery van and licking dripping ice cream from his hand.

Curse the day she'd seen that, because since that moment over a year ago she couldn't get it out of her mind.

They were in a friend group and he was the cousin of her business partner, so a short-term hookup had stupid written all over it.

But…

Merle might be the key to her figuring out who John Jones was.

The sexual attraction that had her distracted, almost frazzled whenever he was around would be a counterbalance to the chaos and confusion she was experiencing as far as her biological fucking father was concerned.

She had three more cards to pull. But she was already convinced Merle would be the key to getting out of this stage and moving into the next one. If he could find out more about John Jones…and if she could find out how Merle's tongue felt on her skin…maybe she'd get through Samhain and the fall without creating a few curses and spells.

The fourth card she pulled was All Hallow's Eve reversed, which immediately made her smile. It reinforced the fact that she shouldn't be doing spells or curses until she had her emotions under control. Who knew what she'd draw into her life if she tried a summoning spell to bring John Jones's information to her.

Unless she was fully rooted in her confidence, there was a chance that the spell could backfire. The universe tended to give back threefold anything negative that was put into it.

Next she asked the cards to show her how she could move past this situation and pulled the Banshee reversed. A warning that sent a shiver straight down her spine. Seeking wrath or revenge could backfire. Her mom's face drifted into her mind. Liberty had to be very careful how she moved forward.

And her magic seemed to be the wrong option. She'd known that deep down, but this confirmed it.

Merle was the only true option here.

She pulled one last card, asking for any additional information and it was the Witch. A sign to use her energy and wisdom to move through this. Follow her gut. She had always believed that her true strength came from the long line of women who'd come before her. Her energy was very feminine, and so was her wisdom.

She wasn't going to be able to use the tools she had relied on in the past but that didn't mean she should ignore her gut or her rituals or practices. Her strength was still the core of who she was.

Her friends were also there to guide her, along with Merle.

She hoped it wasn't her crush that was directing her to him, but either way there would be some outcome that she couldn't predict. And Merle had never given in to her teasing and flirting. Maybe he'd simply be a friend. A good, hot friend. *Maybe not.*

As much as she liked to believe that she had no baggage from the father she never knew, that was a lie. She didn't trust men. Never could. Men took what they wanted and then moved on.

She shook her head as the wind and her conscience warned her that not all men were like John Jones. But Liberty had never been willing to risk her heart or her feelings to find out. Hookups and casual boyfriends were as far as she'd been willing to go in any relationship.

And as she moved through finding her biological father, whether she wanted to or not, she was probably going to have to find a way to trust a man. If she was going to ask Merle for his help, she'd have to believe he could get results. Otherwise she'd fuck up the universe once again.

Finally getting closure was worth the risk.

The very last thing Merle wanted to do was FaceTime with his mom. But she insisted she had very important news to share. So that meant he had to shave, which he really hadn't planned on doing today. It took time to put away the map he'd created for his latest Dungeons & Dragons campaigns. Then he went into the bathroom and made himself look how all of the Rutlands looked.

He put on a collared golf shirt that he'd gotten on their last family vacation when they'd visited St. Andrew's golf course in Scotland. Merle had wanted to explore Celtic sites and visit some pubs, but he hadn't wanted to rock the boat, so instead—just like every other family vacation—he found himself losing to his parents and brothers on the golf course.

God all but spited his dad when Merle miraculously hit under par on the hardest hole on the course, but that hadn't made the trip more enjoyable for either one of them.

He still wasn't sporty enough for his father. Even an achievement that would be boasting material for his brothers wasn't good enough.

He put on a Red Sox baseball cap—his family always supported Boston—and then went to sit with all the lights on and blinds open. His mom hated when he kept his house the way he liked it, dimly lit. She thought he was hiding away behind his computer screen.

She wanted something more…well he wasn't sure what. A different life for him. Neither of his parents ever really acknowledged that he might be happy in the life he created for himself.

He was tempted to have a couple of shots of tequila. But that wasn't smart. He'd probably just take the baseball cap off and let her see his hair, which was down to his shoulders now and *not* trimmed with a number two blade, the same as his father and brothers used.

He still wanted something he wasn't sure he'd get. Acceptance from his parents just for being who he was. A somewhat sloppy, professional computer programmer and gamer who ran highly successful weekly Dungeons & Dragons sessions.

All things that would piss his parents off. They'd never been accepting of anything he'd done. Not even that dumb-luck shot on a prestigious golf course.

His alarm went off and he silenced it as he turned toward

his laptop. His mother thought being on time was late. She'd start the call a minute before the hour.

As soon as he saw that this wasn't a one-on-one call, his pulse raced and he wished he'd done that shot. But it was too late now. He was going on with the entire family, sober and faking it.

That would probably be the story of his life.

He hit the button to answer the video call just as an image of Liberty laughing and teasing him from the day before danced through his mind. She'd transitioned to all-black outfits as fall had officially begun—or as she called it, the season of the witch. Her season. She wore a scoop neck, tight-fitting top over a pair of jeans that she'd painted with stars and moons and the constellations that made up the astrological signs. She told him that she'd placed the constellation of his sign high on her right thigh to keep her warm.

She was always flirting, hoping he'd react. Occasionally he did, just to keep her off guard, but she probably figured he was joking and would never see him as more than Poppy's cousin.

But this was his reality. He was a grown-ass man with a good paying job who owned his own home and still had to pretend to be someone he wasn't with his parents. In short, he was a coward. Still trying to measure up to their expectations when he was with them.

There was a duality to his life and how he saw himself. He just hadn't wanted to bring a woman into that mix and have to explain, *I'm really this guy, unless I'm with my parents and then I have to change how I dress, talk and act so they accept me.*

That's why his relationships were always short and temporary. At some point they wanted to meet his parents and brothers. How could he ever justify that he had to change everything he was for his parents to be comfortable around him?

And he definitely couldn't with Liberty, who exuded individuality and self-confidence without even trying. It was what drew him to her. She'd taken up residence in his mind. A part of him even wanted to believe in her witchy ways, her spells and tarot cards and whispered magic. Maybe she'd cast a charm on him.

But he knew the truth. Before she'd spoken one word to him, when he'd seen her talking to his cousin and heard that loud, carefree laughter of hers, he'd gotten hard and wanted her as his own.

And wanted her to see him not as Merle, the trying-too-hard son, but Merle, legendary dungeon master. The real Merle. The one he was so afraid to let the world see.

"Merle, did you get a haircut? It looks good on you," his mom said.

"No. Why are you asking?"

"Aunt Jean shared a picture of you with Poppy and her friends at the weird shop of hers and it looked like your hair was unkempt. You look much nicer today," she said.

How was he supposed to respond to that? She probably expected him to say thank you. But how was that a compliment?

"Why are we on this call? I have a zoom with my boss in ten minutes," he said.

"That's good. Well as soon as your dad gets back, we can start," his mom said. He noticed his dad's icon appear on screen.

"Now that we are all here, Marcus, do you want to tell him?"

His younger brother looked straight into the camera in

that arrogant way of his. "I got a job as an assistant coach for the Sox farm team."

Of course he did. "Congrats."

That was all he could say as the rest of the family, including his middle brother Manford, rejoiced in having another son who lived up to the Rutland name. Merle smiled and cheered, then made his excuses to leave.

He took off his hat, closed the blinds and turned the lights back off. He shoved aside the feelings that being around his family always stirred. Instead he lost himself in history, reading about real-life battles in medieval Scotland, using it as inspiration for the new campaign he was writing for his D&D group.

This was the third campaign he'd run in the world he created. The one where he felt most at home. And it wasn't lost on him that it was make believe.

Two

Liberty Wakefield was trouble. The kind of trouble that kept Merle up at night and turned him on every time she walked into a room.

He saw her a lot at WiCKed Sisters.

The small witchy shop had three distinctive spaces: the tea shop, owned by his cousin—Poppy Kitchener; the bookstore, run by Serafina Conte; and the magic shop presided over by Liberty Wakefield.

He helped out when Poppy was short-staffed. Of all his family, he was closest to her, and working in her tea shop was a nice way to get out of his house for a few hours. He was a night owl and preferred spending most of his time at his computer writing code or planning his campaigns. As the dungeon master, he wrote the storylines and voiced the different non-player characters when his group played.

He was currently in the Bootless Soldier Tavern, reading a book on different versions of the Hades myth, trying to find some new ideas. After a long month break, they were finally going to start playing again in the last week in September… right when Liberty walked straight up to his table.

She had bright red hair with a slight curl hanging around her shoulders. She was a curvy girl with a full figure and favored blouses that celebrated her cleavage along with stylish waist cinchers over either jeans or full skirts. There was something about her that stirred his senses and made him want to forget that she worked with his cousin and that he was…well, *him* and just go for it. Make a pass, snag a kiss and see where it led.

Maybe that's why he couldn't get her out of his mind.

It wasn't just his imagination. She flirted with him all the time. He suspected it was his nerdy exterior and quietness that made her so bold with him. Flirting always took him aback, so he took his time. Somehow it came off as him being flustered.

"I need a favor," she said as she plopped down across the table from him in the booth.

She picked up the book he'd set down and turned it over in her hands. He noticed the sparkle of the rings on her fingers as she flipped the pages.

"Must be serious since you didn't call me 'nerd,'" he said, because she always did.

She let out a long, ragged sigh, tightening her free hand into a fist and then putting down the book. "It is. And before I say anything else, I need you to swear not to say anything to Poppy or Sera."

Okay now he was worried. "You share everything with them."

"I need to figure this out first."

"What exactly is *it*?" he asked.

"Uh…you know about me and my mom, right?"

"That you're both super close witchy women who don't suf-fer foolish men?" he teased, trying to lighten the mood. That vivacious energy she always had bubbling around her was gone.

She gave a rough little laugh. "Yeah, well she raised me on her own because the man who fathered me didn't want a child and gave her money for an abortion. She asked me when I was sixteen if I wanted to know who he was because he'd sent a letter asking to reconnect… I said no, and that was that."

"Why are you telling me this?" he asked.

"Because fucking Alzheimer's. That's why."

He knew her Nan had Alzheimer's and wasn't doing well. Liberty and her mom, Lourdes, had struggled to keep her at their home and had made the decision earlier in the year to move her into assisted living as her condition worsened.

"What happened?"

She tilted her head forward. "She thought I was Mom and said my biological father's name."

Oh.

"Fuck…that's a lot." He paused, gathering his thoughts. "I'm not sure how I can help."

"Well, I took one of those DNA tests because his name is so fucking generic, because of *course* it would be, and it didn't show anything on my paternal side. And when I type 'John Jones' in Google about a billion of them pop up."

He leaned back, stretching his arms out on the back of the bench. She wanted his tech skills. The ones she was always giving him shit about. She needed him to run a query and find the man.

"So what is it you want from me, Liberty?" he asked.

She lifted both her eyebrows in an exaggerated, exasperated way. "Are you going to make me say it?"

"Hell yes."

"I need your nerdy computer expertise to track down the douchebag."

He shook his head. "You're going to have to do better than that."

She shook her head. "Are you really going to make me ask you nicely?"

He nodded. "And I'm probably going to demand something in trade."

Liberty hadn't wanted to come to Merle with something so personal but, frankly, he was the only person she knew with the skills to find out exactly which John Jones was the asshole who didn't want her. She could just ask her mom but, right now, with Nan getting worse every visit and her mom's online business picking up since Samhain was right around the corner, she didn't want to add to her stress.

Of course the nerd was going to demand his pound of flesh. Fair enough, she always hassled him about…nearly everything. But only because he was sexy in a way that she didn't understand.

He wasn't the kind of guy she usually dated. He was tall for one thing, skinny for another—and as a woman who was born a size fourteen, she usually preferred her guys bulkier. He had a thick mop of dark brown hair which curled around his face, and he habitually wore jeans, an obscure comic book superhero T-shirt and a faded gray hoodie that looked comfy and lived in. He even had thick framed glasses which he only wore when reading.

So…sexy—

Nerdy! Vanilla!

But his eyes were keenly intelligent, and he seemed to feel the attraction between them and understand that they couldn't really do anything about it. Neither of them would be good at a long-term relationship. Neither of them wanted anything more than teasing, and even that, she had to admit, was pretty much one-sided. She would say outrageously sexy things to him and he'd just give her that calm look. Sometimes arching one eyebrow at her in that deadpan way of his, like he was waiting to see if she was serious or just trying to get a rise out of him.

Asking for something in return so suggestively… Well, it stirred her base instincts. And for the first time since she'd read the stupid fucking DNA results, she almost smiled.

She'd tried to pull a tarot card before coming to talk, but she was too agitated and conflicted about what she wanted. The cards had been a mess.

Her mind was spiraling: *Will I find the right John Jones? Do I want to? How will I tell Mom? Will Mom freak out? Will I freak out?*

Yeah, that was why she couldn't trust anything she pulled. And this entire thing was messing with her energy. For the first time in her life she wasn't sure of what to do. That wasn't to say she always made the right choice or decision, but her gut always went all in on a choice once it had been made.

But this thing with fucking John Jones wasn't working. So here she was sitting across from the one person who could help and had no vested interest in the outcome. Poppy and

Sera were too emotionally connected to her to help make this choice. They wanted her to be happy and to have peace of mind where her biological father was concerned. Sometimes her best friends put her comfort before the truth. As much as she loved their protection, she needed to know her father.

"What did you have in mind from me?" she asked.

"You join my latest campaign. One of our players just had a baby and is taking time off from playing. But she'll be back in January," he said.

"Your campaign…? Are you talking about you and your merry band of nerds' weekly D&D game?"

"Technically it's a campaign."

Rolling her eyes, she asked, "How long does it last?"

"This one is scheduled for six weeks. You'd have to create a new character and really play, not phone it in."

"I don't phone things in. You know that," she said. Joining his game for a few weeks didn't sound *that* bad. "It's Samhain in four weeks. I would have to work around the rituals I have planned and my shop has been extra busy."

"We can do that," he said.

"Great. So we good?" she asked. Ready to head to the bar and order herself the largest glass of pinot noir that the bartender would give her.

"Nope."

She looked up and met those large, chocolate-colored eyes of his. A shiver went through her. She almost wished he'd asked for a hookup in exchange for his help. Some reason for her to give into the confusing desire she had for him.

She'd pulled cards and journaled to try to figure out why he was so compelling. But apparently it was simple. That full mouth of his and those strong cheekbones made it impossible to *not* think about how it would be to kiss him. To put her hands on that strong jaw and wrap herself around that tall body of his.

"What?"

"I thought it would be obvious."

Of course. He wanted her to ask him for help directly.

For a minute, she was tempted to just walk away. If she asked, he might catch the truth of what she felt for him in her eyes. It would be too close to admitting that the flirting and the teasing was just a facade to keep him at arm's length. That she actually spent her downtime coming up with reasons to go over and talk to him when he was working.

"Are you really going to make me say it?"

He tipped his head to the side and looked straight over at her as he nodded slowly. "And you should make sure you do it nicely."

"Merle Rutland, you big nerd, will you—"

"That's not nice, witch."

"Who said I was a nice witch?" She winked at him. "You know you want me in your D&D group. I did say I could rock your dungeon, so I guess we'll find out."

"Only if you ask nicely."

"Will you please help me find out which John Jones is my father?" she asked.

He leaned forward and took her hand in his, rubbing his thumb along the back of her knuckles and sending a shiver up her arm that made her breasts full and her nipples tingle.

This was going to be a dangerous game.

"Yes."

★ ★ ★

"Glad to hear it. So when can you start?" she asked. "I know you said six weeks of gaming, but will it take six weeks for you to find him?" She pulled her hand back from his.

"I don't know," he said honestly. "I'll start the search and then keep you posted about the progress."

"Great. Now?" The excited energy around her was palpable.

"Not here. I'll do it from my computer at home. I have better resources on it. But you can start living up to your side of the bargain and creating your character."

"What? I said I'd play. That was it."

"To play you have to create a character where you will get to pick your skills. As the dungeon master, I can help you."

"Was this all a ploy to get me to spend more time with you?"

"You came to me," he pointed out. But she wasn't wrong.

In his family, he was considered the weak one. His mom and dad had both been athletes in college, and his father was now a high school baseball coach and his mom a tennis instructor at a club near their home. His brothers were both semipro players. But Merle had just never been into sports. His father had tried putting him in every one imaginable and Merle had rejected them all. During high school he'd found D&D and started playing online with a group of people he'd never met.

Online, he was enough. He wasn't too nerdy, and in the role-playing world, he rocked. So he wanted Liberty to see him at his best. To see if there was more to her interest in him than just flirting.

"Okay. So what are the options?" she asked.

"Why don't you go buy us a round and I'll pull up the D&D Beyond website so we can start creating your character?" he suggested.

She rolled her eyes. "Fine. What are you drinking?"

"Guinness."

She left and he watched her strut across the tavern toward the bar. She had on a pair of slim-fitting jeans and a sleeveless black flowy top that had moons and stars printed on it. It was made of a gauzy material that floated around as she moved, as if some kind of wind was following her.

His witch.

He knew she wasn't his. But this was his chance to try to change that.

This project was going to be a challenge. People who didn't want to be found were tough to ferret out. And he wrote code for a living. But he had some connections in the hacking world that he could use to help track down John Jones. He pulled his phone out, opened a coders' networking app and wrote a quick message asking for tips as to where to start his search.

Then he took his tablet from his backpack and opened a blank account window on D&D Beyond. What character would Liberty choose? Likely a mage. She really leaned into everything witchy.

Liberty read tarot cards and charged crystals and the like since she was young. Even her mom did online spell casting and had a small shop in town. He'd always been intrigued by it, but he was a practical man. He'd never put much stock in that sort of magic. Hard work and code were the only things he relied on.

She came back, putting their glasses on the table and sitting down across from him again. "So what kind of character am I making?"

He spent the next fifteen minutes explaining the options to her and she chose to make her character a druid wood elf. He made some suggestions for her character's backstory since this campaign was one for his reoccurring group. Then he told her about the other players. He'd write her into the storyline and they'd all meet her during a lighter session the night after tomorrow.

"Where do you play?"

"Usually at my place."

"Where is that?" she asked.

"In that housing development near the outskirts of town."

"You own your own home?" she asked. "I'm still paying off my student loans."

"Yeah, I got a scholarship so…didn't have those. Plus my day job pays really well," he explained.

"Lucky you," she said. "I'm not actually sure why I went to college, except maybe to meet Sera and Poppy. I mean my degree is in business studies so maybe it's useful. But honestly I learned more from talking to Wesley's dad about taxes than I did in four years at U of Maine."

She finished her wine and shifted on the bench, sliding to get up and leave. Liberty turned back toward him, her hair swinging around and her eyes meeting his. "So what's your place like? Is it a real dungeon with lots of handcuffs and chains or what?"

His cock inexplicably hardened at the thought of playing with her in a kinky dungeon. He usually didn't respond to her when she was in this mood. But he wanted things between them to change, so he scooted down the bench until he was even with her and then leaned forward so his forehead almost touched hers.

"Plan to stay late after the session and I'll show you," he said.

Her pupils dilated and her breath came out in a quick exhalation. She licked her lips and he almost groaned out loud.

"Maybe I will, nerd."

"Until then, witch."

She headed out of the tavern and he sat there in a semi state of arousal.

This was the oddest night of his life. And that was saying something. But for the first time, he felt like the things that made him odd were good.

Three

Liberty took a cup of her morning mushroom mud from Sera as she plopped down on the sofa in the back of Sera's part of WiCKed Sisters. The overstuffed love seat was nestled between bookcases filled with new and used books. The room was cozy and truly a reflection of Sera. Old-timey but modern. Book-ish and quiet. And today it was a place to hide.

She should be in her own back room at her altar, making a potion for the morning or taking the time to shuffle her tarot decks for her appointments. But after her reading last night, she had doubts.

The first time she had sex, Danny bragged about it to their classmates—taking something she'd thought was special be-tween the two of them and making it into something else. She'd wanted to put a hex on him, but her mom had come home, saw the open page in her grimoire and done what her mom always did.

She fixed it. She made Liberty a cup of tea and then talked to her about sex and sharing her body and her emotions with a man. From that moment forward Liberty resolved to let no man have that kind of power over her again. And she'd succeeded, for the most part.

Something she'd struggle to keep doing once they were alone at Merle's place.

"You okay?" Sera asked as she sank down next to Liberty on the love seat.

"When aren't I?"

"When you answer a question with a question. So, what's up? Did you get the DNA results back?"

"I knew you two talked about stuff behind my back," Poppy said as she breezed into the room and sat on the ottoman across from her and Sera.

"We don't," Sera reassured her. "I was just trying to figure out what's up. So, Liberty...?"

She took a sip of the mud which was supposed to give her mental clarity and usually did but wasn't really working today. "I got them back. Nothing. No paternal connections at all."

"That sucks," Sera said.

"What are you going to do?" Poppy asked.

She lifted her head and narrowed her eyes, looking over at Poppy. Had Merle told her?

"What do you think I should do?" she asked. Then realized she was lying to try to catch her friend out. Poppy would never lie to her about this. "Never mind. I talked to Merle and he's going to use some of his computer skills to try to find out which John Jones donated the sperm that resulted in me."

"He is?" Poppy asked. "I thought you two were like oil and water."

"That's because you have been distracted by your ex-husband," Sera said. "Those two are like magnets that can't keep apart but one of them always turns away before they connect. This is exciting news."

Liberty shook her head. Sera was the most observant of the three of them. Probably because her friend had grown up in the foster care system and was always watching the people around her to keep herself safe. "How is it exciting?"

"Well you did want to confluence with him…"

Liberty had to laugh and Poppy joined in. She'd created a version of kiss, marry, avoid called Charm, Curse, Confluence that they'd been selling in their shop. When the three of them had named Merle, Liberty said confluence. There was a part of her that was always thinking of that tall, sexy gamer in her bed.

Maybe it was that he was so controlled. He never really let anyone see his emotions. There was so much he kept hidden. Why she wanted to be the one to draw him out, she couldn't explain.

Nan had always said…or used to say, when she'd been herself…that the harder an emotion was denied, the more explosive it would be when it finally was released.

She took another sip of the mushroom mud and closed her eyes, trying not to cry. Nan was a shadow of the woman she used to be—sometimes so vivid and present but other times a distant, angry stranger.

"I did want to. But he's Poppy's cousin and I don't want to mess that up."

"You couldn't," Poppy said.

"You know that's not true," Liberty said softly. "Your friendship with Gemma changed the day you and Alistair got a divorce."

"That's different. She's still friends with him and his family," Poppy said.

"Still, it ended. Men always mess things up," Liberty said.

"Not all men," Sera replied quietly. Her friend had just fallen in love with Wesley Sitwell. He had come on strong, like a total douchebag at first. But then he fell for Sera and her shop. The two of them were practically living together.

Actually, they were the one couple she knew that seemed made for each other.

"So you're not sleeping with him?"

"No. Why would I be?" Liberty asked Poppy.

"Because it seemed like the kind of the thing you'd say to Merle. *I'll shag you if you help me.*"

Liberty shook her head and smiled. "Yeah, well he beat me to the punch."

"He asked you for sex?" Sera sounded slightly shocked.

"No, for a favor."

"A *sexual* one?" Poppy asked.

"Pop, do you need to get laid? Not everything is about sex," Liberty said.

"Maybe. Everything with Alistair is making me nuts. We *are* divorced. Also, we've been chatting online…"

"What?"

"Why?"

Liberty and Sera exclaimed at the same time.

"Never mind that. What did Merle ask for?"

"That I join his D&D campaign. I promised him six weeks in his dungeon." She winked at Poppy. "Make of that what you will."

★ ★ ★

Merle woke up at three in the afternoon, checked his phone for updates on the queries he'd sent about John Jones and saw he had two missed calls. One from his brother Marcus, who was going to be in Bangor for the weekend with friends and wanted to know if he'd like to hang.

Merle didn't but he would say yes. Maybe because Marcus was younger. Merle had always felt protective of his little brother. They'd both been into gaming and had hung out together for a few years before high school. Then Marcus started getting really good at pitching and that was the end of his time at the computer with Merle. Their father had done what he always did: nurtured the talent he saw.

And it had paid off for Marcus.

The second message was from Liberty, asking him to call when he had a few minutes.

He sat up in bed and hit the call icon. It rang four times before she answered. "Don't hang up."

Then he assumed she set the phone down because he heard her talking to someone about the right herbs to grow in their patio garden for protection and healing. He closed his eyes, leaning his head back against the headboard, just listening to the sound of her voice.

Liberty's voice always stirred something restless to life inside of him. Her energy was bright and forceful. She didn't hide any part of herself.

Around her, he didn't have to hide either. Merle imagined her next to him in the bed, her long red hair on his pillow. That scent of her underlined with patchouli, rose and cinnamon. He could almost smell it.

"You there?"

"Yes," he said, realizing his hand had subconsciously drifted down to his cock. "What's up?"

"Uh, did you find anything yet?" she asked.

"It's only been a day," he reminded her.

"Just checking."

She sounded anxious, almost scared. Which made him want to distract her. "So did you do any more work on your character?"

"No," she said.

"Why not?"

"Because my energy is all out of whack. I'm not really sure what's going on," she said. "I've had to concentrate on keeping my thoughts in line to do readings. I don't want my negativity to spill over on anyone."

"How's your afternoon?" he asked. Usually her day was busiest in the morning, tapering off until it picked up again in the late afternoon.

"Just had my last reading, why?"

Why indeed. Now that he *had* her attention… "I need to get some Halloween stuff for my place and thought I'd ask my favorite witch to help me."

"Glad I'm your favorite, but what kind of stuff?"

He laughed, shaking his head. "No idea. Pumpkins, maybe some ghosts and a fog machine. Just thought…"

He trailed off and then heard his father's voice in his head. *Just thought what? Stop thinking and take some action.*

"What?"

"That we could do something together. Seems like you need a distraction," he said.

She cleared her throat and then he heard the clicking of her rings as she turned them on her fingers. "Okay. But if we do this, I'm not going to a box store and buying you a commercial version of Samhain stuff."

"Fine with me. The most I know about Halloween is that it's the one night when it's okay to pretend to be whoever you want."

"Do you pretend a lot?"

"More than I should, but not with you," he admitted.

"Glad to hear it." The tone of her voice was warm and a little bit flustered. "I'll be at yours in about an hour. I assume you just woke up," she said.

"Yeah. I'll be ready when you get here."

She hung up and he checked his work e-mails. He worked for a white knight company that was usually employed to ensure the safety of users in online communities by hacking accounts and tracing IP addresses to make sure that everyone was who they said they were online.

Since there were no work emergencies, he took a shower, then shook out his thick curly hair, letting the curls fall where they did. Because he'd shaved the other day, he didn't even have to trim his beard.

But then he took his time with his clothes. He grabbed a new T-shirt he just got in the mail and put it on over his nicer jeans. It depicted a tiger-sized, hairless blue Sphynx cat from his favorite comic, *Saga*, named Lying Cat. Lying Cat said *"Lying"* whenever she detected someone doing it.

He wasn't expecting his shirt to talk to him, unless Liberty somehow enchanted it, but he hoped it would remind him to stay true to himself.

Liberty called him a nerd, but there was always a note in her voice that softened it. He didn't feel judged by Liberty. Not like his mom, who once threw out his gaming tees to help him "fit in."

He tossed the towel across the room. The last thing he was going to do was start changing for Liberty, who seemingly liked his nerdiness, judging by all her suggestive remarks.

What he did want to change was their flirting and teasing—by taking things to the next level, once and for all. So he was going to keep being himself.

Liberty knocked on his door twenty minutes later. She had a long flowing dress on that clung to her breasts and waist before flaring out at her hips. She wore big clunky boots, part of her signature fall uniform. Her reddish hair was back in a braid, draped over one shoulder and lying over her left breast.

If he were a different man, he'd think she'd cast a spell on him, but he knew that it wouldn't have lasted all the years he'd known her. The only love potion at work here was the essence of Liberty. She captivated him.

That threw him off his game, but he really didn't give a fuck. He liked the way he felt when he was around her.

Her blue-gray eyes were cautious as she looked up at him.

"What is it?" he asked.

She shook her head and hesitated.

"You okay?"

"No. I'm not. I… I have to go and visit my Nan. Mom is out of town and I just got a call that she's… Well she needs me."

"I'll drive," he said, seeing how shaken she was.

"Okay. Thanks."

He put his hand on her arm and squeezed it. She turned and buried her face against his shoulder and he held her, not sure what else to do. She hadn't said what the situation was with her Nan, but it clearly wasn't good.

Liberty hated everything about this. She hadn't wanted to ask Merle to go with her, but secretly she needed him along.

Merle drove the way he did everything, it seemed: with quiet confidence and skill. He had some sort of classical music on, which was giving her mind too much room to imagine scenarios that she didn't like the outcome of.

"Can I put my music on?" she asked.

"Sure," he said, giving her permission to sync her phone to his car.

She did it quickly, skimming through her playlists and finding her "Bad Bitch" one. She needed all the vibes and energy that she got from listening to those songs.

Lizzo's "About Damn Time" came on and she closed her eyes. It blasted through the car—a late-model Audi TT that seemed more suited to an accountant than, well, him. "What's with this car?"

"What do you mean?"

"Why do you drive this? Mostly assholes drive Audis."

"Uh, that's true. I got a good deal on it," he said, then flushed.

"A good deal?"

He shrugged. "I'm not going to apologize for liking to save money. I bought it at the end of the year so they were clearing the cars to make room for the new year's stock. This one has a really good computer in it."

"That's why you really got it, isn't it?" she asked. She needed to be distracted and talking about his car wasn't really doing the job, but it was better than the alternative—which was her putting her hand in his lap and doing something that she'd already decided she wasn't going to do.

"Yeah. I know, nerdy right?"

"Totally," she said, then turned to him. "You don't have to apologize for anything to me, Merle."

"Thanks."

"No, I mean it. I was just teasing you. It's okay to like to save money. My mom raised me that way. I hate that sometimes it seems like the only things of value are the expensive."

He didn't say anything for a few minutes, then adjusted the sun visor. "So do you want me to come in with you?"

She twisted her fingers together. "I don't know. They didn't really elaborate—just said she was asking for mom and I and one of us should get down there."

"How often does that happen?"

Liberty shrugged. Nan had been almost normal for the last few weeks ever since she'd mistaken Liberty for her mother. "This is the first time."

He reached over with one hand and pushed his fingers between hers. He held her hand as he drove, not letting go until they pulled into the parking lot at the care home. She got out and took a deep breath before she lifted her head to the sky and saw what a gorgeous autumn day it was.

The kind of day that Nan would have insisted they spend outside.

She felt tears burning in her eyes and told herself that maybe

Nan would be lucid enough to be the grandmother she remembered.

"I'll go into the lobby with you," he said.

"Thanks," she responded, but she was already feeling as if each step was heavy. Reaching into her pocket, she felt for the rose quartz she'd put in there earlier and rubbed her fingers over it, then reached for Merle's hand. He didn't say a word. Merle simply kept her hand firmly in his the way he had in the car.

The receptionist directed Liberty down the hall to the doctor on call and Merle walked with her the entire time. "I'll wait out here. Just call if you need me."

Merle was a reassuring presence in this place. Part of her wanted to focus on the warmth that he exuded, but there was truly nothing he could do to take away this pain and fear. With her magic so unstable right now, her routines and her talismans out of reach, she was replacing them with people. Poppy and Sera were taking the place of her tarot cards; she was using their advice and friendship as guidance.

And Merle… He was like a protection spell.

Which was ridiculous because she didn't need anyone to protect her from anything.

She had to deal with Nan on her own.

She took a deep breath and went into the office.

"Thank you for coming down so quickly, Liberty."

"No problem. What's going on?"

"She was agitated earlier and we had to use some medicine to calm her down. She's sleeping now, but she said she had a vision and needed to talk to both you and your mom. When we asked her what it was about, she just mumbled stuff that made no sense. I'm not sure if seeing you will calm her down or not."

Nan had visions before she'd started living in the care home. The stronger they were, the more emotions that were tied to them. While not always entirely accurate, there was always more than a kernel of truth to them. "I'd like to see her."

"She's calmer now. If you'd like I'll take you down to her room," the doctor said.

Liberty nodded. When they stepped out into the hall, she automatically held out her hand and Merle grabbed it again. They followed the doctor to Nan's room and when they stepped inside, Nan peered up from the bed. Her blue eyes were cloudy and unfocused.

"Liberty, is that you, girl?"

"It's me, Nan."

"You got a man with you?"

"Yes, this is Merle. You know him from the shop," she said.

"That's right. The boy who watches you with hungry eyes," Nan said with a laugh. "The hot one you pretend not to notice."

"Yeah. That one."

Four

The hot one you pretend not to notice. Was there a better way to describe her confused crush? Merle grinned at her, a hungry and amused look in his eyes sending tingles through her body.

He *liked* that she looked at him. And she liked him liking it.

"Nan, you okay?"

"Yes, sorry to have sent the entire place into a panic. I just had a vision."

Nan hadn't had a vision since they'd moved her to the care home. Maybe this meant that her symptoms were fading and that Nan was *her* Nan again.

Liberty moved farther into the room to sit next to Nan on her bed. Merle hesitated in the doorway, tipping his head toward the hallway, and Liberty shook hers. There was no reason for him to leave. Nan wasn't going to reveal anything that Liberty hadn't told Merle already.

Merle leaned casually against the wall, crossing his legs at the ankle.

Nan put her arm around Liberty and pulled her closer to her side. She smelled of Estée Lauder perfume and mints. Liberty closed her eyes and breathed in more deeply, trying to cement this moment in her memory. She felt the sting of tears in her eyes.

She'd missed this so much.

But she didn't want to dwell. Her rational mind told her no matter how much she hoped that this would last, it wasn't going to. "Nan, what was the vision?"

"We were on Cape Cod in that summer rental we took when you were twelve… Do you remember it?"

She did. Her mom had started making good money on the spells and potions she created for her clients and Nan had begun receiving her retirement money. For the first time, the Wakefield witches had some extra income and they had decided to have a summer vacation like rich people. It was perfect.

Then they'd come back home and gone back to their normal lives. "It was the best. Was your vision about us going back there?"

Nan shook her head. "We were there and Rupert, your grandfather, was there too. We were laughing and dancing under the moon while the waves washed up on the beachfront down the path from our cottage."

Liberty took a deep breath. Why was her grandfather in a vision of the future?

Unless…her grandmother was starting to feel the pull to the other side. They were so close to Samhain when the barrier between the living and the afterworld was at its thinnest. That was probably why he'd visited her. "Nan?"

If Nan felt the pull of the other side, Liberty knew she should just accept that and be happy for her. But she was self-ish. There were still things she wanted to learn from Nan and laughter she needed to share with her.

"I don't know what it means, child. I just know that I saw him clear as day. And you and your mom were there with me."

"Mom will know what it means," Liberty said. Her mother always had an insight or thought that made everything make sense.

Which was why Liberty hesitated to talk to her mom about her father. Lourdes was going to make a valid and succinct comment and then…everything would change. This secret pursuit of finding her father felt more controllable as just that: a secret. With everything going on with Nan and their small, close-knit family falling apart, Liberty needed to feel like she was in control.

"She's probably going to say what we are both thinking," Nan said.

"That you're in contact with the spirit realm and that Rupert is telling you to enjoy this time with your daughter and granddaughter?" Merle said from the other side of the room.

"Maybe," Nan said. "Do you have any experience with visions?"

"Not really. I read a lot of mythology and your vision sort of reminded me of a liminal deity."

"Tell me more about them," Nan invited.

Merle moved into the room and took a seat on the chair next to the bed. "They preside over the thresholds. Kind of a crosser of boundaries. They are believed to oversee a state of transition."

"Like life to death?"

"Not always. They show up during the changes from un-conscious to conscious and use that time to send messages. They can even be gods and goddesses. I was thinking of Persephone coming back to earth in spring. I know that Samhain is a time of renewal for you Wakefields. When you men-tioned seeing Rupert...well, I thought maybe he was trying to tell you something personal."

Nan smiled over at Merle and said something, but Lib-erty couldn't focus. She never realized he had any interest or knowledge in this sort of thing. This was something right out of her world.

But she was beginning to see that there was a lot Merle had hidden from her. Deliberately or not.

Why was he being so open now?

Regardless, she was glad for it. His suggestion lifted the pall that had fallen over her like a heavy gloom. He'd given a reason for her grandfather to visit in a vision that wasn't about death.

She was grateful for that.

She didn't even care if she was being unrealistic to think Merle's suggestion could be right.

They chatted with her Nan for another hour or so before Liberty kissed her good-bye and they left. She wasn't sure what she wanted to say to Merle, but she wasn't going to let this go.

When they got to his car, he leaned against the side of it and shoved his hands through that untamed hair of his. "Sorry. I know my knowledge is about a game and not real life, but I thought it might help."

"It did," she said. Not stopping to think about it, she went and wrapped her arms around him, hugging him close to her.

He smelled of the outdoors and the autumn breeze. The emotions that she'd been trying to keep inside since she'd gotten the call stirred inside of her, and she knew she was going to cry unless she distracted herself.

There was something in the air around her that was making her rethink everything. Wild and reckless. Like her magic and the autumn season.

Tilting her head up, she put her hand on the back of Merle's neck and went on tiptoe, brushing her lips over his.

Liberty tasted of sunshine and bubblegum. He'd felt the sadness between her and her grandmother and could feel that she was struggling right now. Liberty had shifted as soon as they stepped outside. Like she'd shed the hurt and gone into a completely different mode. When she hugged him, his body had gone on red alert. Holding Liberty pressed against his entire fucking body was something he'd been fantasizing about for years.

She didn't disappoint. She wasn't shy or tentative, but he hadn't expected her to be. Her kiss was strong, womanly, taking what she wanted and needed from him.

His dick hardened and he shifted his hips so that she didn't feel it. She needed something from him and he wasn't entirely sure it was physical. A better man would push her away and not let himself get entangled while she had so much going on, but he craved her. He couldn't seem to stop his hands from sliding down her back and cupping her ass. Then he groaned as his hips seemed to move of their own volition, and she thrust hers forward in response until the ridge of his cock rubbed against the center of her body.

God. That felt good. He couldn't help squeezing her ass in his hands. Then she pushed one of her legs between his, making their bodies touch more intimately.

Damn.

He needed to stop. They were in the parking lot of a care home. He pulled away and gazed down at Liberty, her lips wet and swollen from his kiss.

Maybe stopping was what she needed after all.

But then her eyes opened, and for a minute she looked like her old self. Like the Liberty who asked if he had handcuffs in his dungeon while she leaned in close and whispered, *I don't mind being tied up.* The woman who'd been tempting him for longer than he could remember. This wasn't the nervous Liberty who'd come to him in the tavern and asked him to help her find her biological father. This was Liberty in her full confidence and strength.

"Yeah, so that was unexpected," she said. "Almost as much as you knowing about spells to walk between the living and spirit world."

His blood was still pounding in his dick so it was hard to think. She intoxicated him. He should push her away before they went too far.

Merle tipped his head back up to the sky. Clouds were moving in. Maybe they'd finally get that first winter storm of the season as the news had been predicting for the last few days.

"No response?" she asked, lowering her hands and stroking his shaft through his pants.

He had a response for her. No more thinking or holding

himself back. No more lying. He pinned her against the car, her hand trapped between them. "I have a response, but I'm not sure it's appropriate for the parking lot."

"Ah…is being appropriate important?"

He groaned, because it was. He was a rule follower, but Liberty wasn't. She was deliberately pushing him to see how much he would take from her. He brought his mouth down hard on hers, claiming the kind of searing kiss he'd wanted but been too hesitant to demand.

She tipped her head back, playfully biting his lip as she wrapped one thigh around his hips and lifted herself until his hard-on was rubbing against her clit. She held him with surprising strength, her arms wrapped around his shoulders. Nothing felt better than exploring her body.

God, she had a fine ass. He'd admired it many times, but holding her, feeling her thrusting against him, filled his mind with images of her in his dungeon—where he sat on the throne he'd had specially built for his role as dungeon master, with her naked on his lap, treating her to the full, sexy nerd fantasy.

Dammit. He had to step away or he was going to come in his jeans as if he was in high school and not an adult who could take this woman to his house, or even drive up the road to that quiet place near the woods she liked, and make love to her.

He didn't have to do this in the parking lot.

But they wanted to. Despite the risk, Liberty didn't let go. She wanted this. She needed an escape from her reality and he understood that all too well. He wanted to be the man to give it to her.

That was a slippery slope to start down. What if she equated him with fantasy and not reality?

She tore her mouth from his, taking his hand and pushing it up under her blouse toward her breast. There was a frantic energy to her motions.

As if she was afraid to stop and let herself think.

As much as he wanted her, this wasn't *how* he wanted her. When she came in his arms it was going to be because she was so turned on by him—not because she needed a distraction.

He started to pull away. Their eyes met, her bright grays full of longing and need. He cursed under his breath.

"Please don't stop."

He shook his head; he couldn't deny her. Would never be able to. He didn't know if she'd put a spell on him or if it was because she was coming into her full power during the time leading up to Samhain.

But he brought his mouth back down on hers. Kissing her until neither of them could breathe. He felt her moving more urgently in his arms so he shifted his hips, rubbing his cock against her clit, his fingers moving over her nipples as she thrust against him until she came.

Her grip on him tightened and he held her, trying to forget they were still in a public parking lot.

Merle was quiet on the drive back to his place and Liberty wasn't sure what to say. She hated that she was in this place right now. Words were something that flowed easily from her.

"I'm not going to apologize for that," she said at last.

"God, I hope not. I'm still thinking about what it would be like to see you naked and coming."

"Merle."

He slowed the car as he turned into his neighborhood and looked over at her. "Yes?"

A shiver went through her. As nice as the orgasm next to the car had been, she wanted *all* of Merle. Not just some fondling. Something solid to hold on to while the world around her was crumbling into pieces.

A part of her had always looked to Samhain as a time of renewal, a time to lean into her strengths and discover new ones. But this year everything seemed to be tied up with Merle. In what she wanted from him, personally and intimately.

She'd never really allowed herself to need or rely on any man. But here she was, which frightened the bejesus out of her. "I…"

He shook his head. "Liberty Wakefield at a loss for words, no one is going to believe it."

"Don't be a dick."

"I thought you liked my dick," he said, a sexy grin on his face.

She melted.

"I do. Feel like getting it out when we get back to your place?" She winked at him.

Falling back on things she knew worked. Teasing and flirting, pushing until he retreated into himself. But something was different about him, and she really had no idea what to do next. Now that her body was starting to calm down from the orgasm, her mind was whirring and she couldn't control the thoughts spinning around it.

She was a hot mess. For the first time in her life she had no solid idea of who she was. Lying to her mom, having sex in a parking lot, denying the truth about her grandmother and thinking about pushing Merle to practically ravish her in his house didn't seem like her.

Ugh.

Sex and the chaos that was her life right now were entwined in some kind of misshapen braid. Her life wasn't going to follow *any* path if she didn't figure out what she wanted.

Was this thing with Merle only an escape from what was going on around her? Merle deserved better than that from her. She couldn't use him for a sexy distraction. It wasn't fair, and she liked him too much to do that.

This thing between them had always felt fun and light. At its most basic, it was self-protection. She didn't want to be hurt or to hurt him. She was self-reliant, always had been. Until now when uncertainty seemed to be ruling her like the moon in Virgo when Jupiter was in retrograde. *Clarity covered in a cloud of chaos.*

"I'm sorry."

"For what?"

"For pushing you into that. I know you were being, well, you when you suggested we wait. I hate that I'm like this. I can't promise you I won't try to convince you to have sex with me again."

He pulled into his driveway, and a few moments later they were inside his garage. He turned the car off and faced her. "You didn't force me to do anything. I just wanted the first time we were together to be…well not in the parking lot."

"So why did you?"

"You needed me. I get it because I have family and there

are times when it's all too much, so I understand exactly where you're coming from."

"Was it pity?" she asked.

"Never. For the first time you asked me for something—"

"But I asked you to look for my…for John Jones."

"You did, but this was physical. This was you needing someone to help you stop thinking and just feel. And I'm glad it was me you wanted."

His words made her think about how she always kept the scales tipped in her favor. How she was careful to keep her attachments to men and the world around her on her terms. But today she'd allowed them to tip. Revealed a vulnerability to Merle. That hadn't been her intent.

She wanted to find one of his to restore their balance. Even things up between them. And she'd be lying to herself if she denied the urge to feel him in her palm, to make him feel the way she did earlier. She reached for his zipper, but he put his hand over hers.

"What are you doing?"

"Keeping things even."

"They are even."

"How? Because I don't feel like they are."

"You see this T-shirt I'm wearing?"

"Yeah, another one of your obscure comic tees, right?" she asked. But she knew Lying Cat because she'd read the comic when he'd left it in the break room.

Where was he going with this?

"I wore this intentionally today. I wanted to stop…this *game* we've been playing. I'm unsure if you mean it or are just try-ing to get a rise—"

"I think I proved I want more than a rise," she said teasingly.

He smiled at her which made her heart pound and just confused the issue. This wasn't the time for her to let her emotions start ruling her. *Virgo moon with Jupiter in retrograde. Remember that!*

Glancing down at Lying Cat, she had to admit that she owed him truth.

"You'd have to be vulnerable to me."

"Why aren't I? You tease me and whisper sexy come-ons in my ear when we're working in the shop all the time. You must know I'm always a hairbreadth from coming when you're around me. And it's only the fact that we had decided not to do this," he said, gesturing to the two of them, "that kept me feeling like I had any control. But that was an illusion. I've been obsessed with you since the first time you told me you could rock my dungeon."

"Can I?"

"You already have."

Five

"Turn right up ahead," Liberty said. She was still buzzing from her encounter with Merle and wanted something she wasn't about to ask him for yet. She'd never been a woman that men wanted for long.

But Merle felt different. Delving deeper into it wasn't happening. *Fear.* Fear that if she did let him see the real Liberty, with her miscast spells and unsure tarot card readings, he'd run away.

Being strong and sure of herself was fine, but if she let him in too close and he rejected her…well, she wasn't prepared to deal with that. She needed to be chill.

Except she wasn't a chill person.

She was bold and stepped into her feminine power every chance she got. No risk, no reward was usually how she operated.

She wanted things to stay even between them. So she was going to have to find some other way of making him feel comfortable enough to be vulnerable with her.

If only she could get out of her head and enjoy being with him. But that wasn't how she was wired.

"Where are you taking me?"

"Scared?"

He pulled the car onto the shoulder, then put it in Park before facing her. There was an intensity in those chocolate-brown eyes of his that she hadn't noticed before. It sent a chill shooting through her and straight to her pussy, still tingling from her orgasm.

"Stop."

She started to shrug, but he shook his head.

"Either we're the way we were, where you tease me and we do nothing about it or we move forward. I like you, Liberty. I think you like me too. But trying to use witchcraft as a wedge between us isn't going to work. You know I'm not going to hurt you."

"How do I know that?" she asked.

She could never fucking censor a thought before it left her head. She betrayed her lack of confidence, her belief that Merle could drift out of her life as randomly as he'd drifted in.

He had an idea of who she was. A fantasy that she doubted she'd live up to. She wasn't as bold and brash as she presented to the world. Her life was a tight rope over a chasm filled with snakes and sharp rocks and she ran across, slipping and sliding and trying to find purchase every day.

Each night she looked at the moon in whatever phase it was in and thanked the goddess for keeping her on the rope. Merle probably saw what everyone else did in her. Someone walking on solid ground, moving through life as she willed it.

So not the case.

Of course there was nothing random about Merle. Lying Cat proved that. Which was why she'd been doing the smart thing and keeping her distance.

Until fucking John Jones had reappeared and shaken her.

Shook her so hard that she'd gone to the one man she… actually somewhat trusted.

And that fucking scared her.

"Liberty… I'm never going to deliberately hurt you," he said.

But of course he would, because what guy was going to be like *yeah, babe, I'm totally going to make you care about me and then, when you least expect it, leave.*

"Yeah."

He reached out and touched a strand of her hair, curling it around his finger and tugging on it before he let it go. "Until you know it, I'll just keep telling you I'm trustworthy. And you are going to stop trying to drive me away."

"Is that what I'm doing?"

"Isn't it? Or do you just think I'm a huge coward?" he asked.

She hadn't seen this assertiveness from his side. There was a part of her that shoved and shoved simply because Merle didn't budge. When she tried to scare him with her witchiness, he just met her with that quiet acceptance, which then made her be more outrageous. To see if she was too much for him as she had been for everyone else.

Because if there was one lesson that life had taught her, it was that there is no safety.

"You are not a coward. I just do it to get a reaction and you *never* react. Right now I need to see something. To know that you feel something for me," she said. Her words came out in a harsh, agitated staccato. And she was *definitely* agitated.

"Okay. I'm told I'm an all-or-nothing guy. I'm not sure *all* is what you want," he said.

"It's better than nothing," she said.

Then the hand that Merle had been resting on the back of her seat was at the nape of her neck, and he drew her toward him with a light, firm pressure. His mouth came down on hers, hot and hard. He didn't hesitate or ask permission or wait for her response; his tongue gently explored her mouth and her thoughts were stopped in their tracks.

The taste and feel of him was as intense as the full moon in Taurus, his finger stroking the back of her neck as his tongue seduced her with long, languid strokes. She wanted to respond, but he felt so good. Every nerve in her body seemed to tune itself to him. She reached for him, putting her hands on his chest, and he slowly lifted his head and pulled back.

He looked down at her, his pupils dilated, his skin flushed and his lips wet from their kiss. "I want everything you have to give, Liberty. But I want it on our terms. Not strictly yours."

Her mouth was tingling, her nipples were hard and there was that aching, pulsing wetness between her thighs. She was trying to listen to what he was saying, but goddess knew it had been a long, long time since she'd wanted a man the way she wanted Merle.

She turned away and opened her car door so that some of the crisp, autumn breeze would join them. There was only that hot, lingering summer heat, as if nature itself was feeling the tension. It made the desire inside of her that much sharper.

She tipped her head back against the seat and Merle stayed still. Like he did. But he wasn't calm. That kiss had been anything but calm.

How did he do that?

She took a deep breath. "What is it you want?"

"More than a bargain struck because you want a favor. I want to get to know you…"

He hesitated, and she thought he might be afraid too.

"What do you want?"

"To date. To have a chance to really get to know each other," he said.

"You'll still help with John Jones even if I say no?"

She had to ask.

He looked offended. "Of course. I'm not an asshole."

"I know you're not." Everything would be so much easier if he were.

Inside, Merle was the same emotionally over-the-top man he'd always been. But he had conditioned himself not to show it. Growing up, he believed it was better—and maybe safer—for him to be quiet and fall into being the bookish gamer his mom thought he was. It would have been okay if he threw down his bat after getting struck out at home plate, but directly expressing his emotions at home wasn't acceptable.

So he'd adapted to keeping everything inside.

Of course, deciding to let Liberty know he was in his feelings with her and actually doing it…well, those were very different things.

She'd directed him to a small cutout near the side of the birch forest that surrounded the large lake to the northwest of town. Here the leaves had started to change from green into the hues of autumn. Oranges, yellows and browns with dappled sunlight coming through them. The scent was rich, earthy like the woman next to him.

She got out of the car, lifting her face to the sun before saying something soft under her breath. The breeze stirred around them; it was warm in the sunlight and felt more like July than September. He closed his eyes and tipped his head back. He should incorporate a character based on the wind into his latest campaign.

"Let's go this way," she said, taking off toward the left. He double-checked he'd locked the car, then followed her.

"What are we doing out here?"

"You asked me to help you get ready for Samhain, and I am. You need to bring the elements in to celebrate. In a way, you see that with pumpkins and willow brooms laced with cinnamon, but that's just fake."

As they walked through the forest next to each other, it was clear that the scent he always associated with Liberty was from the woods here. "What is that smell?"

She tipped her head to the side and winked at him. "Witches."

He laughed. "It seems more like rosemary and birch, but I always confuse rosemary and thyme."

"It is rosemary. It grows wild here, like a weed. Mom uses it in a lot of the spells she does for her customers, so if I have a slow day in the shop or a day off I come out and gather it for her."

She was more relaxed in the woods than in the car. There was something very elemental about Liberty. In fact, he could easily see her conjuring up a familiar. In his head, a new D&D campaign was already forming—but this one was just him and Liberty.

"Will we need rosemary for my place?" he asked.

"What's your place like? I didn't get to see it," she said.

"Uh… Well sort of empty in most rooms except my bedroom, office area and my dungeon."

She lifted both eyebrows at him. "I *knew* you had one. Please tell me you have something hanging from the walls."

"I do, but it's not handcuffs. I do have a circular wooden shield. I hired some guys to make the walls exposed brick, and then I put down a herringbone-patterned wood floor last summer. There's a large round table in the center and a chandelier that I bought off eBay that's allegedly from a castle in Ireland."

She grinned at him, making him realize he might be going on too much about his dungeon. It might seem silly, but it was the first place that felt like his own. "Yeah, so that's it. Whatever you pick out will look good."

"I'm sure," she said. "I can't wait to see your dungeon. Do you have a fireplace?"

"I do, but it's gas. The dungeon is a converted dining room," he said.

"Okay. Well I'd like to get some fallen branches and leaves to decorate the mantel and your windowsills. Then we can work on a broom for your door," she said. "I'll bring some stuff with me when we play D&D. That's tomorrow night, right?"

"Thanks. Yeah, it is. Mostly it'll be just you and me at my place."

She stopped and made an excited sound as she stooped

and started to push some leaves to the side. Underneath was a small bloom, and she touched it carefully. Again, she closed her eyes and said something under her breath.

He was pretty sure she was doing her witch thing, and he wanted to know more about it. These practices she did were natural, the same way he could code a new algorithm without thinking about the details.

This was magic. Sensual and earthy magic that he'd never encountered before. He wanted to understand it—and not for skills he could bring to D&D or whatever nonsense he'd been telling himself before.

But because it was Liberty. Because when she did it, it made him want to be on his knees next to her, his hands in the dirt, his body brushing hers. He wanted to understand the things she did because, unlike the many sports his father had introduced him to, this actually interested him.

Aside from her innate sensuality, which was enchanting. Magic. It was strange that he was letting himself fall into this world so far from the practicality of his.

She turned and caught him staring. He started to shrink away, but remembered her Nan calling him on it. So he stood there as their eyes met. He licked his lips and she gave him a half smile.

"Come and help me gather some of these leaves. They'll be nice around your place."

He knelt down beside her and felt his shoulder linger against hers. It wasn't what he'd anticipated, but other than sex, it was rare that he touched anyone else. He worked remotely and he wasn't a hugger. So this touch felt more intimate than it otherwise might have.

He inhaled deeply, the scent of the woods filled his nose and lungs and then he noticed something else, something subtle.

Liberty. Part of the woods, total earth mother and moon goddess.

Liberty left Merle when they got back to his place because she wanted to take the leaves and branches home and put a blessing on them before she put them in his house. She felt raw and settled for a wave good-bye when it was time to leave.

Instead of returning to her apartment, she drove to the small row house where she'd grown up. Her mom was meant to be back sometime tonight and Liberty missed her.

She let herself in and started the kettle for some tea before moving to the sunroom at the back of the house where the garden was. She wanted to put herbs and a spell together to give Merle strength and speed when it came to finding her father. But she also wanted protection for him in case her magic got out of control.

These were big asks, and she needed both the grimoire that she'd started making when she turned thirteen and her mother's as well. She wanted all of the Wakefield women with her as she cast this spell.

Merle was doing so much for her even if he didn't know it. Today, he'd been her talisman. He'd asked her to open up so he could get to know her better, but that was already proving harder than she'd expected it to be. Her mind was saying, *It's Merle—trust him*. Kind of. It was more like, *Surely it's okay to trust him?*

But the truth was that she couldn't yet.

Not with this part of herself.

The tarot readings and the crystals she charged were the public part of what she did. That acceptable magic that everyone thought was quirky and cool. But flipping through the grimoire and picking the right candle to light before she started her spell? This was the part that could freak someone out.

For her, this was home. This was the place she felt most herself. Standing in front of the open book, she felt the generations of women who'd come before her. It was as if Mom and Nan were with her, their hands on her shoulder as she found the right elements for the blessing.

Though as much as she had thought it was cool that Merle knew about spirits from other realms crossing into this one, that knowledge was lore that he used in his game. There had been nothing to indicate that he'd accept it in real life.

She lost track of the time as she investigated everything. She wanted to include the branches and leaves into a piece to go on his mantel—a makeshift altar. One of her oldest spell books would have the answer. She flipped through the pages, using her instincts and her gut to find the right spell.

In the middle of her search, she opened a window and was surprised that night had fallen. The wind had been absent all evening, and she was longing for its playful presence to give her some kind of peace of mind. But it was silent.

The sky was cloudy and the earth felt heavy. She closed her eyes as she browsed through the pages of her book. Suddenly, the spine, which had been broken by her folding the cover back over the years, flopped open.

The spell it opened to about spirit-guided writing...was a

little too spot-on for her right now. She was floundering and her feelings had been added to that mix. What she needed was something for Merle. Sexy, nerdy Merle who only knew store-bought Halloween.

The branch she'd picked up was birch and had fallen from a tree that had been struck by lightning over the summer. She ran her hands over the length of it without touching it. Feeling the ghost of electricity in it, but no malicious intent. She said a quick protection chant and then turned to her oils. The ones she liked during Samhain were nutmeg, myrrh and, for Merle, sandalwood. She mixed them in a vial with a carrier oil and then used a dropper to distribute it down the length of the branch.

Next, she pulled herbs from the jars on the wall behind her worktable. She could have done this easily at the WiCKed Sisters shop, but she wanted to talk to her mom, and she was afraid of missing her again.

She already had the rosemary. Next she added sage, valerian and wormwood. She crushed the herbs together in her mortar and then pushed a piece of hemp rope into it. She continued working it with the pestle until the herbs and the oils were infused into the hemp. Then she pulled dried apples, pomegranates and some summer squash and used them to decorate the hemp rope, which she tied, braided and then wrapped around the branch.

Something was missing.

She went out into the garden and found a few small pumpkins to bring inside. The branch had a natural curve to it, and she tried a couple of different pumpkins until she found one that fit naturally into the curve. Then she tucked everything into a wooden crate so she could bring it to Merle later.

Liberty went back into the kitchen and made herself another cup of tea, then sat down at the kitchen table. She ran her fingers over the tiles that decorated the table, which were painted with different symbols for the four seasons. She touched the symbols representing the fall equinox and wondered where her mother was. This was the season of death and rebirth, the beginning of the darkness as they moved toward the shortest day of the year.

It was a time when she wanted to let go of the past—the only way to move forward.

But she wasn't ready to. She had four more weeks until October thirty-first, when she wanted John Jones out of her head. But she couldn't lie to her mom for four weeks. Also, she didn't want to start something with Merle while trying to keep that kind of secret from the one person who was most important to her.

She fell asleep at the table waiting for her mom and ended up dreaming of that Cape Cod cottage. Except instead of just Mom, Nan, Grandpa and her, Merle was there along with Poppy and Sera. All of her family, together.

Six

Poppy showed up at Merle's place at 9:00 a.m. frantically knocking on his door, followed by three text messages and a bang on his bedroom window which finally woke him. When he opened the door to his cousin, she pushed past him into the house and dumped her large purse on the hall table she'd insisted he buy before heading to the kitchen.

"Pop?"

"Sorry. I need to talk and you're the only one who knows everything and I hated to wake you because I know you work nights—"

"It's okay," he said going over and stopping her frantic movements near the sink. He pulled her into his arms and hugged her.

She sighed and then hiccupped a few times before she started crying.

"What is going on?"

"Alistair is going to Gemma's wedding and his family will

all be there. He hasn't told them we're divorced and they want him to make amends with me—probably so they can get on my popularity with Amber Rapp's fans."

Fuck.

Alistair wasn't making it easy for Poppy to move on. When she discovered he'd pursued and married her for the Kitchener tea recipe that had been guarded and handed down to her, it threw her into a tailspin. She'd bought into his whole loved-her-at-first-sight thing. When it crashed, she'd run to Merle who gave her a place to stay and heal.

They'd always been close, and he had Poppy's back then and now. But by going to a mutual friend's wedding with her ex-husband…

"Want me to talk to him?"

"Yes. But what are you going to say?"

"Stop being a douche? It's over? Move on?"

Poppy smiled, though her eyes were still red from crying. She went to the breakfast bar which was the only seating in his sparsely furnished kitchen. "Thanks. But I've already said it."

"Want me to say that we're going together?" he asked after a minute. He hated family functions. But he'd do this for Poppy.

"Ah, thanks. But you weren't planning to go. I thought you gave your parents your invite. I'd… You'd hate it," she said.

He opened the fridge and took out two Gatorades, tossing one to her, which she caught one-handed. Poppy had some athletic skill, though she didn't flaunt it. "But I love you so it's not big."

"It's totally big," she said after taking a small sip of her drink. She made a face and set it aside.

"We can drive down to Boston together it you want and

talk to him. Or I can go by myself… Marcus took a job as a coach to the Sox farm team. I wasn't planning on it, but I'll go and see him first."

"Do you think it will help?"

"It can't hurt. Did you give him any signal that he still has a shot?"

Poppy chewed her lower lip between her teeth.

"Pop. Really?"

She didn't say anything, and he wasn't sure what she needed from him right now. "Am I supportive of you, or pissed off and about to give you the snap-out-of-it talk?"

She laughed. "Both. I shouldn't be talking to him online, but he joined my secret tea society and he's brewing beer or something… It's been a long time and he was being…*nice*. You know, he's only nice when he wants something. And he did all the things I like. I guess part of me hoped he'd finally…" she said, looking down at the countertop instead of at him.

"Don't beat yourself over it. It's natural to hope someone has changed. I do it with my folks all the time. So I get it. What do you want? You could totally hook up without having to go back to him."

"I know. It's just…sex isn't like that for me," she said.

"It's personal."

"Yeah. Not just about the physical. Actually I really don't miss sex per se. I miss intimacy, and with him at least we know each other. Even though he sucked at the end of our marriage, there's all those good memories too."

Yeah. It wasn't like Poppy had ever really pretended not to have the softest heart of anyone on the planet. She cared a lot about everyone. And Alistair wasn't above taking advantage of that. "Let's find you a new man."

"I still have an old man telling everyone we're married. He hasn't changed his socials either," Poppy said.

"So you change yours," he said.

"He'll make me the bad guy. He'll tell everyone—"

"Who cares? The people who know you won't believe it and yeah, I know I'm not online so it's not like I know what that world is like. But fuck him. You should not only say you're not married but start seeing other people and posting it."

"When have I ever been that person?"

"Never. So why do you care what he does online? Why are you letting him control you with this 'she's still my wife'?"

Poppy blinked rapidly and then shook her head and when she spoke her words were low and guttural with the tears that streamed down her face. "I think I still want to be."

"You deserve better," he said. "But if you want him, knowing who he is…then go after him."

He hoped she didn't. Alistair had never been Merle's favorite person and he never would be. He'd hurt Poppy and Merle couldn't forgive that. But it was Poppy's life. If she wanted the guy, then Merle would support her.

"I do deserve better. But what if there isn't anyone else out there who wants me?" she asked.

"There is. Also being treated like shit isn't better than being alone. I live alone and I'm happy," he said.

Unbidden, an image of Liberty in his arms yesterday danced through his head. He wouldn't mind living with her.

"Yeah, you're living the dream with your two decorated rooms and empty house," she teased.

He flipped her off and then pulled out his phone to order breakfast for them. "You going to be okay?"

"Yeah. I need to talk to the girls."

"Why didn't you do that first?" he asked. He seemed like the last choice for this convo.

"Sera and Wesley were at his place and Liberty wasn't at her apartment."

Where was she? Was she seeing someone else?

He knew he had no right to feel jealous, but his crush on her made him feel as if he did. He was putting himself out there, not lying about what he wanted. As simple and complicated as that.

Liberty woke up in her childhood bedroom with a vague memory of her mom helping her to bed and tucking her in. The smell of Italian sausage and garlic wafted through the air. She hopped out of bed and ran down the stairs and into the kitchen. She stopped in the doorway and saw her mom at the stove cooking.

Her mom looked over her shoulder and greeted her. Liberty noted that she looked tired, but it was so good to see her.

"I missed you."

"I figured. I stopped by the care home. Nan told me about her vision and your visit. You okay?"

"No. She saw Grandpa," Liberty said, going to pour herself a cup of coffee from the pot. She rarely allowed herself coffee, but this morning she needed it. Taking a deep breath of the aroma before she had her first sip.

Heaven.

"Yeah. I heard Merle was there."

"Yeah."

Her mom laughed. "So what's going on with him?"

"Mom..."

"Liberty..."

"I'm not sure. I mean, you know I kinda like him. Apparently everyone does, even Nan. She said 'that boy you look at when you think no one is watching' in front of him."

Her mom blinked, and then the saddest smile that she had seen on her mom's face in a long time appeared. "I'm glad. That's her sassy self."

"I felt the same. Yesterday it felt like the dementia/Alzheimer stuff was gone," she said.

"You know it's not going away," Mom said.

She rolled her eyes. Her mom was very practical, always pointing out the reality of things. Like when she was twelve and totally into *Agent Cody Banks*, her mom had insisted on pointing out that there wasn't a bit of reality in it. As if Liberty was going to run off and join a secret agent program... If they'd offered, she totally would have. Still, she lived in the real world. Probably more than her mom realized. "Yeah. I just wanted to hope."

"I know, baby. I want that too."

Liberty wondered how Nan was when her mom got there.

"Was Nan okay?"

"Yeah. Still very clear-minded but she seemed sad. Like she knew that she wasn't always that way," her mom said. "It was hard to see her like that. I'm sure it was for you too."

"It was. I mean Nan has always been the one to comfort me...not that you don't."

"I get it. Grandkids and grandparents have a common enemy—the parent."

"My evil single mom who sacrificed everything to make a good life for me. Yeah, she's the worst," Liberty said with a wink. It was an old joke between them.

And it made that secret she was keeping feel more like a betrayal. Was she lying to herself when she said she was keeping the truth from her mom for her mom's sake? That she even had to ask was probably the answer she was searching for.

"That's me. So breakfast frittata? Do you have time to eat here or do you need it to go?"

She glanced at her watch. It was only nine-fifteen but she had to be at the shop by nine-forty-five and hadn't showered. "To go, I'm afraid."

"No problem."

Liberty ran upstairs, showered and got ready for the day in some clothes she kept in the closet there. Her mom had breakfast ready when she came back down and packed extra for Poppy and Sera too. She hugged her mom an extra-long time.

"Why were you here last night? Was it just Nan?"

Ugh.

"Uh, well I am making some Samhain stuff for Merle and needed some herbs and oils that I didn't have at my place. And I missed you. You've been gone for almost two weeks."

She added the last bit to distract her mom because she'd always had a pretty good instinct when it came to the truth.

"I missed you too," she said. "Why are you making things for Merle?"

"We're hanging out," Liberty said. Totally the truth. "He

asked me to join his D&D group and honestly it might be more fun than I expected."

"That sounds promising."

"For what? It's a role-playing game," Liberty said. Even though her mom never said it directly, she wanted Liberty to have someone to share her life with. Her mom had never found someone. But Liberty didn't feel the pull toward anything traditional.

Her mom was trying to make sure that Liberty had everything she hadn't had. That's what her mom always did.

"It could lead to some real-life stuff," her mom said. "I just want you to be happy. I like what Merle did for you and Nan yesterday."

"She told you?"

"She did. She likes him. Asked me if I'd read his palm yet."

This woman was scarily accurate when she read palms. "Did you read my dad's?"

Her mom went still and her face froze into a mask, one she used when she didn't want Liberty to know what she was thinking.

"I... I tried. I couldn't get a good read on him. Nan said it was because I didn't want to see the truth. Why do you ask?"

Liberty shrugged, telling herself to play it cool, but that wasn't the way she was built. It was on the tip of her tongue to blurt out that she knew his name, but then the doorbell rang, and her mom stood there for only a second before she headed off to get it. It was their neighbor, Imogen.

Liberty let out a ragged breath. She picked up her lunch, half hugged her mom and waved to Imogen as she walked out to her car.

She drove off their street before pulling over. Her hands were shaking. She had to come clean about John Jones to her mom. But at least it was a bit reassuring that mom had opened up a little about him. For a long time, the door was shut. Liberty had been the one to slam it closed, so it hardly seemed fair that she asked her mom to open it again.

But she wanted to know more, and she couldn't until she came clean.

She drove on to the shop and pulled into her parking spot at the back, surprised to see Merle waiting near the entrance. Her heart raced as she noticed he had some morning stubble and his hair was ruffled, as if he'd come here straight from bed.

Merle had no real plan other than to find out where she'd been.

Maybe it was the lack of sleep, but he wasn't feeling mellow at all.

Of course talking about Alistair hadn't really helped things. That bag of dicks gave all men a bad name. Just thinking it made Merle want to punch him. And he wasn't a physical guy.

"Hey, you," Liberty said as she got out of her car. "I was planning to stop by your place later. I went to Mom's last night and finished up your first Samhain decoration. And even though I'm a little wary of spell casting at the moment, I chanced a small happiness spell for you."

She walked over to him with her large purse slung over her shoulder, her hair still damp from her morning shower and hanging around her shoulders. His mind tried to catch up as the truth of what she was saying dawned on him.

He was a jerk for thinking anything else about Liberty.

If there was one thing this woman was, it was honest.

★ ★ ★

"Hey. Poppy stopped by my place earlier and since I was awake, I told her I'd help out this morning. Hoped to see you," he said.

"Of course you would see me here," she said. "What's up with Poppy?"

"Just more from the douche bag. She's going to talk to you and Sera later. She had to go back home because Pickle fell into the water bowl."

Pickle was Poppy's geriatric miniature dachshund. She used to bring Pickle to the shop with her, but lately the old girl had been happier lying in her blankets at home. Poppy had a monitor that kept her alert to the dog's movements.

"Oh. Poor thing."

"Which one?"

"Both of them," Liberty said. She would try to make another potion for Pickle's health later that day. It was funny; her magic seemed to be settling down, or at least she was getting more used to the change that was going on inside of her. She'd been afraid to cast any spells or ask her tarot cards for guidance while her emotions were all over the place.

Yesterday Merle had calmed all of that.

"Yeah. So, full disclosure, I also wanted to find out where you were last night. Poppy said you weren't at your apartment."

She shook her hair as she tipped her head to the side and looked up at him. He stood awkwardly, almost defensive, but she thought—or maybe hoped—that she saw some vulnerability in his confession. "Were you jealous?"

"Did you want me to be?"

"So that's totally a yes," she said.

He shrugged. "You?"

"Well no, I didn't want you to be, but I'm sort of excited that you were," she admitted. Yesterday when she'd tried to even things up, he'd stopped her and she wasn't sure where they stood. In the past, most men dated her when they wanted someone different, a manic pixie dream girl, and then lost interest. Like she was a one-time thing with no merit for anything else.

Merle was different. Wasn't he?

She had to stop doing that. Had to stop putting all men in the same category and expecting Merle to be like her dad had been. He wasn't. He never had been.

"Excited?"

"Yeah. I like it. I'm guessing you're starting to want me for more than an extra player in your D&D campaign."

He threw his head back and laughed. It was a long one that made her heart flutter. "Maybe."

She walked over to him and put her arms around his shoulders, leaning up to kiss him. He tried to give her one of those chaste ones, but she was hungry for Merle and deepened the kiss.

His arms came around her. He placed his hands on her waist, lifting her off her feet so that she rested against his body. It seemed as if time stopped when he kissed her.

In this moment, everything was right in her world. Well, not everything, but enough. Nan was clearheaded. Mom was home. And Merle had been jealous and was kissing her.

She was fully aware that this would pass and reality would be back sooner than she wanted it to be. Nothing lasted forever.

But the autumn wind danced around them, chillier than

it had been yesterday. The crispness made her feel alive and hopeful in a way that only the season of Samhain could. It was the end of one phase and the beginning of another one. Those words resonated in her soul, and as Merle lifted his head, his hands cupping her butt, she stayed pressed against him.

Words weren't the only thing adding to the buzz around her.

"Are you ready for tonight?"

"Do we have to wait that long?"

His cock jumped against her stomach and he groaned. "I meant D&D."

"Of course you did. Well yes, I am ready for that. And for anything else you might bring, Merle Rutland."

She kissed him again before unlocking the back door of the shop. She could feel him watching her as she walked away and was glad she'd squeezed into the tight pair of jeans she'd left at her mom's because they made her ass and hips look damn good.

She wanted him to be thinking about her all day long. Maybe tonight, after the game, she'd see if she could bring some real-world magic to their lives.

Seven

Merle knew his mom hated that he worked in Poppy's little tea shop at WiCKed Sisters. He really enjoyed hanging out with his cousin and her friends. Sera set aside books for him that had to do with D&D, especially anything by Gary Gygax—who was pretty much the father of D&D—and books on war history which some of D&D was based on. But the roots of the current game came from war gaming. The game took some of its inspiration from real-life battles and placed them in a fantasy realm, where the outcome was uncertain.

D&D gave him a chance to create a world that merged his love of history and fantasy together. He liked bringing that world alive for the people. It was a chance to show a different side of themselves.

He was tired, and normally would have resented having to be up at this hour, but he could hear the music that Liberty played in the shop. She had a Halloween playlist going and he had to laugh at some of the song choices. She never went for anything typical, like "Monster Mash" or "Love Potion No. 9." She found music that was evocative and made it feel as if they were really moving into a season of magic.

As a storyteller in the D&D world, he'd never really experienced something as special as Liberty's ability to make the real world feel fantastical. He liked it. Maybe too much. He was trying to justify the feels she was pulling from him. Like he wasn't just someone she was using as a distraction.

Her emotions were big and loud and out there for everyone to see. She hadn't grown up needing a game face, and never was that more apparent than now. She liked him for now, and that was enough.

Liberty was sitting at her tarot table; she'd changed into a long flowy skirt instead of those tight-ass jeans she'd had on earlier. Normally she wore a lot of rings, but when she read cards, she removed them.

He had always been curious about why she did that but had never asked.

He could now. He could probably ask her anything with the tension building between them.

She was giving him all the signs that she wanted to sleep with him and put the benefits into "friends with benefits" and he was…well, *hesitating*. Not because he didn't want her. She'd dominated his fantasies and he wove her badass witch vibe into the NPCs he created for his campaigns.

But more because…he was still Merle Rutland. The odd Rutland. The one who wasn't normal.

That was hard to shake. Even more difficult to deal with than being jealous. He should have leaned into the jealousy, acted the possessive hero and maybe let it burn out the other shit.

"Why don't you ask her to read your cards?" Poppy said as she plopped down on one of the stools at the counter in the back of her tea shop.

He quickly brewed Poppy's favorite tea blend and set it down in front of her before he leaned his hip against the back counter and put his arms over his chest. "What if she reads that I'm…?"

"Super into her?" Poppy suggested as she blew on her tea. "Everyone knows that."

"Even Liberty. So why are you watching her with that intense longing that I thought only existed in period dramas?"

"Why are you poking me?"

She shook her head and shrugged. "I don't know. I guess I want one of us to be happy in love."

"This thing with me and Liberty isn't love."

It couldn't be. Not because he didn't deserve love or any of that shit, but more because he'd seen love firsthand in his family and never wanted to feel that kind of responsibility. To work to make her happy only to let her down and live with her disappointment. To him, love had always been brought in when he didn't live up to expectations—a "we love you anyway." A consolation for his failures.

Liberty deserved someone who would never fail her.

"What is it then?"

"Lust, Poppy. And probably some of that magic that Liberty brings to the world around her. Just listening to the cadence of her voice and the sound of the cards as she shuffles them stirs the energy—"

He broke off, realizing he shouldn't be saying any of that stuff out loud.

"She is magic," Poppy said. "She's the reason we have this shop. I mean we all worked at it and saved, but it was her dream first. She sees the world she wants and then goes out and makes it happen."

He hadn't thought of it that way.

When Liberty's customer left, he glanced at Poppy who nodded at him to go. He left the tea shop and headed into Liberty's section of the store. Sera and her assistant, Greer, were busy in the bookstore, and there were a few customers milling around in front of the caldrons and decks of tarot cards.

But Liberty had left her table and moved behind the register. She looked up as he approached. Her light gray eyes met his and all his words left him.

Why hadn't he taken her up on her sexual invitation yesterday in the car? Why hadn't he let things continue from that sensual kiss they'd shared this morning? Maybe it was the old fear that she was just teasing him. Why was he letting old fear keep him from the one woman he wanted?

Because of this. The softness in her eyes when she watched him. The fact that she'd come to him and asked for a favor regarding her father. He wanted to be different with her—to be himself. But decades of forcing himself to be what everyone else expected him to be had left him stymied. All of this time second-guessing himself was holding both of them back, even if she never saw him as more than a friend to flirt with.

He took the cup of mushroom mud that he'd brewed for her and set it on the counter.

"Ah, I need this. Thanks," she said, inhaling deeply as she wrapped her hands around the mug.

"I figured," he said. "It looked like that last session was intense."

"It was. Were you watching me?" she teased.

"I always am."

"I know. I like it," she admitted.

"I know," he said with a smirk. It was part of who they were. And he wondered if that might factor into his reluctance. He didn't want to change things and lose this. Lose her.

All the charisma between them made him feel more alive than he had in a long time.

Liberty tried not to stare at Merle, but he normally wasn't in the shop this early in the day. There was a zing about him this morning. Whenever she glanced over, he didn't turn away and pretend he hadn't been staring at her. One time he even winked, which sent a little shot of desire through her.

His phone pinged and he pulled it out of his pocket, glancing down, fingers tapping on the screen. A strand of his thick curly hair fell forward. Her fingers itched to thread through it. She should have put her hands in his hair when she'd kissed him, but she'd been too consumed with the feel of his mouth and body against hers.

She set her drink on the counter and took off the rings she wore when doing readings in the store. It was a quirk of hers—she used the moonlight to cleanse and then charge the rings for her readings. Asked the moon to give her clarity and guidance so she could help those who came to her. Not everyone put stock on tarot, and some of her customers booked a session with her purely for the novelty of it. When she wore the rings after, they raised questions. More than once she'd explained her process, which was rooted in her spirituality, and saw judgment and dismissal in her "woo-woo, it's just for fun" clients.

But no matter their intent, she always tried to deliver the most accurate reading she could. She took her rings off and put them in a small wooden box that had been passed down to her from Nan when she turned thirteen. It had intricate carvings of Celtic runes and ancient symbols of protection on it. Nan even added a spell when she'd given it to Liberty. Each year on her birthday, they went up to the top of Hanging Hill and renewed the spell.

Her heart ached. This year Nan might not be able to go with her.

"Good news. I've got a lead on a John Jones who was in the New England area around the time of your birth. I'm running a search to see what it pulls back. Should take about thirty minutes. Are you free for lunch? We could talk then?"

Liberty hadn't been prepared for that. She had half-banished John Jones from her mind, concentrating on this charged back-and-forth with Merle.

Fuck.

That chaos and anger was immediately back in her mind. She was glad she'd taken her rings off. She didn't want them to be tainted by any negative feelings. She turned away from him as she tried to process it.

But it wasn't easy. Of course she wanted to know what he'd found out. That was why she'd gone to him. But knowing would change everything. She still hadn't decided what to do about her mom—

Merle came around and put his hand on her shoulder. He

blinked as if not sure what to do or say. Not that she blamed him. Really, she had no clue what it was she wanted. He'd always been steady—constant. And she flustered him and got a small thrill from it. But that dynamic had changed, and she was so tempted to let him in.

Maybe allow him to see that she was scared. And sad. And anxious.

"Sorry. That's great. I can do a late lunch. I have a reading in about thirty minutes," she said. It was with one of her regulars so she needed to clear her head. Go in the back and meditate. Set up a circle and ask for guidance.

"Can you watch the shop for me?" she asked.

Months of being aloof and keeping her distance…and now she was asking him for favors left and right, acting like a complete mess. She took a deep breath.

"Of course. Should I not run the query?"

"What query?"

"The information search on him. Do you want me to stop?" he asked.

Yes. No. Fucking hell, she had no real idea of what she wanted.

She glanced around her shop, reluctant to think about something so private here. Not in the space she'd created, that leaned into her strengths and the special bond she had with Sera and Poppy.

"I don't know. I need to go and meditate to reach out to my spirit guides. I'll be fifteen to twenty minutes," she said.

"Take your time. I can handle the register until Lucy comes in," Merle said.

She nodded and reached around him, taking her mushroom mud and walking into her back room. The stock room and storage area had a simple hardwood floor. One wall was lined with bottles and vials of herbs and oils that she used to make potions and spells for her customers. Another wall had a long wooden bench that she used as an altar with her cauldron on it. Farther down was the spot where she hand-dipped candles once she added oils to the wax.

This space was her bower and smelled of the outdoors. She looked at the cluster of pumpkins sitting near her meditation pillow and took a deep breath.

John Jones.

She wasn't sure that she *should* know about him, now that Merle might be able to uncover the truth. Of course she *wanted* to know—that was why she'd asked him to look in the first place—but at the same time, she was scared of what the information would reveal and of the emotions it might stir.

She poured a circle of salt and then sat in the middle. Lit a candle for guidance and pulled the herbs she needed for clarity around her. She sank down in a cross-legged position and closed her eyes. The familiar scents of her ritual calmed her mind to a small degree so she could use her chaotic energy to pull down answers from the universe.

Even though they might not be comfortable.

Did she want to know more about her father? Did she want to keep that information a secret from her mom?

And where did Merle fit in all of this? Was she using him as a crutch or a distraction, because it made her feel better to be with a man she knew she could trust while another was fucking up her life? Or was there potential for something…more?

★ ★ ★

Lucy arrived about ten minutes after Liberty disappeared to her back room. Merle hesitated and then told Lucy to let Liberty know to text him about lunch. He went back over to the tea shop, but Poppy was with a customer and her extra staff had arrived, so she waved him off.

With his unexpected free time, he left WiCKed Sisters, walking up Main Street toward the Bootless Soldier after grabbing his backpack. He had so many ideas he wanted to add into the D&D campaign he'd been writing. Seeing Liberty's magic gave him a new idea.

As the dungeon master, Merle played as all non-player characters, or NPCs, in the game; he would roll for them during a session and perform their voices. He had a few regulars that he sometimes went back to from earlier campaigns, but he liked creating new characters as well.

The tavern served breakfast until eleven but it wasn't that busy, so Merle found a table toward the back and pulled out his tablet to start working on his character notes and some new ideas he had for using the music to lure the campaign into someplace unknown. Merle kept his head down and wrote, his fingers moving over the keyboard. He didn't even try to pretend he was setting this particular battle up for anyone other than Liberty. It would lean into her strengths, and the artifact he was going to hide at the end would be perfect for her. Something that she would appreciate finding. It was his way of giving her an outlet to express the combo of sadness and anger he'd seen in her earlier.

"Dude, I knew I'd find you here."

Merle looked up, surprised to see his brother Marcus. "Uh, what are you doing here?"

"Really, that's how you say hello?"

"You said you were in Bangor on Friday."

"Yeah, I know, but… Mom asked me to check on you," he said.

Yeah, right. "Mom doesn't give a crap about me. Why are you here?"

Marcus shrugged and dropped into the chair across the table. His hair was trimmed close to his head, his eyes the same dark brown as Merle's. Marcus shrugged out of his leather bomber jacket, revealing his licensed Under Armour shirt, designed to show off the results of his lifetime athleticism and daily gym sessions.

"My girlfriend is really into that game you play," Marcus said.

For fuck's sake.

"So?"

"She has a group she plays with each week and I really don't know shit about the game," Marcus said. "I remember you tried to show me but it wasn't like, go in and win. You had to eat and sleep and cast spells. Honestly, it was a lot when I was in high school."

"But now that you're twenty-three, it seems less?" Merle asked.

"Make fun if it makes you feel better. I like this girl. She's smart—like scary smart—and all of her friends are into it. Could you help me out with the game? I was going to ask on Friday but I need to concentrate on baseball then."

"Help you out how?" he asked.

"Give me the idiots' notes on the game and what I need to do," Marcus said.

The fact that Marcus wanted to play the game to impress a girl pleased Merle. His brother was used to winning—being the best. After all these years, there was finally something Merle was good at that Marcus couldn't fathom.

"Do you know what edition of D&D they are playing?" he asked.

"I don't know shit."

The first thing Merle had his brother do was text his girlfriend and ask her some questions, particularly to find out if they were using their own campaigns. Turned out they were playing the fifth edition of Dungeons & Dragons. Merle hadn't played that specific edition; he'd at least watched a few YouTube videos.

Together they worked out that Marcus would do best as a barbarian half-orc. The character class that usually raged and used brawn in battles.

"You should probably read the Player's Handbook," Merle said, opening the ebook on his phone.

Marcus took one look at it and shook his head. "Is there anything more…basic? I don't have time to read all of that."

"Yeah," Merle said, opening up the basic rules book which Marcus could download.

"This is what I'm talking about. Thanks, bro."

"No problem. I think you'll like it once you get into it," he said.

"I'm not sure about that. But Talia is really into it and she comes to all my games, so I want to do something that's for her, you know?"

Marcus left a few minutes later and told him they could

skip Friday now. For the first time with his brother, Merle had been himself, and it was exactly what his brother needed. Not another sports analogy or some baseball trivia, but a willingness to listen and not judge.

Maybe he'd gotten too used to hiding from his family, letting those young adult behaviors flavor his attitude toward his parents and brothers. He wasn't sure how his oldest brother would react, or his parents, if he was finally, truly himself.

His mom was never going to like his hair long, but that didn't matter. He'd been doing more than putting on a baseball cap when it came to hiding who he was and what he did. Living two lives instead of one.

Today, as he wove Liberty's magic into his D&D campaign, it no longer felt like something he wanted to do. He wanted to stop being out of sync with everything and start vibing with himself, stepping into his own nerdiness to stop letting others' judgment define him. Talking to Marcus had opened him up to the fact that what he did led to good things.

It was past time that he did that. Past time to stop hiding himself from the world and live as if he had nothing to apologize for.

Eight

Sera and Poppy both came into the back room when Liberty was done with her meditation. The candle and the meditation hadn't brought answers.

Samhain was that season of endings, the time when the lush greens of summer faded. She should be embracing that and the ending of…her childhood.

That's what this was. She was facing her first problem without her mom there to fix it for her. Keeping secrets, balancing lies and trying to juggle Nan's illness and her shop and Merle was a lot. There were times when she wanted to pretend she was still a child and let Mom tell her everything would be fine.

This was something only she could figure out for herself. As a sixteen-year-old, when she'd rejected knowing his name, she'd done it partially out of rebellion, partially out of support for her mom, and maybe a little out of spite for the man who'd walked out of her life before it had begun.

But at twenty-eight, she was making a different choice. She could have ignored the name…

As if. She wasn't that kind of girl. She never had been.

"I'm lost."

The words just came out without thought and Sera and Poppy rushed over as one and hugged her, both of them reassuring her at the same time. Poppy with a "we're here" and Sera with a "we know."

Of course they knew. These were sisters of her heart that the universe had put in her path when she'd needed them most.

"Merle got a lead on my John Jones. There is a chance that I could find out more about him," she said.

Sera stepped around her and picked up one of Liberty's rings. It was made of three strands of bronze wiring braided together and then wrapped around a small obsidian crystal. Sera held the ring in her palm and closed her eyes saying words to herself, but Liberty knew what her friend was uttering.

"Friendship binds us in our hearts and in our lives."

She passed the ring over to Poppy, who took it and did the same thing before handing it to Liberty. For a moment she was overwhelmed by the love she had for these two women. She slipped the ring onto the index finger on her right hand. A sensation not unlike a hug wrapped itself around her body.

"Okay so you've got us with you. What else do you need?"

"I think I need to tell Mom."

"I agree," Sera said. "She's going to be hurt that you haven't yet. Not just about the John Jones part. She needs to know what's going on with your Nan too."

Liberty took a deep breath. Sera had really started to grow into her feminine strength since she began a relationship with

Wesley. There had been a time when Sera wouldn't have spoken up. Liberty loved seeing her friend come into her own. But right now she wasn't sure she was happy with the truth bomb.

Sera was right. But once she mentioned everything to her mom, she was going to face learning more about her father than she could predict—probably from the one source she should have gone to in the first place. She was afraid of learning something that would make her see her mom in a different light.

"I agree with Sera. It's your life and of course we're going to support you no matter what, but keeping this from your mom isn't helping you," Poppy said. "But you can't talk to her now, so we'll go with you to talk to Merle. That way, whatever happens, we're there."

Liberty looked back to the salt circle on the floor and the debris of the meditation and the ritual she'd tried to perform. Was the goddess showing her that her strength was this friendship?

Or was she so disconnected from her authentic self that she needed her friends to make her decisions for her?

The universe had sent her a message. Offered her a nugget of something that could lead to a rebirth. A chance to really face that one part of her past she'd never resolved. That part she ignored and pretended didn't matter, buried in her deepest heart.

All of her life, she tried to say she didn't need to know anything about that man who hadn't wanted her. Pushed it down on Father's Day, when other kids had asked questions on the playground. But a part of her was ignoring that feeling of abandonment that had always dogged her. No matter how much she'd tried to hide it behind her I-don't-give-a-fuck attitude.

She'd developed a hard skin to protect herself against the teasing from others about how her and Mom were two strange witches living without a man. John Jones's abandonment led to financial struggles and emotional ones as well for both Liberty and Lourdes. But they'd gotten through it and were strong. Her home life was good. She'd been so loved and supported by both Mom and Nan that she'd learned to not let that missing man bother her.

She wasn't going to just be passive about this.

She had been angry to hear the way Nan was talking to her mom about that man...about how Mom had loved him and tried to get him to stay... That he'd still walked away pissed her off.

Standing in her back room with the scent of candle wax and rosemary surrounding her, she could finally admit that she needed to find out the truth about her father so she could shove it in his face how awesome she was, and how much he'd missed out on leaving her mom.

Merle read through the search results. Though the query hadn't pulled back one man, but four. Maybe he should have done this before he told her he had found some information.

He just wanted to deliver some results. He'd already admitted he wanted to impress Liberty, and normally this wasn't what he did for a living. But he knew computers and how to find information that no one wanted found. This should have been easy.

These results were, well, lackluster in his opinion.

But they were a start. He was being too hard on himself. Sighing, Merle initiated a more detailed search on the four men and then put his smartphone away.

He rubbed the back of his neck, trying to come to terms with Marcus's visit. His world felt like it was off its axis. Marcus getting signed and the family celebrating was normal. Marcus coming all the way to Birch Lake, which his family sort of hated because it's too quiet and odd, was decidedly not normal.

He was used to being the odd man out. To keeping this part of his life separate from his family. But Marcus, in the way only the baby of the family could do, had swept in and brought the two halves of his life together.

Merle wasn't sure he liked it. D&D had always been his thing. His nerd identity was an armor to keep most at bay. His phone pinged and he glanced down. Liberty texted that she was done and could talk. He replied that he was at the Bootless Soldier and asked her what she wanted for lunch.

She wouldn't want to be away from her shop for too long, and food would give her something other than the information to concentrate on.

Liberty sent back her order and he placed it along with his. She showed up a few minutes later, and his heart skipped a beat when he saw her. Butterflies were rioting in his stomach, and his lips tingled from remembering how hers felt under his. They'd been circling around each other for so long, it felt like they should have already had sex. But everything with Liberty wasn't what he expected.

The truth was, when he and Liberty had sex, it would be intimate and he needed it to be his best—to take things further than they had in the parking lot. He wanted more than that for the first time he orgasmed with her. Sex with Liberty wasn't going to be a quid pro quo thing or scratching an itch.

She plopped down across from him, smelling of autumn leaves, crisp wind and apples. She didn't smile and kept playing with the ring on her index finger. Twirled it around and around before she made herself stop and put both of her hands on the table, leaning forward.

"Poppy and Sera are going to come up here in about twenty minutes, after you tell me what you've found out."

"Why?"

"So I can figure out what to do next," she said.

Merle couldn't help being a little bit disappointed that she was involving her friends in this private moment. But he pushed that thought aside. She had been very clear that the only reason she'd come to him was his computer expertise. Even when they'd visited her grandmother together, it had been because no one else could go with her.

Despite their connection, he wasn't her first choice in any of this. He wasn't her partner, just one of her friends. It was time to stop hiding behind his armor and just ask for what he wanted. Growing up in the shadow of his brothers accomplishments and his parents' disappointment had left him feeling unworthy of asking for what he wanted. No more.

He had to remember that.

"Okay. Did you want to wait for them?" he asked.

"No. Tell me so I have time to process it."

Their food arrived and he updated her about the four men named John Jones who had a connection to Maine and would have been in this area around the time of her conception.

"Four of them?"

"Yes. It's hard to tell since your mom didn't name him on the birth certificate. But I've started a search on each of them. I think we should be able to narrow it down to just one. But uncovering some of the records and information I'm searching for is going to take time. The search is very thorough."

"So I guess that's a good thing. I had hoped it would be just one guy and then I'd be able to decide what to do next," she said. "But this is… I'm not sure what this entire episode is about. Is the goddess trying to teach me patience?"

"I'm not sure that's possible," he said.

She gave him a look from under her lashes. "I can wait for something if I want it bad enough."

He arched an eyebrow back at her. "I can too."

"I know. Well, that's anticlimactic. I was being very over the top, sure that I was going to make a choice right now, but I have more time." There was something almost disassociated in how she was acting right now.

"You do."

Cheering her up was the first step in showing her that he was engaged and present. "So do you think you could tell me more about the goddess and all that? You did promise to help me get ready for Halloween."

"Samhain. I promised to help you get ready for Samhain," she said. "And of course I can tell you. In fact, I've woven a lot of my family history into my druid character for D&D. So you're going to learn about it that way."

"Good. But I thought maybe we could do it one-on-one too. You know, like on a date," he said.

He hadn't planned on asking her, but there it was. A date.

He felt like he was in high school asking Marcy Tanner out the first time. She'd said yes, but he'd been sweating the entire time.

This was better, he thought.

Another delay in getting the information on her father. If ever there was a sign, this was it. She wasn't ready for the information, and now that the white hot anger she'd felt when the DNA test hadn't panned out had waned, maybe it was a good thing. She'd reacted like she always did, impulsively. But with time she was rethinking things.

She still needed to know the truth, but it ticked her off that she wasn't ready like she'd thought she was. The universe gave her an opportunity only to make her hurry up and wait. She finished her lunch, her eyes following Merle's hands as he held his sandwich.

Her body tingled, remembering the feel of them on her skin. How he'd cupped her ass and lifted her against his body in the parking lot. Goddess knew she craved him. But they were playing a long game. There was a lot of comfort in flirting with him. Being a hot mess was one thing. But giving in to her impulses with Merle... Well, it could lead to her getting hurt. She *liked* him. Yeah, that wasn't exactly the news. The more time she spent with him, the harder it was to deny how much like there was in her for this sexy, nerdy man.

He'd asked her on a date.

She couldn't help noticing that he was nervously trying not to look at her while clearly sneaking glances across the table. In the past she'd focused on herself over dating, following in Mom's example. As much as it scared her to put herself out there, if there was anyone she could trust, it was Merle. For her, that spoke volumes. He could have said no when she asked for help. Most people charged a lot of money to do private detective work. But Merle would never turn down a genuine request for help. That strength was probably a big reason why she had started flirting with him in the first place.

"A date?"

"I did mention I wanted that. Maybe this weekend. Just the two of us. None of this 'favor' stuff. Just you and me getting to know one another as more than friends," he said.

"I'd like that. How about an afternoon in the forest and then back to my place for some Samhain fun to fulfill my promise? Then we can get ready and go out on our date," she suggested. With everything going on, she hadn't really had a chance to enjoy the beginning of her favorite season. Liberty wouldn't let that stand.

She needed to slow down and immerse herself in autumn. She'd been in such a hurry to get here that she hadn't even picked up any leaves on her way; she'd seen a particularly large rust-colored one that she wanted for her mantel. It was like she was losing pieces of herself to this obsession with getting information about a man who didn't want her.

A man who meant nothing to her.

Why hadn't she seen that before? Why had she allowed the fact that she had a name to drive her into this frenzy?

"Okay. But what will we be doing with the pumpkins?"

"Decorating. It'll be fun. I'll get some more for your place too. Tonight I'm going to bring over the altar piece I made for you from the branches and foliage we collected in the woods the other day."

"Great. But I don't have an altar."

She shook her head. "Disappointing. We can figure something out. Do you have a countertop?"

"I do."

"I'll make it work," she said. "Now to the D&D session tonight. Should I wear something druid-y?"

"If you want to. No one in the group dresses like their characters. I tend to wear jeans and a T-shirt. But there isn't a dress code," he said.

"Disappointing," she repeated. "I was picturing you in some tight leather pants and an adventurer's shirt...maybe a medallion nestled in the deep V."

"Sorry to keep letting you down—and just to manage expectations—I don't own a pair of tight leather pants," he said.

"You don't? I'll put that on my gift idea list. I was just thinking how much fun it would be to dress as my character."

"There's a group that does that. I haven't been, but if you're interested I can see when they're meeting up again."

"What group?"

"LARPers. Live-Action Role Players," he said.

She stole a potato chip from his plate. "Why haven't you done that? Seems right up your alley."

He was so good at world building and character creation, she wanted some recognition for him.

His face got tight in a way that meant he didn't want to talk about this. Part of her knew she was using Merle as a distraction from her own messed-up life, but also, she wanted this for him.

"I tend to keep D&D private."

"That's not D&D, right? Are you embarrassed to do your

nerd thing out in the open?" There was something so cute about seeing him almost blush when she asked him. It made her like him a little bit more.

He sighed. "Yes. I am. Plus my mom is on Facebook so if anyone tags me in pics, she'll see it and then it'll become a thing."

She had started out teasing him, but it sounded like there was more to it than that. "So?"

"So, I'm not the perfect son, Liberty. I don't have the relationship with my family that you have with yours. Even my hair and the fact that I haven't cut it in ages causes discussion at every family get-together. So as much as I've wanted to try to meet up with the LARPers, I haven't done it."

Merle gave off all the confident vibes when she saw him, so realizing he was actually shy about his interests angered her. Merle deserved better than whoever had made him feel this way.

She'd never empathized with him more. All of her life she'd boldly shouted her differences to the world because she knew she'd never fit in. But she'd assumed that Merle did the same.

She reached over and rested her hand on his, which he'd clenched into a fist. "Screw them. I like your hair, and I'm not sure what they'd want to discuss about it. And if you want to do the LARPers thing, I'll go with you. Until then I'm looking forward to D&D and seeing you in action."

Nine

Screw them. Merle liked the sentiment and Liberty's defense of him.

They finished their lunch and left the tavern. Standing awkwardly by her, he wasn't sure what to say next, but he didn't want to go back to his place. He was ahead on his projects for work and could catch up overnight if he needed to. "As you said, you haven't helped me get ready for Halloween…"

"I haven't, you're right about that. I have another hour before I have to be back to the shop for my next client. Let's go and get some pumpkins and we can carve them later today."

"So pumpkins are authentic?"

"Yes," she said. "Samhain is a season of endings and preparing for rebirth. Some endings include death and spirits. Carving pumpkins is a ritual connected to them that goes way back."

"How do you know all this stuff?" he asked, impressed with her knowledge of something that he had only ever thought of as a chance to get candy since his mom didn't allow it the rest of the year.

"It's part of our family tradition. In our household it was bigger than Christmas," she said. "I bet your family did Christmas big."

"You'd be wrong. We do draft day big."

"Draft day?"

"Yes, that's the day when sports teams recruit players. It's sort of a big deal. My dad is a high school baseball coach so he's had a few students over the years go on to play for major league teams," Merle said.

His dad took draft day seriously. The other holidays? They were just days that his athletes weren't practicing and Merle's mom felt the same way. She was a tennis pro at the club near their house. She said the holidays made her students sloppy and it took her a few weeks to get them back to where they'd been.

"Well... I guess that's...that's weird, right? I mean, no judgment."

He arched one eyebrow at her.

"Okay, totally judging your fam. Do you think like that? I mean, you're in good shape, but you don't seem overly sporty to me."

He smiled at that. "I'm okay. I don't like sports, but I don't suck at them."

"I'm guessing that's a good thing given the family you've grown up in," she said.

"It isn't," he said as she led them to the local grocery store off the main street, a co-op supplied by local farms. They had a huge pumpkin patch outside the entrance that included bales of hay, cinnamon "witch" brooms, gourds and so many different varieties and sizes of pumpkins. Because of Birch Lake's past and history with witches, there were a lot of traditional Halloween—and Samhain, he assumed—items set out.

"Why not?"

"Because I have potential and don't live up to it. If there is one thing Coach hates, it's wasted talent," Merle said sarcastically, having heard countless lectures on that subject every year he could remember. It was the refrain of his life until he left home. Talent didn't mean dick to him. He wanted to pursue something that was for him, and not because his father's rotator cuff injury had kept him from playing baseball after college.

A part of him had always felt selfish for thinking that, but they already had his middle brother Manford, who played baseball in college and went on to become their assistant head coach. And, of course, Marcus could keep the Rutland baseball dream alive too. It had just never been his dream. And while he had a fast arm and could pitch, he'd hated every moment on the field.

There was so much pressure not to fuck up and ruin the game for the entire team. Merle could handle pressure and did all the time in his day job, but he was the only one who had deal with the screwups. He could fix code in no time at all. But if he missed a pop fly or got tagged out, there was no way to go back and undo it.

"Wow, really? Do you call your dad 'Coach'?" she asked.

"Yeah, when we were growing up everyone called him that. We had kids from the team over a lot," he said.

"That's…" She trailed off and shrugged.

"What?"

"I don't know. I was going to say odd, but I didn't have a

dad growing up so I have no way of knowing if that's normal or not," she said.

"It's not." He followed her through the pumpkin patch until she stooped next to a larger one and he did the same. Up close, he could smell her perfume and see the way those individual strands of her hair were made up of brown, gold and red. He almost reached out to touch her, but hesitated. One touch wouldn't be enough for him.

He wanted more from her. And he wasn't going to have it if he kept checking himself. He carefully took some of her multicolored strands in one hand, running them through his fingers.

She tipped her head back so she was staring up at him. Her lips parted and those bright gray eyes locked with his in a combination of dare and desire.

It was a challenge.

One he always backed down from...but not today. He shifted forward slightly, slowly, allowing her time to pull away or push him back before his lips touched hers. The corners of her lips turned up before they parted and her tongue brushed against his. She leaned slightly toward him, her hand resting on his thigh, her fingers gripping his arms as she used him for balance.

He deepened the kiss, a feeling of relief and white-hot heat coursing through him as he gave in to the urge to touch her. She tasted faintly of cinnamon and sage. God, he wanted her more than anything.

He tried to keep things light and keep it cool. Just a kiss. They were in the public pumpkin patch, so he had to keep his wits and only take this one kiss. Otherwise he'd be tempted to worship her on the bed of leaves and vines below them. But he couldn't help letting his lips fall to her shoulder and stroking her collarbone, innocently revealed by her scoop neck top. Her skin was soft and his fingers were calloused and sturdy from years of gaming and typing.

Their eyes met. He wanted to say something profound, but his mind was a messy jumble of heat and joy and an image of her naked in the pumpkin patch. He heard people coming toward them. Liberty just licked her lips and nodded.

"I think you should get this one," she said, patting the pumpkin.

He stood up and took her hand, drawing her to her feet, and her breasts brushed against his arm. *Just be cool, just be cool.* Which was almost fucking impossible as he felt himself harden in his jeans. Then she turned her hip, brushing against his crotch and she smirked over her shoulder at him as she felt his erection.

She was *teasing* him again.

And he wasn't at all upset by that.

There was something magical about pumpkins. Liberty had always thought that Disney had picked a pumpkin for Cinderella's coach deliberately. Pumpkins were used in spells to conjure protection, prosperity and abundance amongst other things. Merle was carrying a large pumpkin and she had two smaller ones that would make a nice cluster at his place. On the little front porch he had.

That kiss set fire to her. Maybe it was the thrill of being so close to the earth in that patch of pumpkins that made her feel that way. But there was something even more ancient and elemental that sparked inside of her when she touched Merle.

It was such a change from when he talked about his family. Her family inspired her passion and had really grounded her. She'd always known that she'd use the gifts that all Wakefield women inherited to help others. Purpose found her.

Now she wasn't sporty at all. Goddess knew she couldn't catch anything to save her life. But still, she wondered how growing up in a house where Merle didn't fit in had affected him.

She glanced over her shoulder and he met her gaze for a long minute. He was getting bolder. Which simply made her want to tease him more. Especially after she grazed his cock when she'd brushed against him. She remembered the way it had felt in her hand in the parking lot when she'd stroked him. What would it feel like to break this tension between them and feel him inside of her, indulging in every ounce of pleasure? Yet she also enjoyed the dance of being so close to him, of tasting him and touching him, keeping them both wanting.

Perhaps it was some latent restraint coming out to play. Or she was just scared to move forward with Merle, to plunge them both into uncharted territory, where she was at risk of getting her heart broken and losing her drive.

There was something more to Merle than just being this long, lanky guy with great hair who kissed her like he was ravenous. He only let her see what he wanted her to see. And didn't they all? But was he doing it because she was something mysterious for him? Something to play with until the shine wore off?

Was she doing that thing she always did, where she tried to find a flaw in a guy so she could walk away?

Probably.

She'd never realized how often she'd been aware of men dating her and hooking up with her because she was different. Or how much she craved feeling needed just for herself.

"Like what you see?" Merle asked when they got to his car and placed the pumpkins in the trunk.

"You know I do," she said, turning into his body since they were both standing so close. The trunk was open, blocking them from anyone who came around the back of the shop. He'd left his car behind WiCKed Sisters too. "I only have about five minutes before I have to get back to work."

He had one hand on the trunk lid as he leaned in, putting his other on her waist, guiding her more firmly into his body and bringing his mouth down on hers again. There was a solidness to Merle that she'd never noticed until she was held against him. He was a skilled kisser, his tongue easing into her mouth slowly, deliberately, and that banked fire that had been burning started to grow.

He tasted faintly of apples and smelled deliciously woodsy. There was a comfort in that as he drew her body closer to his.

His kiss was thorough, and she wanted him more than one kiss should make her want any man. But this was *Merle,* her good friend, her bestie's cousin, her coworker, and things were different with him. One wrong move and she could lose him.

His fingers traced a pattern against her waist, and her skin tingled through the fabric of her shirt.

She put her hand on his face and felt the stubble of his whiskers as she rubbed her fingers over it and sucked his tongue deeper into her mouth. She grazed the hard shaft pressing against the front of his jeans and felt her body practically clench and melt at the thought of taking him inside of her.

His hips rocked against her hand. Goddess, she wanted to put an end to the years-long foreplay that had dominated their relationship. Denying herself and running from the truth had to stop.

She tore her mouth from his and looked up at him. His eyes were half-lidded, his lips slightly wet from their kiss and his face was flushed.

"I…uh…"

"Come with me," she said, pulling him back from the car, closing the trunk and leading him to the back door of her part of the shop. She unlocked it and then opened the door before turning to him.

He licked his lips, following her with those hungry eyes. Enough time had passed. This slow dance they'd engaged in was coming to an end.

Samhain was working its magic, moving her from one season of her relationship with him and into the next.

She held her hand out and he threaded their fingers together, nodding as she stepped up into her shop with him closely behind her.

He closed the door and they were surrounded by the darkness of her back room. The scent of the candles and oils and the herbs she used to create her custom witchcraft materials surrounded them. But all she felt was the heat of Merle's body so close behind her. It was intense. The buildup of tension and desire emanating from him staggered her as she took a deep breath, inhaling his scent and all she wanted in this moment was him.

"Wait here. I have to let them know I'm back and can't be disturbed."

Merle surveyed Liberty's back room. It was one of the few places in WiCKed Sisters he hadn't been to before. Liberty guarded this place like it was her sanctuary. Poppy had mentioned that she liked to keep the vibe pure in here. And he wasn't sure what that meant, but as he looked around the room, he had to admit it felt like Liberty.

There were all the smells that he associated with her. Sage, rosemary, earthy tones of wood and wax. There were oils on the counter that she used to make her candles. He walked over to them, catching the scent of cinnamon and ginger—a warm autumn mix that she'd been wearing since the middle of September.

He took a deep breath, trying to concentrate on her space rather than on the fact that he was minutes away from having her naked in his arms. Thank god he had a condom—had been carrying one around since the other day after the visit to her Nan's. On the small chance he'd be adventurous.

But neither of them was ready for more than sex. They were still essentially friends.

"Back."

He turned as she closed the door that led to her shop and locked it. The bustle of energy and life that was always inside WiCKed Sisters disappeared. Leaving only the two of them.

He grinned.

"Disappointed."

"In?"

"I had hoped you'd be naked, lying on my meditation pillow, when I got back," she said.

He glanced down at the small square pillow. "How would I fit on that?"

"Fantasies don't deal in reality," she said.

"So you fantasize about me?" he asked as he toed off his shoes and started undoing the buttons of his shirt. Her wish was his command.

"I do," she said, sauntering toward him. He'd never really noticed it before but she practically glided across the room.

"Stop."

"Why?"

"I want to give you your fantasy."

She paused, nodded. "Go for it."

He shrugged out of his clothes, dropping them in a pile. He glanced at that magenta-colored meditation pillow and then back at her. But she was staring straight at his erection. Which got even harder as she watched him. He moved awkwardly at first, given he wasn't Magic Mike, but the appreciation in her eyes and the way she watched him slowly made that fade. He was so ready to see her naked, to have her back in his arms.

As he sat on the pillow, she licked her lips. Unsure what pose he should take, he leaned his arm on the pillow and bent one leg so he was reclining.

She watched him as if he was made purely to please her. He lifted his hand and beckoned her with the crook of his finger. But she didn't move. Instead she started removing her clothes. She undid her jeans and with a twist of her hips and shimmy of her legs, she let them fall to the floor before stepping out of them. Then she pulled her blouse up, revealing her skin. There it was. All of those gentle curves that made his fingers tremble with the need to touch her as he watched it fall, landing on top of her jeans.

She stood there in a lacy black bra and the smallest, tiniest panties. Her hips were full and curved, her waist defined, her stomach a slight bump. Everything about her was beyond reality. Her breasts were full and her nipples were pressing against the lace of her bra. His blood started racing through his body, and he felt his dick jump, wetness blooming from the tip.

He growled as she reached behind to undo her bra, her back arched. The dark pink of her nipples, then the small birth mark on her left breast, drew his eye. He stroked his finger over it and followed the red mark left by the band of her bra. And then she pushed her panties off before coming toward him. He could barely think. He wanted to get to his feet, but it was clear she was in charge here.

She came down on one knee in front of him, her hand moving to stroke his erection as he began to rub her nipples with his fingers. As she leaned forward, he felt the warmth of her breath against his cock as she licked the tip. He thrusted his hips forward, temporarily entering her hot, waiting mouth. Then he eased her away temporarily as he sat up and lifted her with him, pulling her lips to his. She straddled his waist, her moist pussy against his cock, shifting so that she was almost riding his shaft.

Lifting her breast, he took one nipple into his mouth, sucking deeply on her as his hands ran up and down her back, finding her ass cheeks, cupping them and drawing her forward. The scent of patchouli, cinnamon and rose was so much stronger here.

The brush of her hair against his arm as her head fell back was cool and soft. Balancing herself with one hand on his shoulder and the other between them, she let him maneuver his cock toward her center. The wetness of her against his bare skin rocked him to the core. The fire running through his veins was consuming him. Before he got too close to the edge, he tore his mouth away, reaching for the condom in his pants pocket.

He ripped it open and slid it on as she shifted. Liberty was already straddling him again as he positioned himself at her entrance. Their eyes met as she lowered herself on him. He couldn't breathe for a minute, not until he was fully buried in her.

That fire burned brighter and stronger.

For the first time in his life, he was out of control and he didn't give a fuck. His hands were on her hips, urging her to move and move faster. Driving her toward the center of the inferno so he wasn't alone. So that when they both came, they'd emerge from it together.

He lowered his head, wanting to taste her again, to draw her very essence into every fiber of his being. She rode him, but not fast. She took her time, as if this moment could last forever, but he felt that tingle down the back of his spine and his balls tighten. Dammit. He was going to come. He could try to delay it, but he was fucking Liberty Wakefield. His body didn't want to wait. Not when she was everything he fantasized about come to life.

At least he could bring her with him.

He reached between them, finding her clit and rubbing it as she kept rocking on him, taking him in and out of her slick body. He felt her start to tighten around him as she threw her head back, moving faster against him. The moans she made were getting quicker and faster.

He dug his fingers into her buttocks and pulled her hard against him as her pussy quaked around his cock. He grabbed her hips and drove himself into her harder and faster, coming on the second thrust as she let out a low moan. He kept stroking until he was empty and she collapsed against his shoulder. The heat of her breath tickled his neck and felt so right.

This wasn't something he could walk away from.

She wasn't.

And he was going to have to sort out a lot of other things in his life to have a chance of keeping this bold, ballsy woman.

Ten

Merle was in her most sacred place. This was where she let her hair down and didn't have to keep her guard up. What had she been thinking? Pussy still spasming, she realized she'd just had the most jaw-dropping sex with him here. If she needed further proof that she was in the middle of a maelstrom, this was it.

She protected this back room as if…it was her heart. This was the one place that she owned—she rented her apartment and her mom's house was her mom's space. This little room at WiCKed Sisters had been curated to bring together all the parts of herself. Here, she could let herself be free, even if she was alone.

And as she lay naked against Merle, his arms wrapped around her and his exhalation moving down her back, it felt… well, different. Changed.

As much as she was driven by the phases of the moon and by the cards she pulled from her tarot deck each day, she liked to plan.

Since the moment that Nan had muttered the name of her birth father, *nothing* had gone to plan.

Abso-fucking-lutely nothing.

But this might be the most off-course she'd ever been in her life. And the most excited.

"Stop overthinking this."

She tilted her head to the side and met his gaze. Those big chocolate eyes of his still seemed shielded to her.

She scrunched her face up and shook her head. "I'm not."

Yeah, that's it, Wakefield. Lie. Because that's always served you so damn well.

"You're digging your nails into my side," he said dryly.

Fuck. She let go and shifted back on his thighs so she wasn't crowding him. "Sorry."

"It's cool."

Except it wasn't. Merle was already making her behave differently, and this was one change she hadn't expected. She liked sex and had a lot of it over the years. But she didn't attach emotion to the act. It was like casting a spell or charging crystals. Just one more thing in her life that gave her pleasure.

So why was she sitting here trying to figure out what he was thinking? Why had she brought him in here? Why was she still sitting on his lap staring at him?

She put her hand on his shoulder and stood up. Time to take action. Merle rose next to her. The room smelled of sweat and patchouli. She was either going to have to burn sage and clear the energy from this room or confront the image of him sitting naked on her meditation pillow every time she came in here.

"The bathroom's back there," she said, pointing toward the

corner that shared a wall with Poppy's teashop and her back room. She'd just be cool, casual, chill.

Except when had she ever been chill about anything? She was used to emoting. To letting everything she felt come out and then dealing with the consequences.

Merle didn't move, as if he wanted to say something but hadn't worked up the courage. She almost felt more comfortable watching his awkwardness because that was the Merle she was used to dealing with.

She put her hands on her hips, her shoulders slightly back, and watched his eyes drop to her breasts.

Okay, it might not be the most feminist of ideas, but she could totally use her body to distract him until her mind figured out what to do next.

Merle shook his head. He stooped to pick up his T-shirt and handed it to her. "Put this on or I won't be able to think or talk."

"Is that a bad thing?" she asked, taking the T-shirt from him and pulling it over her head. It smelled of his cologne and wasn't even baggy on her.

He groaned.

"You look way better in that shirt than I do," he said. "Not sure this was a good idea."

She smiled then, because he sounded the exact way she felt at this moment—wanting to be sensible and make a plan, but still tingling from sex and craving him again.

"Glad you like it. I'm keeping this shirt," she said.

"What would you do if I said I'm keeping you?" he asked.

Blood rushed to her head, her pulse pounding loudly in her own ears. "You can't keep a person."

"I meant… I want to keep doing this."

"Sex?"

"Sex. And lunch and pumpkins," he said.

"You did ask me out on a date, and I said yes," she pointed out. Most men would assume she was the one who wanted more dates, that her desire to connect with them was a forgone conclusion. But Merle wasn't most men.

Clearly neither of them was good at dating. Somehow, she'd always assumed that, because he was Poppy's cousin and they had a big, seemingly close family, Merle would be more experienced.

"That's right, but how do I know you didn't just say yes because you wanted to keep things even between us?" he asked.

"Oh."

She'd forgotten she'd said that. Was that what this was? The moment he'd mentioned it, she'd felt vulnerable after the visit with Nan and the orgasm he'd given her. At this stage, maybe it would be better not to bring him in too deep.

"Nah, it's not that," she said. "I don't know *exactly* what it is, but not that. I'm still going to go on the date with you and all the other stuff we've been talking about."

He rubbed his hand over his chest. Drawing her eye to the light dusting of hair on his torso. Funny that she hadn't noticed it before in the heat of the moment. There was going to be more things about Merle that she missed too.

Discovering them would be very exciting.

"What is it?"

"Do you know?" she countered.

"Nope. In fact, dating you is going to be a first for me."

"I know you've had girlfriends before. You brought one

to the Not-Valentine's Party. But that's not me. We aren't official or anything yet."

"Cool."

His face didn't agree with his mouth. If there was ever a man who looked less than cool with it, it was Merle. As if he was just as uncomfortable as she was with labels.

Or was she projecting?

"You totally don't sound sincere," she said. "Lying Cat would be calling you out."

He shrugged. "You're not wrong. I've never dated someone who knew my family."

"And that's a problem?"

"Poppy will be hurt if we hurt each other," he said.

"Yes, she will. But think of how happy she'll be if we don't," Liberty said. She wasn't a pessimistic person by nature. She considered herself a realist, but she secretly leaned toward optimism. As her mom always said, why start something you assume is going to fail?

As usual, Liberty kept him off balance, and there was a part of him that wasn't sure he could trust it. He had used Poppy as an excuse. The truth was, his cousin was the easiest piece of this puzzle. She had her own issues with relationships and would never hold it against him or Liberty if they dated and it went nowhere.

So why was he over here giving Liberty half-truths?

Because he could be a fucking wuss when it came to people who mattered to him. He didn't want to lose. Ironic.

Her friendship was something he was coming to count on. Liberty gave him space to be himself. Never judging.

If things didn't work out, they'd probably get over it. He was doing her a favor, and she'd be in his life forever regardless because she and Poppy weren't going to fall out over anything.

Really, he was evasive just for himself. Because if they got together and didn't work out, he'd be devastated. Another failure when he never had a steady relationship unlike his brothers.

That was it.

If he meant what he said earlier, he had to man the fuck up.

Dammit, he'd never sounded more like Coach.

"It's not Poppy," he said.

"Then what is it?"

"My family. I like you, and if we date, Poppy will mention it to her mom, and then my mom will know."

She shook her head as she walked over to him and punched him in the shoulder. A solid punch. Was there anything she couldn't do? "Are you embarrassed by me?"

"No. I'm embarrassed by me," he said, rubbing his shoulder and then looking around for his underwear, because this conversation was hard enough without being stark naked.

He found them, then realized he was still wearing the condom and shook his head. "Give me a minute."

Merle stalked to the bathroom, got rid of the condom and washed himself before putting on his boxer briefs and going back out to Liberty. She'd pulled on her jeans, still wearing his Vox Machina T-shirt.

He slowly pulled up the fly of his jeans, as if by drawing it out Liberty was going to pretend she hadn't heard what he said and stop waiting for him to explain.

Of course, since this was the real world, that's not what happened.

"Merle."

Just the sound of his name and he felt a grin tug at the corner of his mouth, despite the fact that this was one of the hardest things he was ever going to have to say. She just wasn't budging.

"Okay. Well the thing is, I'm not like this with my family."

"Is this the haircut thing again?" she asked.

He shook his head. "It's an everything-about-me thing. I have to be a certain way when I'm home. So normally when I date, it's local girls, and it's not serious. I never talk about it with my family."

"Okay. So…that's a couple of things to unpack, but firstly, you're serious about me?"

Of course she'd go for that.

"Yeah. You have to know I've wanted you since the first moment I met you. And you push and tease me and keep me completely off balance…so yeah, I think this is serious. That's exactly why I don't want to move too fast. If I share you with my family, then I have to share who I really am and…things could get rough. I don't want you to be a part of that blowup," he said.

That was the thing about being vulnerable. He didn't want to be alone in this. If she wasn't serious, then he'd still hook up with her when she wanted—their connection was too good to deny it—but he'd have to try to stop himself from caring any deeper for her.

Easier thought than done.

But there it was.

She tipped her head to the side and he noticed some stubble burn on her neck. He hardened a little bit at the thought
of kissing her again. Even though he'd been preaching about
going slow, that might not be possible. He'd left a temporary
mark on her, and he wanted to do more than that. To claim
her. To tell the world that this vibrant, charming, strong
woman was his.

"I'm not sure," she said. "I mean you're probably right, but
at this moment, everything I've ever known or believed about
myself seems to be in flux. My magic is wonky, I'm lying to
my mom and afraid for Nan. I've always said I never wanted
to know the cocksucker who was her sperm donor, but at the
same time, I have his name and I'm anxious for you to find
him…and then there's you."

Then there was him.

"And?"

He searched for a calm he wasn't feeling. He had a lifetime
of hiding his emotions from his parents, and he hoped that
he was able to do that here with Liberty. That she'd think he
was going to be okay whatever her answer was.

But it was obvious she wasn't buying it.

Because—and this was more comforting than he'd
expected—Liberty was actually looking at him and saw him.

Could that be answer enough for right now?

"And… I don't know. I like you. I brought you back here
into the one place that's most *me*," Liberty said, gesturing
around. "Of course my explanation is all about me too, right?"

Shaking her head, she closed her eyes. Why was it always
easier to admit to the vulnerable stuff that way? "I'm scared,

Merle. So much is happening in my life and I don't handle change well. I can't be anything other than who I am, but I'm not always nice and the situation with Nan and now my dad is really testing my limits.

"I don't want you to see the real me and decide I'm not what you expected," she admitted.

"You're always more than I'm anticipating, and I have never been disappointed by that. I get it though. Life would be easier if this was just about hot hookups."

That sweetness that was at Merle's core made her smile, his words wrapping around her like a warm breeze in summer.

She took another deep breath, not allowing herself to delve too deeply into that comfort. He said he wanted the truth and could handle it. "I like you, but I'm not sure if I'm using you like the rituals I usually do to keep normal. Instead of drawing a card, I'm texting you. Instead of thinking about the next moon phase and asking for guidance, I'm falling into your arms. What if I'm just using you?"

Her words sounded harsher than she'd intended, but there was no use in lying. The fact was, as much as she wanted to own her feelings and live in the moment, right now she couldn't.

The past was dominating every action and inaction. And that really pissed her off. Why should a man who had abandoned her and her mom get any of her thoughts? He'd changed her behaviors and her belief in herself.

It was hard for her to face, but there was no way to hide from it.

Merle nodded in that contemplative way of his and then stepped closer to her, pulling her into his arms against his bare chest. Her cheek rested on his skin. The scent of his cologne was much stronger here, subtly mixing with his natural smell, and she closed her eyes, trying to identify the individual notes to distract her body.

She wanted him again.

Wanted to push him back down on the meditation pillow, maybe light a sensual candle that she sold in the shop and get naked. Except more sex would be a distraction from what they needed to say to each other.

"I can handle that. Thanks for the honesty," he said.

"Yeah, I'm not ever going to lie to you," she replied. She stopped herself from saying that she didn't lie at all, knowing that she was keeping the truth from her mom at this moment. "I do want to date you, but take things slow."

"Good. Me too," he said.

"So about your family…"

Yeah, change the subject, Wakefield. That's the way to get out of her own head. Put the ball back into his court.

"My family." He sighed. "Well, I guess I'm not one hundred percent sure it will be an issue."

"Why not? Birch Lake is a small town and Poppy will notice we're dating. Unless you were suggesting we keep this from her?"

He stepped back. "No. I'm just pumping the brakes. My immediate family is complicated. Poppy can keep a secret. And until you know if I'm just a fun distraction from your problems or something more, I'm going to let things ride with them."

She wrapped her arms around her waist to keep from punching him again. "Are you that wishy-washy about me?"

"No, I'm not. But if you're not sure, then I just want to wait until you are," he said.

"What if I never am? This thing with your family shouldn't be a change you make for me or any other woman," she said. "If you're someone else around your family and you don't like it, then you need to change for you, dude."

Dude. Goddess knew that wasn't what she normally would have said to him, but he was right. Until she could determine if this was real or just a distraction, it would be wise to be cautious.

She heard faint laughter in her mind and shook her head. Even the goddess couldn't let her live that one down.

Yeah, cautious and her didn't really go together.

But this was Merle.

She truly liked him and cared about him. She didn't want to hurt him just because she needed someone to make her forget her problems.

"You're right, but I don't know how to do it," he said, lifting his hand and scrubbing it through his hair.

"Break it down for me," she said.

"It's going to take longer than you have," he said.

"You're running away," she pointed out. Though he was right. In about ten minutes, her assistant was going to knock on the door. Liberty needed to prep for her next tarot reading and she had two regulars who were coming by for their autumn rituals box later that afternoon.

"Maybe I am," he said.

"Okay, for now. I'm not going to drop it," she warned him.

"As if I don't know you at all," he said back. "What the hell am I going to wear out of here anyway?"

"Hold on," she said with a giggle, then went over to the boxes of new merchandise that she'd ordered for the shop. There were some tees and she found a purple one in his size. She tossed it to him.

He looked down at the WiCKed Sisters logo and slogan emblazoned on the front of it.

It's Time To Be WiCKed.

"Nice," he said. "I was hoping for one that said I've been confluenced."

She flushed as he pulled it over his head. "Why?"

"Oh, I know you keep saying you want to confluence with me." He paused, a mischievous look on his face. "Was it everything you thought it would be?"

And more.

"I thought for a dungeon master there'd be more kink, but otherwise yeah, it was good."

"You want kink?" he asked. "My dungeon does have a few tricks and toys in it."

She couldn't tell if he was joking or not. Or if she even wanted him to be joking. But she was already thinking about Merle putting her in handcuffs and ordering her around in his dungeon. She kind of liked it.

Her nipples hardened against the T-shirt. She had to get her head back into work before they started this cycle all over again. Soon.

Walking over to him, she went on tiptoe and bit the lobe of his left ear. "Maybe I'll let you take me there."

She kissed the side of his neck and then stepped back. "But for now I have to get back to work. Later, Merle."

He leaned in close, the heat of his breath sending shivers

through her, and whispered, "When I get you in my dungeon, you're not going to want to leave."

He dropped a quick kiss on her lips and then winked at her before he stepped out the back door of her shop.

Eleven

As the shop closed that night at six, Poppy and Sera lingered by the front door. Liberty glanced over at them. Something was up.

"What?"

"Did Merle find your dad?" Poppy asked. "We wanted to ask you all afternoon but we've been so busy."

"It's so mad," Sera said. "I'm trying to keep up with making the grimoire covers you suggested but they're flying off the shelves. Wes found me a printer who did a sample print run and I'm going to check it out tonight. If they're good quality, I'll order a batch for our Samhain event."

Liberty forgot that she told them about her dad. She'd almost been afraid they knew she'd had hot, rocking sex in the back room. Which was silly when they'd definitely cheer her on for it. But no, they wanted to talk about her dad.

She really was detached from her normal. This was something they routinely did. Catch up with each other and offer support in hard times. She glanced over at the large table at the front area of Poppy's tea shop and saw that it was set with three cups. She took a deep breath.

It was as if by learning her father's name, she'd lost who she was. Lost where she belonged in this world. In her world. Today was her day for lots of realizations, but she had no idea how to push herself back to where she'd been now that she'd cracked herself open.

She glanced down at her watch. Two hours until she had to be at Merle's for D&D. It was time to renew her ties with Poppy and Sera.

"Tea and talk?"

"Yes. You've been so…not yourself lately," Poppy said carefully.

"We were planning an intervention if you tried to flake on us again," Sera said.

"I'm sorry, girls. I just—this thing with my dad has me flustered. And with each step I take to figure out what's next I just keeping getting blocked, and then I get back up and try something else," Liberty said as she followed them over to the table.

They sat down and Poppy muttered a few words under her breath that she'd learned from her grandmother, her own little spell. Then she poured each of them a cup of tea.

Steam rose from the fine bone china cup. Liberty put her hands around it, absorbing the warmth as she inhaled the fragrance. It was Poppy's autumn blend and smelled of pumpkins and nutmeg. She took a deep breath and some of the tension in her soul dissipated.

She'd needed this.

She'd been so afraid of hurting anyone with her anger that she'd been keeping those she loved at a distance. Maybe because she was lying to her mom, she was trying to punish herself.

"Maybe the universe is telling you to let it go," Sera said.

"Probably, but I hate being told what to do," Liberty reminded her.

They all laughed. "There are times when you have to adult it, you know. Ask the tough questions and be honest with your answers."

Again, Sera came in clutch with the advice that she needed to hear. Not that Liberty wanted to. But Sera was making a lot of sense.

"What questions? Because right now all I've got for sure is, who the fuck is the man who knocked my mom up?" Liberty said.

Poppy and Sera exchanged concerned looks and her stomach sank. This was an intervention. Her friends had been talking behind her back. For a second, she was mad. But then when they both looked back at her with those gentle smiles and love in their eyes, she let out the breath she hadn't realized she'd been holding.

These two women were sisters she trusted to be honest, steadfast and have her back always.

Sera chewed her lower lip for a minute. Liberty's friend had a hard time being tough with people who mattered to her. After growing up in the foster care system, Sera was used to people leaving and had developed a habit of saying the right things to make them stay.

"Firstly, why aren't you telling your mom? The fact that you've kept this from her makes no sense."

"I know. I almost told her last night, but she didn't come home until late and then this morning… I just couldn't."

Poppy reached over and put her hand on Liberty's, stopping her before she took her first sip. "Why is that? Ask that as you drink."

Poppy was going to read the tea leaves in the bottom of Liberty's cup when she was done. For the first time since she'd done that ritual in her apartment and felt her magic swirling out of control, a part of her relaxed.

She had been denying herself one of her greatest strengths. This friendship with these two women. Not only had she cut herself off from her mom, but her grandmother wasn't reliable anymore as reality shifted around Nan and her mind played tricks on her. Liberty had always found her strength from the feminine bond and she'd let that wane.

She closed her eyes, so many thoughts jumbling in her mind, trying to find the thread that connected them all. Why was she afraid to let the women in her life come on this journey to find her father?

Why was she determined to do it alone?

She had never been alone. Not one moment in her life. She'd been surrounded by love and magic from her earliest memory. Liberty even found Poppy and Sera when she'd left to go to college, creating a new threesome in her life of chosen family. They had always supported her. And yet she'd given them only the barest parts of the truth as she tried to figure out why hearing her father's real name at this point in her life was throwing her into a tailspin.

She wasn't sure, but she needed answers. To stop hiding from her friends and her mom. To stop fearing whatever it was that they would say to her.

Was that what was keeping her silent? Was she afraid that her friends would tell her something that made this all go up in flames?

"Dude, you invited another player? The party's getting kind of big," Darren said as he arrived at Merle's.

They'd been roommates in college and had stayed close. Darren lived in Bangor and usually drove over early. They usually had dinner and beers before they played D&D with the rest of their friend group.

Darren hadn't played D&D before college but joined when Merle started this local group. Darren ran a small sporting goods store in Bangor that had been in his family for generations.

"It's Liberty."

"Liberty Wakefield…interesting."

Darren knew that Merle had been into her for a while. He was one of the few people that Merle trusted and the two of them talked about everything. Darren's family relationships were complicated too, so he understood things other people just didn't.

"That's one word for it," Merle said. He hadn't really had time to process everything that happened today. But that was the effect that Liberty had always had on him.

He wasn't ready to discuss it with Darren, so he wanted to change the subject, but since Liberty was new to the group he had a feeling everyone was going to be asking about her.

Merle really should figure out what he was going to say about it. They weren't dating exactly, just…sort-of-dating.

Darren laughed and patted him on the back. "I picked up a pizza in town. Let's go out back and eat it before it gets too cold."

Merle grabbed two cans of Guinness from the fridge and led the way. His house was a work in progress, but his backyard was finished. He'd put in a seating area, a grill and a large table where they'd played D&D all summer. Darren sat down and took a slice after Merle handed him a beer.

"So, Liberty?" Darren said.

"She asked me for a favor, and since Mandi can't play because of baby Grace, I figured we could use a sixth player who was here for the campaign. In exchange for my help with her project, Liberty's filling in for Mandi. She's only going to play for six sessions," Merle said. Somehow after all she'd said to him in her back room this afternoon. Six sessions—one session per week that lasted three to four hours—seemed way too short an amount of time.

He wasn't sure she'd figure out what was going on with her dad in that time. This might be a longer journey for her. He wondered where he fit into that path or if there was room for him.

He was bringing her into his life and opening up more to her than any other woman and she was…hesitating.

Then again, so was he. In that way they were already a perfect match.

"Sounds reasonable. And the others are totally going to buy that," Darren said.

"But not you?"

"I know you too well. This is Liberty, who you've been into since Poppy introduced you to each other. She's like the one person I've seen rattle you. I can't wait to meet her."

This could be awkward. He wasn't used to having people from the different segments of his life cross over. Darren had heard him talk about his cousin and her shop but he'd never been to it, and they'd never met.

There was potential crossover between the D&D crowd and the witchy crew. But after a lifetime of having to keep his lives separate, it was his default to separate, to protect himself from the worst.

As Darren started talking about their last campaign and things he was going to do differently this time, Merle sat with the fact that he'd never faced those anxieties and kept all of that behind when he'd left home.

Well, fuck.

Had it just been an impulse to bring Liberty into this part of his life? In reality, he was still more comfortable showing people what they expected him to be.

Brutal as it was, he fit himself into what the different parts of his life needed. Keeping each part separate might have started in high school, but it had become a habit, the way he'd structured his world.

Even Darren. They bonded over drunk nights in college and then the long walks they'd taken to sober up and get over their hangovers. Both of them had felt like misfits in different ways. There was no one who knew him better. And Merle had kept him tucked away from his family.

Even Poppy.

Frankly, there wasn't a good reason for that other than habit and fear. Liberty meeting his family would be like letting a genie out of its bottle, and there would be no going back.

But what fear could he still be carrying out here in Birch Lake, where he felt the most at home?

Perhaps he didn't feel at home anywhere.

He didn't trust people to like him when he was himself, when he wasn't being the man they'd come to know. The man that Liberty knew was one degree away from how he felt inside. Still a fumbling nerd—that was never going to change—but more comfortable in his own skin, less frantic about hiding his interests.

It scared him to imagine anyone seeing all of him, even the disappointing pieces. But hearing Liberty say that she wasn't confident that he'd like her true self made him want to try. To prove both of them wrong.

"Merle? You okay?"

He shrugged. "This is the first time I'm letting two people from different parts of my life meet."

"I noticed you tend to keep college and D&D friends away from Work Merle and Family Merle," Darren said, giving him a sly smile. "But it's cool. I'm looking forward to seeing you with the one woman you've mentioned to me."

Merle shook his head. "I didn't mean to do that—keep you separate."

"I know. Your family fucked with your head. Luckily mine is just a hodgepodge of weirdos," Darren said.

Darren's family were all very different and yet they all accepted each other. It was one of the many things that Merle envied about his friend.

"Thanks," he said.

★ ★ ★

Poppy saw a boat anchor in her teacup after Liberty had finished, which meant to slow down.

It was not the time for action, according to yet another magical sign.

Well the universe was doing a good job of keeping her in this holding position. The anchor appeared in sector two—the teacup had three sectors when you looked at the bottom of it, and the leaves tended to cluster and take different shapes in the three different areas.

At first, Liberty wanted to argue that maybe it wasn't an anchor, but it was clear. Sector one was an arrow. Fast paced and frustrating times. That certainly didn't help.

Sera suggested, and Liberty agreed with her, that the fast pace and frustration was all coming from her. That she was trying to force this knowledge of her father to appear right away when she really needed time to adapt to it. Time for the goddess and the universe to figure out what was next for her.

Finally, in sector three was the candle. That represented help arriving from friends when one didn't know what to do. Fitting since she'd been also thinking about how grateful she was for her friends when she'd finished her tea.

"I'm not sure what's next," she said.

"Tell your mom," Sera said.

"I agree. It's eating you up keeping it from her. Whatever she says to you about this, it can't be worse than whatever you've made up in your head," Poppy said. "Believe me, I know. When I told my mom I was getting a divorce, I thought she'd be all 'told you so,' but she didn't."

"Of course she didn't. She might have looked at you all

judgy," Liberty said. But she was mostly joking. Poppy's mom was very aware of her place in society and what her friends would think, but she was always there for Poppy.

"Yeah, I know. But she just nodded. She told me that I lived in Poppy's World and saw everyone else as their most...idealized self. She was glad I'd woken up," Poppy said. "Which immediately made me wonder if I'd made the wrong choice."

"You didn't make the wrong choice. We all thought it was good that you divorced him too," Sera said. "He led you on. You know that. I don't care what your mom said about Poppy's World. Alistair played on that and romanced you for a tea recipe. What a dick. If you'd let me give him that spell—"

"No. I agree it's good I divorced him. Especially since everything with Amber Rapp put us in the spotlight," Poppy said.

"Now he's trying to weasel his way back into your life because everyone wants your tea," Liberty said.

"It's more than that. We've been chatting in my online tea society and things are...amiable."

"I do need to tell Mom. I hate keeping this from her. I can't talk to her about anything because all I can think is that I know his name and how hurt she'll be that I didn't come to her earlier," Liberty admitted.

"Yeah, I bet it's hard," Poppy said. "Just do it."

"We'll come with you if you want, but you and your mom might need to discuss him by yourselves," Sera said. "I'm the least experienced with parent stuff, so whatever you want."

"Thanks, but I do think you're right. Mom and I need to talk. I'll do it tomorrow," Liberty said.

"Why not tonight?"

"I'm playing D&D with Merle and his group. And I don't want to miss it," she said.

Poppy gave her a cheeky grin. Sera laughed. "I'm happy to hear that. So…?"

"So that's it. We are going to go on a date this weekend. And we hooked up."

"Yay. It's about time," Sera said. "I like you two together."

Liberty did too. But with the recent massive sign from the goddess that she still wasn't herself, and her own doubts, she wasn't sure she should be starting anything with him. Because she did like him. She didn't want to hurt him.

When she was at her most unpredictable, it was a dangerous time emotionally.

But for tonight, she wanted to pretend she was her old self and just enjoy flirting with Merle. The uncertainty of how she was going to navigate a relationship with him alongside Nan's deterioration and finding out more about her father was a big ask. She wanted tonight for herself.

She was curious about this other part of his life too. He talked about D&D a lot in the shop because he was always getting books from Sera or asking Liberty about which crystals were best for healing and other properties—all in the name of whatever campaign he was designing. And she'd been intrigued. Well, if she was honest, she'd been more intrigued the first time she'd seen his butt in those jeans he habitually wore. But his interest in the arcane teased her. Made her wonder if he could understand her.

There was so much about Merle that drew her in and she'd been smart to keep him at arm's length, because if their encounter in the back room had shown her anything, it was that once she'd let him close it was hard to push him back out.

She'd spent the afternoon feeling as if he were still with her. Maybe it was the lingering scent of his cologne on her skin or the slight tingling that spread on her lips and throughout her body. But as much as it scared her…she'd enjoyed it.

Enjoyed how he helped her calm her frustration and how he showed her that maybe the past wasn't where she needed to be looking for answers to the questions she had about herself.

Maybe she needed to be present. With him. And that was more than she knew how to handle at this moment.

Twelve

Darren and the others played D&D like a sport. They had their own kits with them that included notebooks, dice and tablets for online resources. Sometimes Merle used a tool from a D&D website called Roll20 to set up their sessions, especially when they were all playing online. Because this was Liberty's first time playing with the group, he set up a small session starting in a tavern so she could be introduced, and so his regular players could get used to their new characters as well.

With each new campaign, everyone made new characters. For this first session, Merle started the story with each of the characters reading a sign seeking participants who were interested in helping to find an ancient treasure.

Each session Merle wrote with a clear objective to move the story along. But in D&D, nothing was set in stone. Players made choices for their characters, at times pushing the narrative in a different direction. For tonight, he wanted Liberty to have a chance to learn to play the game and experiment with her character's strengths.

But it was only the first part of a journey that they would continue over the next five sessions.

Liberty looked gorgeous tonight and Merle struggled to keep his attention on the game. He wished he'd taken more time when she was naked in his arms earlier. She wore a scoop neck top and a long flowing skirt with her hair loosely hanging around her shoulders. He could tell she'd taken time to get ready to meet them because she had put on black eyeliner and the deep red lipstick she wore when she was going out.

It made it almost impossible for him not to keep staring at her mouth as she chewed her lower lip and read the character sheet in front of her. But as more of his friends arrived, he had to start making introductions.

Liv and Johnny came together. They were both local to Birch Lake. Liv's new character, Brilla, was a dwarf cleric. Clerics were crucial because they could heal others. When their group went on a new campaign because Darren always rushed into combat without thinking and took massive injuries.

Johnny created a sorcerer named Sylnan who was half human, half elf. He'd been born with his magical powers but cast out from his family because he was only a half-elf. The different types of characters gave players a chance to explore surprisingly emotional backstories.

Darren was a barbarian goliath named Kravoi whose main skill was killing and crushing things. He had a lot of strength and could "rage," which meant he went into a berserker killing phase—he usually used it when they got backed into a corner. It could only be activated once at the start and it took all of his energy, but as Darren leveled Kravoi up, he'd get more rages.

Then there was Misha who lived in Bangor and was zooming in for the session. Misha's character was a dwarf bard named Runselle who used the lute to cast spells and enchant people.

Liberty was playing as Jocaryn and she had chosen to be a wood elf druid, leaning into nature spell-casting powers. No surprise really since she'd picked something that suited who she was in real life.

"Why did you pick a druid?" Misha asked. "I was one last time and loved having their powers."

"I figured since I'm a witch in real life it might be easier for me to figure her out. But when Merle told me about the fantastical things I'd be able to do, I wasn't sure that was the case."

Since Merle had been playing with Darren for about ten years now, he had to regularly change his style to keep things fresh as the dungeon master. Darren always put in something unpredictable to surprise him, like a spell where he could conjure animals. During a battle with a troll, Darren even kept conjuring eight of any animal the rules allowed.

"Wow, this is impressive, I know I've been teasing you about your dungeon, but I had no idea you had… What is this table, exactly? It looks like something from a medieval feasting hall," Liberty said, leaving his living room and moving into his dining room, grazing her hand over the polished tabletop.

"It is," Darren said. "We built it last summer. He got the plans from some dude in the UK who makes furniture replicas."

"Nice," Liberty said, uncertainty in her eyes.

All of the regulars took their seats while Liberty looked at him. He gestured to the seat between himself and Darren. Everyone was getting their stuff out including the boxes they used when they rolled all of the dice. He handed Liberty an embroidered velvet pouch he'd bought on Etsy for her with a set of dice inside. He knew she wouldn't have her own dice yet. The pouch was big enough to hold her notebook, dice bag and a pen.

"Thanks," she said as she sat down. After a moment she looked over at him again and mouthed "What do I do?"

Even though Liberty had been emotional lately, she'd never seemed so lost. He smiled reassuringly at her. He wouldn't let her fail at this.

"Keep out your character sheet that you printed off from D&D Beyond. You can reference it while we're playing. Then get your dice out. We'll all roll as we start to play," Merle said.

She did as he said and he shifted back into his chair, a large wooden one designed like a throne. He was nervous for Liberty to see him tonight—not scared per se, but he wanted to impress her. Wanted her to really see him and what he was passionate about.

Then again, maybe she would see him for the giant dork he was and she wouldn't like what she saw, which he hoped wouldn't happen.

But the truth was that he couldn't hide from her anymore. He wanted her to know every part of his life even though it scared him to be crossing these lines together.

Darren helped her get ready for her first roll as Merle took a deep breath, ready to DM. As soon as Misha was ready on Zoom and the others looked at him expectantly, it was time to begin. He had an LG TV mounted on one of the walls that he used for the zoom sessions. He'd built a model of the tavern that was placed in front of him so he could move things around during the game. He slipped into his deep narrator voice, commanding the attention of the group.

"Welcome to the Broken Axe Tavern. It's a late summer evening. Samhain is upon us. The changing of the seasons is stirring something in the mountains and bringing a strange vibe to the place tonight. Misha, you're already in the tavern, introduce yourself and describe your character, and then tell us what are you doing?"

She described her half-orc bard as having gorgeous green skin, long red hair that matched her braided beard. "Probably entertaining the locals. I am singing a song of seduction, trying to score with whoever is there. Who do I see?"

Adrenaline rushed through him. After weeks of planning and preparation, he looked forward to seeing everyone's reaction to the battles he had designed.

"There's a few people around, two humans and a dwarf. You can roll a performance check to see if they're interested."

"Oh, they'll be interested," Misha said.

"Are they though?" Liv asked.

"Roll to check and see how it's going," Merle said. Relaxing into his DM role and letting the energy of his friends guide him into the scene, focusing on being in the world where he felt the most at home, he stopped trying to impress Liberty and just played.

Liberty wasn't sure what she'd expected the game to be, but it was way more fun than anything she'd imagined. She loved seeing this new side to Merle. His friend group wasn't what she'd expected either.

There was a lot more to Merle than met the eye. His friends

were clever and funny—totally expected because of what she knew about Merle. But there was a level of bawdiness that she hadn't anticipated. Merle was also pretty quick-witted. He was always so chill in WiCKed Sisters that she'd pictured him as a shy guy, but here, with this group, he was relaxed with a self-deprecating sense of humor that kept everyone laughing.

She'd learned quickly that no one took themselves too seriously, but they also played the game with heart. She loved the vibe in the room.

Merle was...amazing as the dungeon master. She hadn't realized how talented he was with storytelling and doing different voices. Being new, she quickly noticed that the campaign he had them on tonight—defeating an unknown menace outside the tavern—had been designed for her to test out and try different skills with her character.

The tasks were probably easy for most of the other players, but they were all really good at helping her out. When she wasn't sure what to do, the others would all make suggestions. They often positioned their characters in a way that gave her chances to try different spells and moves.

She forgot about all of the worries she'd been carrying around since she'd learned the sperm donor's name. This was the first time she felt light in the longest time. She felt like that was a little bit unfair to Sera and Poppy's moments of support, but they were both too connected to her to give her a chance to relax and just be fun. Until her chaos magic was tamed, her friends were feeling the vibes she put out in the universe and right now they were straight up wild. But tonight with this group of strangers, she let herself sink into being Jocaryn.

Merle's deep voice wove the story around them. These strangers were becoming her friends.

Now that a troll was attacking the tavern, the group all took turns working together to defeat him.

"Roll to hit," Merle said.

There were seven dice in the bag that Merle gave her. But they mainly used the d20 for most of the encounters, which was a twenty-sided die. She took it and threw it on the table. It rolled and landed on five and everyone groaned.

"Is that good?"

"Not really," Merle said. "You get distracted by Misha's song across the room as you cast your spell, and when you aim it, it hits the rafters behind the troll and splinters rain down, but you don't do any damage. The troll is straight up pissed now."

Merle rolled a sixteen when it was the troll's turn and the troll threw a large heavy bench at her. In her mind she could see the scene. Merle had a great attention to detail. The energy in the room was palpable.

"I tell Misha to stop trying to seduce the troll and get to helping me. Then I duck behind the table that Darren's barbarian knocked over for shelter and try to hide."

"Roll to see if you make it."

She rolled a pretty high number and the other members high-fived her. She made it behind the table and was safe until her next turn. The night progressed until the trolls were all defeated and the session ended. She was surprised to see that four hours had passed since they'd started playing.

"What'd you think?" Merle asked later, when everyone else was gone and it was just the two of them. They had moved from his dining room into the living room and he'd grabbed his laptop to check on the queries he was running about the different John Joneses.

"Honestly, it was way more fun than I'd expected," she said, curling her legs underneath her as she sat next to Merle on the couch.

His fingers were busy on the keyboard of his laptop and as she watched them, she shivered, remembering how they felt on her skin. She wanted him again. Hell, she had since the moment he'd left WiCKed Sisters that afternoon. She toyed with the hair at the back of his neck, twirling her fingers through it. It was soft and curly.

He looked at her. "I'm glad you had fun. And I want to check on the John Jones thing, but you're distracting me."

"Is that a bad thing?"

"Depends on how quickly you want to find John Jones."

She didn't stop touching him and shifted a little closer. John-fucking-Jones wasn't going to take this night away from her. She'd given that name too much power since the moment she'd learned it. There was a part of her that wished it had never happened. But until she talked to her mom, until she learned the truth, she could lose herself in this.

Merle closed his laptop and set it aside, half turning toward her. He slid his arm along the back of the couch, his hand falling to her shoulder. Those long fingers of his moved idly against the skin exposed by the neck of her blouse.

"I just realized why my magic and my life has been so fucked."

He raised one eyebrow. "Are you seducing me or are we talking?"

"What? Like I can't do both," she said, as she straddled his lap and sat back on his thighs.

"You might be able to, but I'm not sure I can," he said.

She smiled and tilted forward, putting her hands on his shoulders and leaning down very slowly until their foreheads touched. "Aw, are you that kind of guy?"

"The kind who gets distracted by a sexy woman sitting on his lap? One hundred percent," he said.

She laughed and then kissed him. She meant for it to be light and quick, but as soon as their lips met, his parted hers and she came undone. There was no controlling herself. He tasted good. He felt good. He *was* good. That was something she'd never found in her previous encounters with men. Merle was a decent person.

And unlike the few men she'd allowed into her life, she was almost convinced she could trust him. For her that was a lot.

Liberty was unpredictable tonight. To be honest, it was the first time since she'd sat down across from him in the tavern that fateful day that he'd caught a glimpse of this confident impulsivity. This was the woman who'd been tormenting him for more than a year and he hadn't realized how much he'd missed her.

How much of this reaction was simply due to him no longer hiding a part of himself from her? And how much was the fact that the harder she tried to find her biological father, the less progress she made?

He wanted it to be because of him.

He wanted to be enough for her.

It was funny. Once he'd seen a therapist in college after

he'd started drinking too much for one semester. His dad had arranged a tryout for him on the baseball team, and his mom had guilted him into going, telling him it would make up for a huge physical fight he'd had with the old man in high school.

Like he'd told Liberty, he wasn't *bad* at sports. He was actually pretty good, and his school was a Division Three so he didn't need to be major-league ready anyway. The college coach had offered him a spot on the team and...he took it. Thought maybe this was his chance to fit in.

But he'd been miserable and the drinking had led to him being cut. When Coach found out, he was disgusted and said he shouldn't have expected anything else.

Merle's therapist later told him that he had to be enough for himself and stop trying to live up to his family's expectations.

Was he doing that with Liberty?

But she was the one kissing him. Her hands were in his hair while she was on his lap, which made it hard for him to concentrate on anything other than how to get his pants open and her skirt up.

She shifted back on his lap as if reading his mind, her hands going to the buttons on his jeans. He rested his hands over hers. "I don't have a condom out here. Let me go and get one."

She shimmied off his lap, brushing every part of his body with hers until she was standing next to him. Everything felt like it was on fire—a raging inferno. She lifted her skirt and pulled her panties down, then stepped out of them while she wriggled her eyebrows at him. Only Liberty could make a wriggle erotic and sexy. "Hurry."

He was on his feet instantly and dashed for the bathroom, before fumbling for the drawer where he kept the box of condoms and taking one out. He glanced in the mirror. This was literally the most sex he'd had in more than a year. Twice in one day.

He just grinned at himself as he headed back into the living room. Liberty was kneeling on the couch, and she'd dimmed the lights so that just one lamp on the end table was still on; she sat in the glow of that warm light looking ethereal.

He couldn't take another step. She had her eyes closed and her arms were spread out, reminding him of that famous Italian portrait of Venus rising from the sea. She was chanting something; it was low, and her voice was husky. The melody was soft, seductive.

His dick hardened even more if that was possible. He should have shucked off his jeans when he'd had the chance, but now he was too focused on getting to Liberty to worry about paltry things like clothes. He half walked, half ran to the couch and sat down next to her, undoing his jeans and freeing his cock.

She opened her eyes.

Their gazes met and he couldn't help the wave of emotion that rolled through him in that moment. Yes, lust was a big part of what he felt for her. But damn if he didn't really like her more each day. The fantasy of a woman he'd only dreamed of touching like this was coming true.

She licked her lips.

"Get what you needed?"

"Not yet," he said, putting the condom to the side where he could easily grab it before lifting her onto his lap. She smiled as she shifted her hips against his shaft, sending shockwaves through his body. She was wet and ready for him. But he wanted to take his time.

She put her arms around his neck, her hands in his hair again. He glanced down, realizing that she'd removed her bra from underneath her blouse. This woman was a genius. He gently cupped her breast, rubbing his forefinger over her nipple as it stiffened under his touch. She made a soft moaning noise in the back of her throat, then took off her top and tossed it aside.

He groaned as he massaged her breasts and leaned forward to bury his face in them. One of her hands gripped his hair while the other teased his cock as she moved the tip of his dick against her clit. She shifted on his lap rocking her hips against him.

He turned his head and took one of her nipples into his mouth, sucking on it as she kept rubbing herself against the tip of his cock. He felt his dick throb and knew he wasn't going to last much longer, so he had to make this count. He sucked harder on her nipple, releasing a guttural groan of pleasure from her sweet mouth. Liberty started to move more quickly against him and then threw her head back, letting out a long, low moan as she came. She collapsed against him for a minute.

He never wanted to let her go. She'd put some kind of spell on him and he didn't want her to stop.

Her breath was hot against his neck, fanning the flames pulsating through him. Her curves were lush and intoxicating as he rubbed his hands up and down her body.

"Merle, I want you inside of me."

Spoken right into his ear, making him harder. She let out a surprised laugh as he reached between them, trying to get the condom on quickly.

"I want to be there."

She was back on his lap in a tangle of limbs. He cupped her ass as she shifted around until he was poised against her entrance. He pulled her down and thrusted up, immediately feeling the heat of her against his dick, both of them too excited to hold back. He'd almost forgotten how tight she was as she took him all the way inside of her.

Merle didn't know how long he'd last now that he had her ass in his hands, his dick inside of her and his mouth full of the salty-sweet taste of her skin. God, there was something about Liberty that always went straight to his core.

Having her naked in his arms felt so right, like the one thing he didn't want to lose. He drove himself harder and faster into her as her nails dug into his shoulders. She whispered into his ear.

"Deeper."

He drove up into her until she tightened around his cock. His name was a long low groan followed by a whispered *"Now,"* as she came. The feeling of her orgasm was enough to send him flying. He drove into her a few more times before he came hard and fast.

She collapsed against him again and he held her as their breathing slowed. There was no going back to the way things used to be between them. He wasn't going to be able to settle for keeping her in one segment in his life, for just being friends with incredible benefits.

And if she wasn't ready for it, he'd be there for her anyway. He was already too entangled in Liberty to let go.

Thirteen

Merle's bed was huge, like king-size. He'd invited her to stay the night. Normally she wasn't a clinger—she always needed her space. But tonight she'd said yes. So Liberty sat across from him at the foot of the bed wearing one of his T-shirts and shuffling the tarot deck she always kept in her bag.

"Tell me again why you have so many baseball shirts if you hate the sport," she invited as she shuffled the cards. "It seems strange that you're keeping them."

She felt mellow, which wasn't usual these days. It seemed like, for the first time in a very long time since Nan had gotten sick, the energy of the goddess was flowing through her and around her. She'd felt out of the flow for too long.

There were times when it seemed she hardly knew anything about Merle. Like all the shit she thought she knew before she'd come to D&D tonight was just superficial, surface. It was slowly dawning on her that there was an entire world of his that she'd never explored.

What did that say about her, that she'd just thought he was her friend's hot cousin? Had she been objectifying him without meaning to?

Probably. Doing that had kept Merle in this safe little box, but she'd let him out of it and now…she was intrigued by everything about him.

He rolled his eyes and shook his head. "I don't hate baseball. I hate the way my father is obsessive about it. And I have a lot of tees because I played as a kid."

"You were on the Yankees?" she asked, looking down at the logo on the shirt she wore.

"Yeah, the Western Mass Suburban Yankees. We were league champs two years in a row," he said.

She saw the way he sat up a little straighter when he talked about their wins. He was proud of his team. Which just made her wonder why he hated the sport and his father's passion for it. "Did you suck on the team?"

"No. I'm actually a pretty decent pitcher. I was even scouted for some traveling teams, but…"

Like she was going to let him leave it there.

"But what?"

"I was a teenager and hated my parents for pushing me to do something that I didn't love." He paused, a pensive look on his face that faded before he cocked his head to the side. "What about you? Why the cool down on looking for your dad?" he asked.

She shifted on the bed, almost drawing her knees up into a crisscross position. He'd lashed out because she'd cut close to something real. And that was what she wanted. For him to drop the barriers he built. She wanted to see all the different facets of this man who had become her lover, who was quickly becoming a close friend.

Seeing him struggle made him more real in a way, but also reinforced that she didn't have to try to always be Strong Liberty with him.

"Don't be a dick. If you didn't want to say, then just tell me that. I could get hating the sport if you sucked at it and couldn't live up to your parents' expectations, but it sounds like you were good and enjoyed that about yourself. And deny it if you want but you sounded…well, proud of winning the league championship."

He scrubbed his hand over his face and the slight stubble that was on his jaw and cheeks. "Sorry for being douchey. Baseball is…"

"If you say complicated one more time, I'm going to leave. Life is complicated. Find another word," she warned him.

"Very well. Baseball is my dad's thing, and he got three sons who could follow in his footsteps and maybe go further than he had. When I was little…it was fun I guess, but to be fair I didn't know anything else. And then my brother came along and he's got so much natural talent, and he loves the game, and it became their thing. Dad is really judgmental and competitive and would say things like, 'why can't you be more like Manford?' and I finally just stopped trying. I liked the game, but as a game, not a way of life."

"Why?"

"He had his phenom and didn't need me. It happened around middle school time, so I was starting to actually realize there were things I liked better than baseball. Which pissed my dad off. He sort of ignored me until high school, when he said he thought it was a phase. Then when I was a sophomore he pushed me to try out for the high school team. I refused, we had a physical fight, he hit me and I... I punched him back. My mom got in the middle of us and my dad said some shit about how I was a loser. I said something about being just like him, and it went downhill. After that no one tried to make me play baseball anymore."

Wow. Well shit. That wasn't what she'd been expecting at all. She reached over to touch his leg right above his knee and give him some support. He covered her hand with his, linking their fingers together. He squeezed.

She lifted her head and their eyes met and she felt something pass between them. Something deeper. And that uncertainty she'd felt toward both her situationship with Merle and her messy life seemed to drift away. Not completely, but she felt a connection to him that she hadn't before.

To a man.

It was different than any of the other connections she'd felt in her life, and it scared her. Growing up in a household where she'd been praised for her independence and being different, she'd thrived. Meanwhile Merle made his own path and found his own way. This house, with the decorated rooms and D&D dungeon, gave him a place to indulge his passions.

"That sucks, Merle. I had no idea."

"Why would you? It's not like I advertise it," he said. "That's why I have a love–hate relationship with baseball. Sometimes I crack open a beer and watch a game on TV, but then Coach will put something in the family chat about it, about which player fucked up or failed, and I get pissed again."

"You're in a chat with him?"

"He's still my dad."

"Did he ever apologize?" Liberty asked. Because that man totally owed Merle one.

"No. I didn't either. We just ignore it. He asks about my job. My parents are very happy I have a good paying one. They just don't ask about anything beyond it. I'm still their son, and they are still my parents."

"I guess. But I would have hashed that out with my mom," Liberty said. "I would have at least kept being passive-aggressive—"

He snorted.

"What?"

"You're never passive-anything. You would have been aggressive-aggressive until she talked."

"True." She chuckled at how well he understood her. "Thanks for sharing that."

"You kind of left me no choice. Now, are we talking about John or are you reading my cards?"

Merle hadn't meant to share all of that. Talking about that time in his life always made him angry. He had worked hard to get around his anger and resentment. It was his first therapist who suggested he start playing D&D. Creating campaigns and channeling his frustration into role playing really worked.

After the fight with his dad, he'd resorted to passive-aggressive behavior at home and needed an outlet at school. He was picked on often enough, so it hadn't been hard to find a fight.

Looking back it was easy to see that he'd been trying to get attention and maybe punish himself. He'd been constantly frustrated at that time. He hated being at home and there had been so much tension there…he'd become the worst version of himself.

But his parents didn't notice him. At that point his parents were just happy he wasn't in his room all the time. So it had really worked. In a way, that fight with his dad had been the moment he'd become a man.

It set him free from always trying to please someone who was never going to be satisfied, no matter what he'd done. He hated that he'd given into his violent side and become more like his dad than he'd ever wanted to be. Which was why he worked so hard to keep his family separate from everyone else in his life.

"Parents are complicated."

"They are," she said. "Let's do your cards."

He'd never let her read for him before, and to be honest he wasn't sure he wanted her to analyze his cards. What if she saw something that made him less attractive, a warning that she shouldn't be with him? Was that even a thing? He should have texted Poppy and asked her about this before he'd agreed to it.

Facts had always been his true north, but tonight he was starting to see just how many times he'd been ruled by emotion. The respect he had for Liberty and her witchy side was growing stronger. She deserved a man who could appreciate it, and Merle wanted to understand it. This entire night hadn't gone at all the way he'd expected.

"I'm nervous."

"Why?"

"I have no idea what a reading is and how it's going to affect me," he admitted.

"Cards aren't good or bad. They just offer a possibility," she said, shuffling them again. "Usually when I draw something it resonates with an opinion or thought I already had. Like when I was trying to draw to find out about what to do about my father, the cards were all over the place and I knew… well, that I didn't know what I wanted to do."

"So you came to me?"

"Well I tried the ancestry thing first," she said. "Then yes. I decided magic wasn't going to help me, so I needed to look outside, and the world of computer detective work seemed logical, and you're good at it."

"And you wanted to get in my pants," he added.

She tipped her head to the side. "Maybe I did."

"It worked."

"It did. Are you trying to flip the script and distract me from reading your cards?"

"Maybe. I'm nervous. I think I'm doing good tonight, and what if you flip over a card that makes you…"

He trailed off. No way was he going to say *What if you get one that makes me look like a loser.*

She leaned over and put her hand on his leg again. That warm touch sent a shiver up his body. He'd been alone too long with just hugs from Poppy and quick grasps from his short-term lovers to sustain him. Liberty's touches were different, sexy and affectionate at the same time, and he craved them.

"It's going to be fine. I was thinking I'd do a spiritual council spread for you. See what your ancestors are advising you. What do you think?"

He had no idea if that would be good or not, but he wasn't going to argue with her. "You're the expert."

"That's right, I am," she said, winking at him. "This is a Samhain oracle deck. It's sort of a version of the traditional Rider-Waite deck that's themed specifically to witches. I've been using it a lot lately." She handed him the deck. "Shuffle it until you feel like it's ready and then spread the cards out in front of you."

He took the deck of cards from her. They were bigger than a normal playing card deck and had red foil around the borders. He shuffled them a few times, not really certain if he'd know when it was ready.

"Close your eyes and just concentrate on the deck. Ask your ancestors for some direction."

"Like what?"

"Maybe, 'Am I on the right the path? Should I talk to Dad about the fight?' Whatever you want some guidance on," she said.

"Do I have to tell you what I ask?"

"If you want to, but you don't have to," she said.

He closed his eyes. He wanted to ask if things with Liberty would work out. But that didn't seem like something he'd want to share with her this early. Then he thought about his parents and this lingering pain he had with them. That felt like the safer option.

Should he talk to his parents about the past and about who he truly was? Should he ask them if they could love him for who he was and not who they wanted him to be?

As that thought coalesced in his mind, he finished shuffling the deck. He spread the cards out on the bed in front of him and Liberty put her hands on his.

She breathed with him and, in a soft chant, she asked him

to pick a card as their hands hovered over the fanned-out deck. He just let her voice guide him, hesitating over one card, then another until he'd picked three.

Liberty set the three cards aside in the order he'd chosen them and then gathered the deck, placing it back in a box that she'd carried them in. She moved the three cards between them, still face down.

"So the first card will be what your ancestors want you to know about the question you asked."

"I asked them if my parents could love me for who I am and not who they wanted me to be."

"Okay, let's see what the ancestors have to say about that. The second card will clarify why they told you the first thing, and the last one will guide your actions," she said.

He found himself holding his breath as she reached for the first card. Liberty glanced up at him, and then shifted to her knees dropping a soft, comforting kiss on his lips. "Whatever the cards say, your gut will know the truth. And your parents are the ones who are missing out if they can't love the man you are, Merle. Never doubt your worth."

Liberty's relationship with her mom had never been perfect, but the one thing she'd always known—even now when she was avoidant—was that her mom loved her no matter what she said or did. When she eventually came clean with her mom about finding out her biological father's name, her mom would be mad and disappointed, but Liberty would never doubt that her mom loved her.

She hated that there were parents out there so stuck in their own lives that they couldn't see their children weren't meant to be a direct reflection of them, but instead their own living breathing beings trying to figure their own shit out.

Liberty's mom had given her a gift by nurturing who she was and by being brutally honest about her own flaws. Nan had too. Neither woman had acted like they knew what they were doing all the time, which gave Liberty the freedom of knowing she could mess up.

And she had. Many times.

Tonight felt like she'd stumbled into the right place at the right time, but her ancestors had pointed her at Merle for a reason.

A logical man to help calm the chaos she found herself in. She liked it.

She flipped up the first card and laughed when she saw it was Nature Spirits reversed. Nature Spirits were playful. This card was the perfect first card for the questions that Merle had asked.

"This card urges you to be silly and playful in order to lighten the mood and see the problem from a new perspective."

Merle's brows drew together as if he were trying to figure out how to be playful, or he wasn't sure how being playful would help.

"How does that feel to you?" she asked.

"I'm not sure. I don't know how being silly would help anything. My parents really aren't into anything that isn't focused on bettering yourself."

She took a deep breath, letting go of her own protectiveness toward Merle and reading the cards as she'd been taught. Liberty needed to be impartial here. What Merle needed was to stop giving this discussion so much weight. "If I drew this card, I would try to think of something silly I could do so I'd be relaxed and comfortable before I spoke to them. To help remind myself that I can make the situation feel less important even if I can't change other people."

"So the ancestors are telling me to stop stressing? Wow, that's something I've never thought," he said sarcastically.

She mock punched his shoulder. "You may have considered it, but you've never done it. Your ancestors are telling you to let go of your worries. Maybe you should trust them," she said. "Ready for card number two—that will tell you why they've advised you to be silly?"

He flashed his eyes to hers and then nodded. "Sure."

The Black Cat reversed.

Hmm…

"The Black Cat…isn't that bad luck?" he asked.

"No, it's not. This is your reminder that you have more than one chance to get things right. Actually, I think they are telling you to take a leap of faith."

Merle leaned back against the headboard, stretching one arm up above his head and sort of leaning into the curve of his elbow. "I don't know. I mean this seems like the cards are telling me to talk to them, but it's not actually saying if they'll accept me."

"There is no card that will tell you that," she said, shifting around until she was sitting next to him. She put her head on his shoulder and dropped his arm down around her. "They love you or they don't. They'll accept you or not. What you need to do is find peace with it. Right now I think you're afraid to ask anything because of the answer. Your ancestors are telling you to take the chance with this card. Show them who you are, not in anger this time, and see what they say."

Wow. Whenever she did a reading, she was drawn to interpreting the card's meaning in her own life. It was easier to see things when she was looking at another person and not herself. The universe was sending a clear message.

"What's the last card and its meaning?" he asked.

"This one is why have your ancestors told you what they have which is meant to guide your next action," she said, flipping over the last card and nearly smiling when she saw it was The Veil.

"Perfect. They have offered this advice because you have been lost in a fog. Either you are seeing through old eyes, looking at a new situation, or you are allowing yourself to fall into old behaviors. The ancestors believe it's time for you to move on," she said.

She looked up at him again. He was still so nervous; it endeared her in a way she didn't expect.

He swallowed. "What if I don't?"

"Then you don't. The cards aren't going to bring down doom on you if you don't listen to them."

"Did I sound ridiculous when I said that?"

"A little bit. It's just something to think about. So maybe you could introduce your parents to someone you are dating. Maybe you don't cut your hair when you go see them. Something to introduce the conversation without being too direct about it."

"Yeah, maybe," he said.

He didn't sound convinced, but it would take time. Merle didn't jump the way she did to make a snap decision. He was one for thinking every detail through before he made that choice. And whatever he did decide, it would be something he could live with.

Unlike her, running to find out more about the man she'd never wanted to know and then getting scared when the information was so close. Living with the outcome of that search wasn't going to be easy. She'd put things in motion on an impulse and now she wasn't sure how to deal with the results.

She put her hand on Merle's cheek and languidly kissed him, inviting him to end this trip to the spiritual realm, because sex made her stop thinking. His arms wrapped around her as he rolled her underneath his large frame, deepening the kiss.

Seemed he might need the distraction too.

Fourteen

Merle lay next to Liberty as she slept, working and checking on any new leads for John Jones.

It was funny how they both had certain things they wanted to avoid. It was impossible not to notice that she was using sex to distract him, to keep from answering any of the intimate questions she didn't want to entertain.

Because he'd been so open about his parents, he almost thought it would make her talk about hers. But his issue was different. He'd grown up with both of his parents and had somehow, over time, come to believe they didn't really give a shit about him. Liberty only had one parent but never questioned her mom's feelings.

Poppy sometimes said he was exaggerating. He saw her point. His parents did call him once a month and they always talked for twenty-five minutes. His brothers were different; he mainly talked to Marcus because Manford was busier, and even Man usually texted a couple of times a month to chat.

They didn't talk about the hard things, but they were still brothers and stayed connected.

Liberty didn't know if her dad was a dick or not. She knew nothing about him, other than he didn't want to be in her life… So yeah, he got why she might not want to talk about it.

But he was struggling a little, because tonight it had felt like they were growing closer. If she really wanted his help, she was going to have to ask for more. The last thing he wanted was to shoulder his way into her life and have her shove him out.

He opened another window in Linux, entering the information he'd pulled on the first of the John Joneses who might be Liberty's biological father. The code he used was pretty common in hacker circles, but it would pull from sources and databases that most people were unaware of or couldn't get access to.

Liberty was curled next to his side, sleeping. Her hair was spread around her pillow in a halo and a few strands curled around her neck, grazing her breast. His heartbeat sped up at the sight and he felt that warm feeling in his stomach. Yearning.

God, he really hated that he wanted her this much. This need to have her in his bed—not just tonight, but more and more—even though he might just be a distraction, wasn't what he wanted. He didn't want to go all in while she was still figuring out her own life.

So he had to keep his emotions in check.

Which had never been an issue before. Maybe it was the anger that had pushed him away from his family, or the techniques he'd learned in therapy, but he never really had a problem keeping a wall up between himself and others.

Then again, that wasn't working too well for him either.

There were a few people he'd let in over the years like Poppy and Darren. Now maybe his brothers, and of course Liberty. He wanted to play like he was cool with whatever she decided she could handle. But from the moment he'd seen her in her black clothes, her creamy pale skin and that fiery red hair, he'd been drawn to her.

There was no more chill where she was concerned.

He ran some more codes and eventually found a reference to a John Jones in Birch Lake. He started tracing further and found it was a library article that hadn't been placed in a public database. Maybe the library would have it in their old files. He opened the notepad on his computer and dropped the snippet he'd been able to read into it.

There was a grainy photo accompanying the scanned article. When he tried to zoom in on the faces, all he saw were pixels and shades of gray. He copied the photo into the file anyway.

Liberty made a soft sound in her sleep and slid closer to him, her arm coming up as if to grab him, so he closed his laptop and set it on the floor next to the bed. She embraced him and he switched off his light, turning on his side to pull her into the cradle of his body.

"Merle?"

"Yes," he said.

"Did you finish working?" she asked sleepily.

"Yes, go back to sleep," he said.

"I can now that you're here," she said, rolling back on her side so that he could spoon her. He wrapped his arm around her waist. Trying to still his racing heart. But it wasn't working. He wanted those words to be more than something she said when half-asleep. For him to be one of the reasons why she could sleep at night. Hell, he wanted to be her white knight and he didn't even believe in shit like that.

He gazed down at her in the dark. The faint light provided by the night-light in the bathroom didn't really give him enough illumination to see her features, but it didn't matter. He'd memorized them long ago.

More than anything, he wanted this to be real.

He was so afraid it wasn't.

Just a temporary aberration, a moment where their lives had hit a crossroad and they were both walking it together until things diverged again.

Her pushing him to talk about his parents had forced him to admit out loud, and more so to himself, that it was past time to resolve things. He was tired of always feeling like he didn't measure up. And he wanted to be able to bring women home with him—if he still wanted to go home. He wanted to be able to be himself around his parents and be accepted.

That was a big ask and something he'd been afraid of…until he had Liberty in his arms. Now it was something he had to do because he wanted his life to be in order so he could be the best version of himself for her.

Fifteen

WiCKed Sisters was busy, which Liberty was thankful for. She'd recently begun making brooms to sell in her part of the shop and they were flying—pun totally intended—off the shelves. She loved this time of year, and working with herbs and crystals for the customers improved her mood.

Her good mood was definitely going off of the success in the shop and *not* because she was sleeping with Merle.

Well, it wasn't *just* the sex—which was great—that was responsible for this feeling of...she wanted to say joy. But joy couldn't be sustained. Her mom had always advised her to strive to be content instead of happy. Content was something that could be maintained through her life, and joy was temporary.

But Liberty had never been even keeled. She was more like a gremlin from that '80s movie her mom loved. Once she felt something, she turned into a monster until she was done emoting and then calmed back down.

What she felt for Merle was undefinable.

Which would be totally throwing her off her stride if it wasn't Samhain. Her excitement for the new season was keeping her from completely losing the plot. Maybe she was changing, she thought as she wove some rosemary leaves into the broom she was making. Rosemary was good for mental stimulation, purity, love and protection.

She even made brooms for Poppy and Sera. Poppy's had a lot of rosemary in it because she still seemed unsure of what to do with her ex-husband. Liberty knew she should get with Sera and find a way to coax Poppy out of the shop and up to Hanging Hill. A girls night ritual would do them all a lot of good. She glanced at the moon phases calendar that hung on the wall next to the register.

Tomorrow night was the waxing moon. That would be perfect for an attraction spell to help usher some answers into Poppy's life. To distract her from Alistair, who was being very charming…but Liberty feared it wouldn't last. So did Poppy, but she didn't want to admit it.

She finished the broom she was working on and then headed over to talk to Sera first. Poppy was on the phone behind the counter in the tea shop. Between her ex and her family, Poppy had been very busy lately and Liberty felt a pang as she realized just how much she was missing the time with her friends.

Sera strained at the book press, twisting the machine down to flatten the signatures she'd put into her handmade journals and grimoires.

"Hey, you seem like you're in a good mood."

Liberty chuckled. "Is that strange?"

"Sort of. You've been off since J.J."

Sera was right. She had been off, and it wasn't that everything was back in place inside of her, but something had shifted. It felt like things were still shifting around and would be for a while.

"I'm different."

"Different good? I mean, it seems good, but change is scary," Sera said.

"Yeah it is. But this feels right. Anyway, can you go out tomorrow night?"

"Girls night or couples? Wes is in Bangor checking out some old books and won't be back for a few days."

"Girls night," Liberty said. "Let's go to Hanging Hill."

"Perfect. I've been working on something for the two of you and it's almost done," Sera said. She reached over and hugged Liberty. "I've missed this."

"Me too."

"I know it's sort of me a little bit, and I love spending more time with Wes, but he's different than you two."

Liberty wasn't sure what Sera was trying to say. "Are things going okay?"

She chewed her lower lip for a minute and then nodded. "Yes. And that's what scares me. I thought I'd worked through most of my being abandonment issues, but the more I start to depend on Wes the more fear seems to creep in."

This was totally one of the reasons why she loved her friends so much. They weren't #blessed. They were real. Women who weren't perfect.

"Hey! Are you two dishing the good stuff without me?" Poppy asked as she came over.

"Just saying I'm a big scaredy cat about relationships—still, nothing new," Sera said. "Liberty suggested we all go up to Hanging Hill tomorrow night for the waxing moon."

"Oh, tomorrow?"

"Yes. Can you go?" Liberty asked.

Poppy pressed her lips together. "I'm supposed to host the Secret Tea Society online chat tomorrow…"

"Didn't you say Alistair was part of it? That man owes you way more than one favor," Liberty said.

"Good thinking. I'll message him now."

"How's that all work? Do we still hate him? Or has he actually changed?" Sera asked.

"I'm not sure. He's been different lately." Poppy took her phone from her back pocket, typed out the message and put her phone away.

"You definitely need a girls night," Sera said. "We all do."

"Yeah, I do." Poppy sighed. "I thought I was over him, but…"

Liberty really didn't like Poppy's ex, but if her friend still had feelings for the guy then she would support her. But if they got back together and it turned out he was courting her just for his family's business again, Liberty was going to pull out Nan's dark magic book and on the next dark moon she'd put a curse on him that would make him rue the day he messed with her best friend.

"Great. Let's do an attraction ritual," Liberty said. "I need one. I'm still not sure what to do about the sperm donor or Merle. And Sera needs answers about Wes."

"It's not about Wes."

"It is about Wes if you think he might leave."

"It's me that's the problem," Sera said, rolling her eyes.

"What are you talking about?" Poppy asked. "You're perfect and he loves you. I mean, you can totally see it when he looks at you."

"But what if he stops looking at me like that?" Sera said.

"Why would he?" Liberty asked. "He's moved his entire life to Birch Lake and even opened his shop on Main Street to be closer to you. That doesn't seem like a guy who's planning to leave."

"I know that. I do. Rationally I feel so loved by him, but there's this tiny spark of doubt inside of me that I don't deserve to be this happy and this loved."

Poppy and Liberty moved as one to hug their friend close. Liberty had no answers; whatever they said to Sera wasn't going to be enough. It was going to take years of Wes loving her before she felt secure. And years of them loving her.

"We haven't left you," Poppy said quietly.

"No, you haven't."

"That's because we're family," Liberty said. This was what family was. Not some unknown man who had never wanted to know her. These women had been drawn into her life during the hardships, the rough patches, the imperfect places. They had nothing binding them to her other than the love they'd all created. One thing that her father had never given her.

Liberty had finished her last tarot reading for the day when she heard the bell on the shop door ring. She glanced up to catch her mom standing there. She looked tired but put on a smile as though nothing was wrong.

The love she felt for her mom washed over her. She missed

her and had only herself to blame for the distance between them lately.

She finished helping her customer, hoping she looked chill and calm on the outside, because inside she was very aware of the secret she still kept and how wired she was the last time they'd seen each other. Her mom was talking to Poppy and ordering a chai tea as if it was a normal day.

She didn't have to be close to know the order; it was what her mom always got—she liked the way that Poppy mixed her own blend of spices with the water and soy milk. Liberty knew so much about her mom, but there was still so much she didn't understand. Hell, she was keeping more secrets from her mom than ever before. There was probably just as much her mother didn't understand about her either.

It wasn't like she wanted to start spilling everything, but she needed to tell her mom the truth if she wanted to make progress on finding her father. And her mom would tell her. Liberty believed that.

Part of moving on was actually letting go of the past. She'd thought she had let it go a long time ago—not just the ache of missing a parent, but its impact on her relationships. She had nothing but respect for her mom, who'd never moaned about being a single parent. She taught Liberty to stand on her own. But looking back, it was easy to see that at some point that lesson had changed, as if life had become black and white where men were concerned.

Her mom hadn't dated at all when she was growing up. As an adult, Liberty eventually realized that some of her mom's late nights involved going out with men, but those men had never been brought home or invited into their family and rituals.

It was only since things with Merle started heating up that Liberty saw it. Things were changing.

Merle showed her that not all guys were like her father and the other short-term men in her life. But she also totally had to admit that it was a little bit her. The reason why those men had been short term was because she never opened up to them or asked them for more.

She'd chosen them because they didn't want anything permanent. Sera admitting she was still afraid to be left by Wes, even though the guy was totally obsessed with her and knew that Liberty would curse his ass if he hurt Sera, had been eye opening.

Fear didn't just disappear because you willed it to.

Liberty had always been bold and brash, showing the world that she wasn't a woman to be fucked with. But inside...inside, she'd been small and scared more times than she wanted to admit.

"Hey, baby girl," Mom said as she came over.

"Mama," Liberty said. Her mom held one arm open and Liberty went in for the hug she'd been missing. She'd been so busy avoiding her mom, trying to figure this out on her own. Her fear of confronting the messy truth had forced her to cut herself off from everything she'd always known.

Fuck.

Maybe her magic wasn't in chaos, maybe it was just her. Fucking with her own head and believing the worst thing would happen, because she was scared.

"What's up? And don't try to play that nothing is," her mom said.

"Mom, every time you say 'play' like that you sound like you're forcing it," Liberty replied with a smile.

"I'm not. I'm a cool mom, remember?"

"Since when?"

"Poppy and Sera, I'm a cool mom, right?" she yelled across the store.

"Definitely," Poppy said.

"The coolest," Sera confirmed.

"See?" her mom said to her.

Liberty just shook her head. "They were being nice. More importantly, I need to talk to you."

"I know," Mom said.

"That I need to talk, or what I need to talk about?" she asked.

"Just that you need to talk. I've been trying to figure out what's wrong, but when you get like this you're hard to read," Mom said. "Is it Nan?"

"Partly," Liberty admitted, watching over her mom's shoulder as Sera locked the shop door and turned the sign to Closed. "Let's go sit down."

She led the way over to Poppy's tea shop where there were tables and chairs. They sat down while Poppy brought over a pot of tea and a new cup for Liberty before squeezing her shoulder and then entering Sera's bookshop section to leave them alone.

She appreciated that her friends were close by and drew strength from their bond. It was past time to discuss this with her mom.

"So it's bad?"

"No. I mean maybe. I don't know." She took a deep breath and centered herself. "Nan thought I was you during one of my visits," she said. That was probably the best place to start.

"Oh. When?" Mom asked. She wrapped one arm around her waist and sort of held herself for a moment.

"Back in the spring. She hasn't done it again," Liberty said, wanting to hug her mom and at the same time not have this conversation. Her emotions were swirling around because she knew that this was hurting her mom, and she hadn't even gotten to the part about her sperm donor.

"Well it's good that it hasn't happened again." Her mom had a steady look on her face, but Liberty noticed her hands shaking. With a long sigh, she sat her mug down on the table, and her eyes were watering as she rapidly blinked to keep from crying.

"Uh, Mom, are you okay?"

She shook her head. "Not really. I'm worried about Nan."

"But she's doing better lately," Liberty said, trying to reassure her, but also looking for some reassurance herself. If her mom thought Nan wasn't going to get better, then it would force Liberty to acknowledge it as well.

"She is, sweetie. You're right. But she's never going to get better."

Liberty had been in denial, but she couldn't be anymore. Mom needed her now more than ever. Nan's deteriorating state wasn't something that she could pretend was going to change anymore. The move to the care home had been hard on her mom, and Liberty had tried to pretend… She couldn't do it. She didn't want to admit to herself that Nan wasn't going to get better.

Liberty felt like a bad daughter for not being there for her mom.

"So why'd you wait to tell me?"

Tears choked her as she tried to find the words. But the truth was hard to get out. How was she going to say that if she'd told her mom, then she'd have to admit that Nan was slipping further away from them? And the subject of her father was going to hurt her mom too. Enough time had passed. She couldn't wait any longer.

"I didn't want to hurt you," she cried.

"Baby, you never could," Lourdes said, coming around the table.

Liberty stood up, allowing her mom to hug her tightly. In her mother's arms, with the comforting scent of her lilac perfume, Liberty took a shuddering breath and spoke into her mother's shoulder.

"She thought I was you when you were pregnant, and she told me that I had to get rid of that John Jones or she was going to kick you out of the house," Liberty said. The words just spilled out in a rushed jumble.

It felt like her head was full of yarn and the room was tilted off-kilter. The embrace changed and Liberty stepped back. Her mom's face went pale and she put a hand to her throat.

"Oh."

Oh?

Lourdes was struggling to process everything. Liberty knew she should give her mom space, but her emotions were all tangled into some complicated knot, and the words that had been trapped had freed the dam.

"Mom, why didn't you tell me Nan didn't like him? Why

didn't you at least see if I wanted to know his name now that I'm an adult?"

"That never really mattered, and you didn't want to know about him when you were young. When did that change?" her mom questioned. There was no emotion in her voice which was so totally not like her mom.

This wasn't what she was expecting. Was there more to her parents' relationship that had yet to be revealed?

Sixteen

"Mama?"

"Give me a minute," her mom said as she stood up, angling her face away from her daughter.

"Is there more to the story than I know? I asked Merle to try to find him on the computer."

Her mom looked back, eyes wide with tears, and Liberty could tell that pushing this any further wasn't going to bring her any answers. She was hurting her mom. But she was hurting too. It felt like there was more to the biological father thing than her mom had let on. That was why she'd been so reluctant to tell her mom about it in the first place.

On some level, it was clear that her mom had kept important information from her, and that felt like a betrayal from one of the few people she was supposed to trust unconditionally.

"Why?"

"Because I did one of those DNA tests—"

"I mean why didn't you just ask me?" Mom sat down at the table again.

Ah. Now it was time for her to get real.

"Because we burned that letter he sent. We pushed him out of our lives," Liberty said quietly.

Inside she was scared, and angry, and didn't know how to cope with this. She wanted to be ballsy and use her sass to defend herself, but she couldn't. Her mom had always been her soft spot, even in moments like this where she just assumed that Liberty shared the same opinions.

Her mom never wanted to talk about this man. Liberty assumed at some point her mom would give her the agency to have a change of heart without projecting her own pain onto her daughter.

"I'm sorry, Lib. What do you want to do?"

Her mom reached across the table and took her hand. There was such comfort from that touch. For a moment, the wise goddess who'd always been able to guide Liberty through everything was in that touch. But Liberty was mad. Mad that she'd made it seem like the reason her biological father had left was purely because her mom had gotten pregnant. Liberty had assumed that he was a jerk, that he didn't want her, but was he just a man afraid of commitment? Was she really just collateral damage?

"What was your relationship like? Did he hurt you? Why did Nan not like him? Would he have stayed with you if you'd gotten rid of me?" Liberty asked the questions in quick succession, in case this was her only chance. There were more in her mind but that would do for a start.

Her mom pulled her hands away and rubbed the back of her neck.

"Okay, you want everything, and I will tell you, but please

remember I made the best decisions I could at the time. Looking back on it, I can see places where I should have made different ones, but in the moment the choice I made seemed the best," Lourdes said. "Want some more tea?"

"No. I want answers."

"I'll give them to you. I promise," Mom said. "I've always loved your fire and your spirit, but you really could work on your compassion. I need a minute."

Liberty hadn't given her one. There was a validity to her being upset. Her mom had gotten a lot of information at once and needed time to process it. She could trust her mom. Which was what the mother-daughter relationship was for.

"Sorry, Mama. Let me get you some more tea. Poppy made a new blend for me that I think you'll like. Take your time."

Her friends had both gone into the back of Sera's shop, but she knew they were still close by.

"Thank you, baby girl. I'm sorry, it's just… I hate the woman I was. Since the moment I learned I was pregnant with you, I vowed to stop being the worst version of myself…"

Liberty went over and hugged her mom. Her hair smelled of vanilla and cinnamon. So comforting that she wanted to rest there for a minute. To hold her mom and let her know—

"Mom, I get that you weren't always my mother. You are, and were, your own person too. More than anyone else, I get what it's like to feel like the worst version of who you could be and react without a filter. But if I've learned one thing from you, it's to own it and move on. Sounds like you did that with my dad," Liberty said.

She touched the teapot Poppy had brought and realized it

had gone cold. She left her mom to her thoughts to go and make another pot.

What should I do?

She needed to take action and figure this out. Pull a card and finally get some clarity. This time, the deck would speak to her. Liberty was ready.

She set the teacups on the table and went back to her shop where she'd left her Rider-Waite tarot deck. She returned to the table and sat down across from her mom again, shuffling it. Mom seemed to relax for the first time since Liberty revealed the truth.

"What are you asking?" Mom took a sip of her tea, putting her hands on the table.

"If I should let this go," Liberty said.

Her mom took the cards, shaking her head. "That's not the right question."

"I thought there was no such thing as a bad question for tarot," Liberty retorted.

"There isn't. But that won't give you the answer you're seeking. You should ask something like, 'Will I gain anything from knowing this?'"

Liberty shook her head and took the cards back, trying to maintain her composure. "You can ask that. I want to know more. I just don't want to hurt you by pushing."

Her mom gave her that sad mom smile that Liberty had seen a lot growing up. Being friends with your mom was great in many ways, but in some ways it made the tough things even tougher. "You can't hurt me. I'm afraid I might hurt you."

"Why?"

"I can't… I can't talk about this now. I'm sorry, but I need some time."

Her mom was shutting down. Was her biological father a dangerous man who'd hurt her mom? It had never occurred to her that maybe her mom had a bad experience with him.

"Okay," she said. She had never seen this side of her mom and it scared her. This wasn't like Nan slowly forgetting that you ate soup with a spoon or that they'd always lived on Cherry Lane. This was something else.

It was hard to see her mom through a woman's eyes instead of as the child she'd always been. This woman needed time, and Liberty knew if Sera or Poppy had asked for it she'd give it. She had to do the same for her mom.

Liberty quickly rose to her feet, grabbed her bag and left the store. Her mother was still at the table, looking…

She thought she had no destination in mind, but wasn't surprised when she realized she was on her way to Merle's house.

Merle had a new work project that should have been keeping him busy and his mind occupied. His boss had given him an assignment that was almost too easy, so he was running a few programs in the background while working on some details for the next session for D&D. At least that's what he was supposed to be doing. But instead he was thinking about Liberty.

He'd texted her over an hour ago and she hadn't gotten back. Their official date was quickly approaching and they hadn't agreed on a time. As much as she was into the entire Halloween thing, he didn't think she'd ghost him. That wasn't her style. Plus she knew she'd see him at WiCKed Sisters this week as Poppy was going out of town, so maybe—

The doorbell rang, interrupting his thoughts. He got up to answer it, only stopping in the kitchen to toss out his Gatorade bottle. When he opened the door, he was surprised to see Liberty looking like she was about to cry.

Her hair hung around her shoulders in a wild array, her eyes were wide and she was restlessly shifting her weight from one side to the other.

Something was wrong.

"Come in," he said, stepping back and inviting her inside.

She marched past him, tossing her bag on the kitchen counter. She opened the fridge and looked inside. "Do you have anything to drink?"

"Tequila. But what's going on?"

"I told my mom I knew my dad's name and asked her to tell me about him. The truth. After agreeing to answer my questions, she freaked out and asked me to give her more time," Liberty said.

Oh, that explained her energy, but he felt like something else was going on. He couldn't drink while he was working, but she needed him. He closed the distance between them as she closed the fridge and leaned back against it.

He opened his arms to offer a hug and she shook her head. "I need to drink or fuck or fight or run somewhere far away. I'm not sure what to do."

"Okay. Let me text my boss and get the rest of the night off," Merle said.

He sent the text and his boss gave him the thumbs-up, telling him to take whatever time he needed. Merle went to the cabinet where he kept his tequila bottle and took down two shot glasses. He usually had lime and salt when he did shots but he hadn't been the grocery store in a while. Almost dating a witch had his regular schedule on pause.

"Do you like tequila?" Not everyone did. If she said no, he'd run out and get what she wanted. Which made him realize, he needed to keep stuff in his place for her if they were almost-kind-of-dating. But maybe it was too soon.

"Yeah, it's fine. I can't do shots though," she said. "I mean I can, but they make me throw up."

"Sure. I've got ice," he said. He pulled down two of the fancy glasses his mom gave him when he'd moved out and filled them partially with ice, then poured a hearty amount of tequila into both of them. He handed one to her.

She took it and lifted it to her mouth, taking a long swallow and then placing the glass down on the counter. Her hands were shaking again.

He had never seen Liberty like this. What could he do to help her?

"Let's go sit on the couch. We can talk."

She shook her head.

She was too wired, so he thought about what he did when he was pissed and needed to get some aggression out.

"Want to play Call of Duty? You said you needed to fight. You can kill people in the game. Might help you release some of this anger."

"I've never played before."

"It's not that hard. Want to try?" She kept twisting the glass in her hands. It was easy to see that her mind was racing. He wanted to distract her, calm her down and help get that look off her face.

"Yes."

They moved into the living room and he set the bottle of
tequila on the coffee table next to his glass while he got out
the controllers. His were the Xbox Elite controllers, another
badge of his hardcore nerd status. He spent a lot of time gaming, which was a healthy outlet for his competitive streak that
he'd inherited from his father. He handed the second wireless
controller to Liberty.

He loaded the game and then talked her through the basics
of how to play. She was awkward at first but got the hang of
it pretty quickly.

Once she was ready, he joined a co-op multiplayer game
and they were on the same team. She took sips of her tequila in
between shooting and respawning. She was quiet so he wasn't
sure this was helping. Though he was the top shooter in their
match, Liberty was number five. Not bad for a first timer.

"Want to try your skills against me, witch?" he asked.

She gave him a hard stare. "How?"

"We can play one-on-one."

"One-on-one, nerd? You sure you can handle it?"

"I'll give it my best shot," he said sardonically.

"You're on," she said.

They played three matches and at first Merle went easy
on her, but she quickly called him on it. It wasn't long before she was killing him with frag mines and then laughing
at his defeat.

It was good to see her laughing. Something tight around
his heart loosened and he draped his arm over the back of the
couch as they both agreed to end the game. She tucked her leg
under her as he handed her another glass of tequila.

"So…?"

"Mom was totally shut down," Liberty said.

Not really something he expected from Lourdes. Liberty's mom was a lot like the daughter she raised. "I guess she was surprised."

"Maybe. But she's always been so open before. Why isn't she now? Was she only saying she was open because I didn't want to know anything as a kid?" she asked.

She wasn't expecting an answer. Which was hella good because he really was out of his depth, struggling to find the right thing that would help Liberty. But he didn't need to.

She picked up her controller. "Want to do that multiplayer thing again? I have some ideas on how we can work as a team."

He picked up his controller and got them into a lobby for the next match that started in thirty seconds. A glance at her confirmed she watched the TV intently, ready for the game.

Maybe he didn't need to respond. Being here, listening, might be enough.

He focused his attention on the game and they played until the match was over. Their team lost, and Merle was expectedly the top scorer on their team and second overall in kills during the match.

"Want to play another round?"

"Sure."

They played and drank tequila for another two hours, getting lost in the low-stakes competition. Liberty was getting better at the game and she talked randomly throughout it. Mostly about her mom. Telling him stories from when she was growing up.

Merle had always admired the relationship that Liberty

had with her mom and the stories made him a little envious. They were very close.

"One time we went to my cousin's wedding in Bangor when I was eight. I was really into being a little witch. So I wore my favorite forest green dress with these big sleeves and Nan had sewn crystals into the bodice. It was so cool."

"I bet it was," Merle said.

"Anyway, Ali… She's like my mom's cousin's daughter. I don't know what that makes her, but she was obviously super popular at her school and she just kept…" Her voice trailed off.

A lifetime of not fitting in and being low-grade bullied told Merle what had happened. "What did you do?"

"I hid in the house in this small, dark room. Today I'd tell her to go fuck herself, but back then… I felt like a druid goddess when I got there. But that was gone.

"So Mom found me. Taking my hand, she led me back out to the party and onto the dance floor. Nan and Grandpa joined us and we danced in this little circle and soon more people started to join us. It was magical.

"Mom never said anything to Ali or even to me but she showed me that if I was confident in myself than the opinions of others didn't matter."

"You're lucky you had her."

She told him another particularly funny story about the time that she'd been called to the principal's office for putting a hex on her bully and how her mom had defended her. It was clear to him that their relationship would survive this hurdle. Maybe he should take that mindset into his own life before it was too late.

★ ★ ★

Liberty was feeling a little bit tipsy and a lot more mellow than when she'd arrived at Merle's house. He'd given her space and distracted her which was what she'd needed. Merle was a great guy. He made her feel excited and safe at the same time.

Now, Liberty was still mad at her mother. She wasn't ready to be reasonable about it, even though she knew she should be if she wanted the answers to her questions.

"She has been there for me," she admitted as Merle poured some more tequila into her glass and then into his own.

"So…what's different now?"

"She's hiding something," Liberty said.

"Are you sure?"

"Yes. She was being all…not her. Moody and avoidant. That's how I know, and she said she was afraid of hurting me by telling me about John Jones. How could she hurt me? I already thought he left because he didn't want me."

Merle shrugged. "I don't know. Parents have their own things that don't always make sense. Fuck, my parents never make sense to me, and they never want to talk about anything difficult. But your mom, from what I've seen, isn't like that."

Merle was right. Which didn't surprise her. He was smart about people, even though he struggled with how others viewed him.

But she wasn't ready to let go of the hurt that her mom had caused. It wasn't realistic to think her mom would suddenly want to talk just because she had made her mind up to start the discussion.

Liberty tried to put herself in her mom's shoes, something she'd never really done, mainly because they had always been a team. This was the first time that she felt like they weren't. And it wasn't even because of anything her mom had done; it was what Nan had said.

She'd told Lourdes to leave John Jones. Why? What could he have done to make her Nan so angry? And what was it that her mom was reluctant to tell her?

"So what's with you and your parents anyway, since you mention it?"

"Nothing."

"Nothing?"

"Yeah, nothing," he said. "We're talking about you and your mom."

"So that's a no-go zone?"

"For tonight. I already told you about them. So I wouldn't say no-go exactly," he said, taking a long sip of his drink and emptying his glass. "I just haven't figured out how I want to approach them yet. And I'm more worried about you."

There was always more. His family rattled him. But she understood why he wasn't ready. You can't force an epiphany.

She put her controller on the coffee table next to her glass. Merle rested his head against the back of the sofa. He'd taken off his glasses and had his eyes closed. His long, shaggy hair curled around his face. Reaching out, she pushed her fingers into his hair. There was something homegrown handsome about Merle's face. It proclaimed his health and strength with his strong bone structure. Those full lips though, they drew her in.

"Merle?"

"Yeees?" he said in an exaggerated way that made her giggle.

She'd definitely had enough tequila.

"Why not just let me cry or convince me to go and talk to her?"

"It didn't seem like what you needed. You left her and came to me," he pointed out.

"Naturally that meant tequila and gaming," she said as she straddled him. He stayed reclined on the couch but put his hands on her waist.

She leaned forward to rest her head on his shoulder, closing her eyes, inhaling the familiar scent of his aftershave and something basic that was just Merle. It was so odd that the one constant that she could really count on at this moment was a man. This one.

Merle somehow figured out the exact thing that would get her out of her head and give her a chance to be aggressive.

It wasn't lost on her that she'd come to his place instead of texting Poppy and Sera like she normally would. They probably overheard everything in the shop if they did stick around in the back room. But tonight she'd needed to be with someone who didn't know her mom. Who wouldn't take her mom's side and tell her that she was being a brat or try to see her point of view.

And Merle was that person.

His hands roamed up and down her back and she felt his erection stir under her. She shifted closer.

"Are you okay now?" he asked her.

Merle was the kind of guy who never wanted to take advantage of her. He was one of a kind. *Chivalrous*. That resonated deep in her soul. Made her like him even more.

She hugged him tightly. Up to this point, she lived her life with no regrets, and that wouldn't change just because of the situation with her mom and John Jones.

"I could be better, but I'm good."

"I'm glad," he said, tipping his head to the side and bringing his mouth to hers. He kissed her slowly and tenderly. She felt a decadent warmth spread throughout her body, and she couldn't decide if Merle was the best thing that ever happened in her life or if it was just the tequila making her feel that way.

Then she decided it didn't matter. Right now, he was here, and she didn't want to hold back.

Seventeen

Samhain.

She took a deep breath as she stepped into the apple orchard. It was old, not ancient, but her mom had brought her here to pick apples when she'd been young. The same couple still ran it. Merle took her hand in his as the entered the orchard. She'd never brought a guy with her before. But why would she?

After tequila and sex at his place last night, she'd needed to get back to normal. Talking to her mom was step one but Liberty hadn't been up for that today. More time with Merle was somehow refilling the well of her soul and making it easier for her to take that next step. When she was ready.

This was the season of the last harvest and she liked to cut and dry the apples to use in a wreath for her kitchen with other branches and herbs. But she had also brought Merle here to use an apple for divination. Sort of. Mainly to see what she could expect from this relationship with him.

She wanted to see what happened when they were here together. It was the kind of fall day that she loved, after all. The leaves had started changing on the trees. As they drove to the orchard, the countryside was blanketed in oranges, rusts and browns. The breeze was chilly but the sun was warm. She'd worn a pair of black jeans and a burnt copper-colored scoop neck Henley under her long black cardigan.

Merle rubbed his hand over his face; his beard had started to grow back in, and she liked it. He looked so rugged and, if anything, more *Merle*. Though he was good looking cleanly shaved, she was used to him with the beard. "Do I have something on my face?"

"No, I was just thinking I hadn't had a guy friend. Probably ever. Sort of like Ford."

Merle shook his head. "Sera's old guy friend who died?"

"Yeah. I mean they had a shared interest...for them it was books, for us it's—"

"Sex. I'm pretty sure Sera was never having sex with Ford."

"Of course she wasn't. And I thought our friendship was based on us both being oddballs, not just sex," Liberty said.

"Oh. Well, I guess you're right. We are both different," he said.

She could tell he appreciated that. She did too. It was cool that they were both genuinely enjoying each other's passions and sharing them. She never would have guessed she'd love gaming or D&D. He'd shown her things not to change her, but to share who he was too. It made her feel more seen.

He never treated her as just a friend. This crush that they both had was clearly becoming serious.

She was lying to herself when she pretended it wasn't.

The card she'd drawn this morning hadn't really helped

with navigating these feelings. She'd asked if she should watch her back around Merle, if she was in too deep, and pulled the Witch from her Seasons of the Witch deck. The card urged her to allow the fire in her belly to awaken. Letting her passion guide her. Which made her feel like her magic was returning even more, like the chaos was calming down.

So she'd followed her instincts and invited him to come apple picking with her. They'd planned to go on a date for a while. Along with her witchcraft, she needed apples for the upcoming harvest festival the WiCKed Sisters were sponsoring in the park the Saturday after Samhain. In just two weeks.

This season, she hadn't been taking the time for the rituals she normally did. Part of it was because she usually did them with her mom and Nan. This year, that wasn't possible. Anger and sadness warred inside of her. Why was she like that—allowing her secrets to separate her from her family? Why couldn't she be more like Sera who accepted change and rolled with it?

Liberty thought of herself as someone who embraced change, but deep down, she knew that was BS. She'd never embraced it. Instead she'd stopped and screamed her way through it. Maybe her chaos hadn't come from learning her biological father's name and the potential change there. Maybe she used that as a distraction from what was truly coming.

Nan's health was deteriorating, and everyone saw it. Liberty had suspected that was why her mom had been going out of town so much lately. Her mom was so defensive. Was it because that time had been hard with her and Nan? Was that why she didn't want to talk about it?

If her life were less chaotic, she'd love to return the favor for him. He'd really helped her out and she wanted to return the favor. Help him figure out his life. But honestly, right now she wasn't sure she was in any position to do that.

"So apples? I thought pumpkins were the Halloween thing."

"They are, but apples are important too. Tree of knowledge and all that," she said with a wink. "It feeds my inner Eve."

He laughed, a deep booming sound that made her feel light. "How many are we picking?"

"Just a bushel. I ordered a bunch more for the festival so kids can do apple bobbing," she said. "I just wanted to pick a few for our homes."

He reached for her hand and carefully pushed his fingers through hers, clasping them together. A tingle went up her arm. He held her hand so securely. It was sexy, the way that she felt connected to him. His big hand wrapped around her smaller one was something new to her.

When she was with him, she didn't feel like she had to take care of herself. Even with her mom, she was always taking care of herself. One of the greatest gifts her mom had given her was independence, but it was nice to be cared for, to feel like Merle would be there to catch her.

Picking apples wasn't something he'd ever pictured himself doing. He wasn't a fan of bugs and dirt and picking through rotten apples. But he was having fun with Liberty.

The afternoon was sunny and they had wandered deep into the orchard until they were alone. He hadn't allowed himself to dwell too much on the other night, wanting to just be present and live in this moment with Liberty, without putting too much significance on their date so it wouldn't pressure her.

Too bad casual and low-key wasn't who he was. There was no halfway with Liberty. He'd been all in even when he'd been trying to play it cool and agreed to take things slowly. No one made him feel he was enough like Liberty did.

Plus being with Liberty let him pretend his own issues didn't matter.

His parents were bugging him about coming up for a celebration dinner for his brother who would start his new job with the coming spring season. But he'd put them off.

Liberty shifted and the black cardigan she wore swung around her as she turned, hugging her curved hips. She noticed his frown and arched both eyebrows at him.

"What's up? I was going to try to tempt you into getting naked with me after this, but you don't seem in the mood," she said.

"I'm always in the mood to get naked with you," he said.

"You know, I'm not just with you for the sex. You can talk to me if something is wrong."

"Disappointing."

She laughed and he couldn't help the way his body reacted to that deep, husky sound. It made him almost forget about the angst going to dinner with his parents was causing him.

"Ha. So?"

"It's nothing. My folks want me to come to Bangor to celebrate Marcus getting signed to coach the baseball team," he said. "I was thinking about the cards you drew, and I'm going to do it. Just go as myself."

"Want me to go with you?" she asked.

"Would you?"

"Yes. I'd love to meet your parents, and I'm definitely a

ice breaker kind of person so you can chill. I'll even be extra witchy if you need me to."

Need her.

He hated to admit it, but he did need her, probably in ways he was still figuring out. But bringing her would mean… "I'm usually a different person with my family."

"You said they're sporty. Is it some sort of competition thing?" she asked, rubbing an apple on the lapel of her sweater and taking a bite. Juice dripped down her hand and she licked it off before offering the apple to him for a bite. "Do you have to hit a home run or something before your dinner?"

But honestly, all he could do was stare at her hand and the bit of juice she missed. He wasn't thinking of anything but this sunny October afternoon and this woman. He bent and licked her hand where the remaining bead of juice was and she let out a ragged breath. Her other hand drifted up to his hair.

She pushed her fingers into his locks, rubbing his scalp, and he took another bite of the apple. More juice dripped onto her fingers. He licked her hand until it was clean. When he stood up, his erection was throbbing in his jeans. Her blue-gray eyes stared into his as he moved closer to her. Her pupils were dilated and her skin had a rosy flush to it. She licked her lips and then lifted the apple to her mouth and took another bite of it, right from where his bite marks were.

A groan ripped from his core as she seduced him with this apple. *"Woman."*

"Man," she said, tipping her head to the side, a strand of her red hair falling over her shoulder.

There wasn't as much juice this time, but some still dripped down into her palm. She held her hand out to him and he glanced around, making sure they were still alone, then pulled her behind one of the trees so that they'd have some extra privacy. He quickly undid the three buttons at the neckline of her top and took the apple from her hand.

Licking the juice from her hand like it was his last meal, he leaned in close to her and he took another bite of the apple, his body buzzing with heat as a splash juice dropped onto her chest. He watched as the small amount moved down into her cleavage.

"Sorry about that," he said, his voice husky with need. This witch would be the death of him.

She arched one eyebrow at him. "Better clean that up."

He lowered his head between her breasts and captured the apple juice with the tip of his tongue. Placing his hands on her waist, he heard the apple fall to the ground as her hands rushed to the waistband of his jeans and lowered the zipper. She pushed her fingers into the opening and touched his shaft through his underwear, and he knew that he had to have her.

Now.

Merle turned so his back was against the base of the tree. He undid the fastening of her black jeans, immediately cupping her through her panties.

She moaned, that feral uninhibited sound she made when she was in his arms. Liberty gripped his hair and used it to pull his head free from her breasts. Her mouth met his hard as he moved her underwear to one side to finger her, her hips grinding frantically against his hand.

Her hand stroked his cock to the same rhythm. He was frantic and felt like he was going to explode. But not before he gave her what she deserved.

He found her clit, rubbing it until he felt her shudder with growing pleasure. She sucked his tongue deeper into her mouth as her hand worked his dick harder and faster. He realized too late that he was going to come and tried to draw his hips back, but she held on, lightly biting his lower lip. She let out a long low moan as she orgasmed against his hand and he came with her.

He held her, trying to catch his breath, to remember where they were. But the only thought that he could keep in his head and the only thing that mattered was that Liberty was the most beautiful person to him, and he wanted to pleasure her forever.

Playfully, she grinned at him. "I think this is going to be a good apple season."

"Definitely."

She dug a packet of tissues from her purse and they cleaned up as best they could. She took his hand in hers and he stopped her, pulling her back into his arms instead.

He'd always been an island, always been the only one he needed in his life, but this witchy redhead with her bold advances and flashes of vulnerability had changed him for good.

Liberty told herself she had no expectations from life. She prided herself most days on taking complete control of her destiny. It was harder lately with Nan in the care home, the sperm donor's name out in the universe and her own magic being so in flux. But the only way for her to fix it was to take action.

"Now that my pulse has stopped racing, we can get back to the topic of me going with you to dinner with your family," she said. They just finished picking two bushels of apples.

She was carrying one and Merle was carrying the other. As they came closer to the front of the orchard and the checkout stand, they came across a couple of influencers—or maybe they were just teenagers—taking pictures of themselves pretending to pick apples.

Which made Liberty smile despite herself. Most people didn't realize how many of the seasonal traditions they had were based in basic magic. That was probably why the traditions continued as long as they had. The meanings were still there, even if most people were unaware of them.

"Uh, are you sure you want to go?" he asked.

She stopped and put her bushel down. Her arms hurt because she wasn't used to carrying that much weight around. Merle usually carried the heavy boxes for them at the store.

"Do you not want your parents to meet me?" she asked.

He set his bushel on the ground too, shaking his head. "It's not that."

"Then what is it?"

"I told you, I'm usually a different person with them. What if I can't turn that off after all? And you like *this* me. I don't know if you—"

"Stop right now. You don't have to be anyone but yourself. With me, with your parents, with the world. Why do you think you have to?"

He rubbed his hand over his jaw and gave her a chagrined look. "Habit mostly."

"Maybe it's time to break it. You act like the man before isn't…what exactly? Good enough?"

"Uh, well my hair is too long. My clothes are too nerdy."

She started to laugh but realized he was dead serious. She

moved closer. "I already told you that I like your hair and your nerdy T-shirts with comic characters hardly anyone knows. But if you wore something different, you'd still be you underneath, wouldn't you?"

The guy who could handle anything and was calm in every crisis was nervous. It floored her because their time together had helped her lean into her own weaknesses. She wanted to give some of that to him as well...

"Nerd," she murmured softly, using the term as an endearment. "You are the one guy I count on. The only man I would trust with the name of my father. You don't have anything to be ashamed of or hesitant about."

"I'm not ashamed of who I am," he said.

"Then what?"

"I don't know. I think I'm afraid of being rejected by my family. Not very manly right?"

"Fuck that. Everyone is afraid of something. It's not just women who get scared, and I'm not going to judge you for your fears when it took me months to tell my mom what I discovered with Nan. Don't ever think it's not okay to be afraid," she said.

"Yes, ma'am. Or witch."

"So what's the worst that can happen? That's what my mom always says."

His brow furrowed and she knew he was running different scenarios through his head, taking her question literally. Dude liked to be prepared for any outcome.

"They could say they don't want to see me again."

"Okay. How would that be bad? You are torturing yourself into being what they want, and if they reject you, why would you want to be around them?" she said. "And before you answer that, I'm sorry. We all want our family to love us for who we are."

"Yeah…that. That's what it is."

She had no solution for him. Not that Merle was looking for her to solve it. "I think, partially, that's why I waited so long to talk to my mom. I knew I was rocking the relationship and the dynamic she and I have always had. We hate the sperm donor. And here I am trying to find out who he is. Maybe bring him into our lives. But I want to know. And Mom is going to have to come to terms with it.

"For you…if you truly are faking who you are with your mom and dad, then I think you should stop. They deserve the chance to see the man you are. And if they can't see how special you are, that's on them."

"I really don't deserve you," he said, pulling her into his arms and kissing her.

She winked at him. "You're right, you don't."

Liberty and Merle picked up their bushels of apples. The autumn breeze stirred around them, playing with her hair, and she tipped her head to see the sliver of the waning moon in the sky.

It was the moon cycle for both grounding and release—grounding her goals and beliefs and releasing what didn't serve her. Two things that she'd been trying so hard to keep at bay. Finally, she felt ready to move forward. Her magic was back in balance with her spirit. Blessed be.

Eighteen

Tonight Liberty was determined to move forward and get ready for the upcoming Samhain celebrations. There was a new energy buzzing inside of her from the orchard with Merle.

But her most recent visit with Nan had been eye opening. Things were going downhill fast.

She pulled out her copy of the Wakefield Witches Grimoire. Since she'd been young, her mom and Nan had guided her in writing down all the advice and information they'd given her. She traced her finger over the first page, which she'd created when she was six. It read "Liberty Wakefield awesome witch." But she'd spelt awesome like *awzoom*.

This book was so much a part of her family that it instantly made her feel stronger and happier just by opening it. She flipped through until she got to the page she was looking for. Liberty's grandfather died when she was eight and Nan walked Liberty through making a healing poppet for him.

She wanted to make one for Nan. Her mom had been right

that Nan wasn't getting better, so Liberty wanted to prepare and help herself accept what was on the horizon. She had stopped by the fabric store in town on her way home from work and purchased a light yellow fabric and gold thread. Both of them had healing properties inherent in the color that would enhance her spell.

She lit the gold candle that her mom had blessed for healing rituals. Even though Nan's illness wouldn't go away, their family recognized that death, or acceptance of it, could be a form of healing.

Then she gathered herbs to stick inside the poppet, the ones she'd collected at her mom's before their fight. She laid the yellow fabric flat on her altar in the back room which she'd used to create the occasional poppets for her customers. She bundled together rosemary, bergamot, echinacea and peppermint for good health. She hesitated and then included in lavender, mugwort and parsley which were used to ease depression and anxiety.

She was feeling overwhelmed and took a deep breath of the candle. The wind was quiet today, which made her unsettled. The wind was always around her, guiding all of her rituals. Shaking herself off, she traced the doll pattern and stitched it together doing her own version of the ritual, remembering Nan happy and healthy. Then she stuffed it with Poly-fil, the herb mixture, a charm from the bracelet that Nan always wore and a note that had her intention written on it.

Let Nan be healthy and happy.

She finished stitching the doll and then recited the healing chant three times over the poppet. She closed her eyes and meditated on seeing Nan happy and healthy for the rest of her days until the candle burnt down.

Maintaining her vision was hard though, and she had to force it more than once. She kept seeing Nan in the care home, not back at their home. Liberty didn't like the vision of her Nan in that place away from her family. Eventually she opened her eyes, pulling her phone toward her and opening the photos app, finding her favorite selfie of her and Nan. It was from last Samhain. They were dressed in their long black dresses and wearing pointed hats. They were both smiling at the camera.

That was what she wanted.

Nan back home and smiling with her. She put her hand on the doll as she looked at the photo. Happy Nan. That's all she asked for.

There was a knock on the door and she glanced over to see Sera standing there. They'd been so busy after the waxing moon ritual a few nights ago that they hadn't had time to hang out. But the ritual had been fun and Liberty felt they had all been clear on their intentions for what they wanted to attract into their lives.

For Sera, the acceptance that she was worthy of being loved.

For Poppy, a man who loved her for herself, not for how she could make him successful.

And for Liberty, the answers she needed, that would come to her when the time was right.

"Hey, got a minute?" Sera said.

"Yes, what's up?"

"I wanted your opinion on the grimoires. I used a binding company that Wes knew and I think they turned out pretty good. They couldn't use the gold foil, it was taking too long, but Greer, Wes and I are going to foil some of them by hand to have some special editions," Sera explained.

Liberty got up from her altar, running her hand over the poppet before going over to her friend. Sera didn't enter her back room during rituals.

Unlike Sera's back room, which was crammed with bookcases and a couch and chair where they all hung out, seldom did they come into her room unless it was to get ready for a moon ritual or a private tarot reading. Liberty liked her space to be sacred.

"You can come in," Liberty said.

Sera nodded, and the scrunchie she'd used to hold her hair back must have snapped because her hair suddenly fell around her head in a riot of curls. Sera let out a defeated sigh. "My hair is nuts today. Must be the energy in here."

Liberty laughed loudly. She'd been so in her head, thinking of the negative, that she'd completely missed out on the good things that were around her.

"It doesn't look bad," Liberty offered.

"Thanks, but it feels huge, and honestly with the humidity… I'm pretty sure rain is coming because it feels like my hair is growing by the minute," Sera said, walking into the room and handing the grimoire she'd been holding to Liberty.

Liberty looked at the cover, which featured a design that she'd helped Sera create. They incorporated the WiCKed Sisters logo into the design. Sera had thought they should leave a space on the bottom of the logo where they normally had the words "books, spells and tea" blank so that the purchaser could add their own name or slogan.

The covers were solid and thick, and Liberty was sure that Sera had paid extra for that. The printer had thankfully been willing to do it to their specifications. Sera was considering using him to do some other types of journals if the quality on this project was good.

She opened the first page and gasped. The endpapers had a surprise design. Sera had hand-lettered the three sayings that were displayed over each section of the store. The bookshop's was "Words Are Magic." Hers was "Destiny Awaits." And the tea shop portion was "Tea Fixes Everything."

"I love this," Liberty said.

"I figured the Amber Rapp legions would like it. I've asked Merle to add it to the shop website," she said.

Merle.

He had been in her life even before she'd started sleeping with him and seeing him all the time. Through the store, and even before, through Poppy. It was like fate had tied them together. She glanced over at the doll she'd made for her Nan and felt a pang in her heart. There were new people in her life to love and learn from. Maybe that's what the goddess was trying to tell her through her acceptance of Nan's deteriorating health. That no matter what, love would find her, and she would return it. Her heart felt a little light.

But she was still determined to do everything to keep Nan healthy and with them for as long as she could be.

She handed the book back to Sera. "These are really good. I think any witch who buys one will treasure it."

"Thanks. What were you working on?" Sera asked.

"A poppet for Nan."

"Is she okay? I mean, I know she's not, but is she worse?"

Sera asked, coming over to the altar and looking down at the doll.

"I don't know. Seems like she's not improving. The doctor did say that at least it's not worsening. But I have..." She stopped, a sob catching in her throat. "Sera, I don't want her to stay the same. I want her to go back to who she was."

"Lib—"

"I know it's not realistic. I just don't want to see Nan like this. I want her at our house, muttering spells and singing chants as she dances around the living room. She can't even stand anymore. She's always in bed or in her chair," Liberty said, feeling her voice crack.

The fears she'd kept locked inside were all spilling out. The emotions that accompanied them were ripping her heart out.

"Nan's the one person who loves all of me. Even mean me," Liberty said.

"She's not the only one," Sera said. "But she's been there the longest besides your mom."

The goddess must have placed Poppy and Sera in her life in preparation for this moment. Perhaps creating this new chosen family was the next part of her journey.

Destiny was a funny thing. Believing that she controlled hers was always a bit rash and against her better judgment. But she'd done it just the same.

She touched the doll again. Was she trying to wish something into existence that Nan might not want? Would Nan want her to accept this changing of seasons?

Of course she would. Nan would be the first one to point out that she'd always be with Liberty through their spells and memories.

"Thanks, Sera. I guess... I was so caught up in Nan's health and in finding out more about my father. I've been a train wreck. But I think it's all really about Nan. I'm not ready to let her go," Liberty confessed.

"I can't really help with that. I have no idea what that's like—to lose a family member, but I do know that when someone leaves you, something else comes into your life. Not better and worse, just different, and that can be enough. Sometimes. Plus you always have the memories," Sera said.

Greer appeared in the door and called Sera back to the bookshop to help a customer. Liberty watched her friend leave. She'd take the doll to Nan tonight and talk to her about it.

That didn't bring her any closer to solving her other worries, but it was a start. Her phone pinged and she glanced down to see it was a text from Merle, asking if she was ready for their date with his parents. She told him she needed to stop at the care home on her way out of town but was ready otherwise.

It was time. She quickly changed into her one fancy black top; it was sheer so she wore a black bra underneath, pairing it with a skirt that cinched in at her waist and flowed around her hips. Determination to face her fears made strength flow through her, which she would use to help Merle tonight. She'd lead the charge to help his family see what a fabulous man their son was and how much they were missing.

Something was different about Liberty tonight. Her hair cascaded around her shoulders and a small, black velvet choker was around her neck with an onyx set in sliver against her creamy skin. The scoop neck of her sheer blouse drew his eyes to her skin and the dangerous curves beneath the fabric.

He couldn't help but notice that she had a black satin bra under her shirt. That would be explored more later.

"Will this do?" she asked, twirling and letting the full skirt flare out around her legs.

Yes. Hell yes. Everything about her would more than do. God, he wasn't sure he was ever going to be the same after her.

He was wearing a pair of dark jeans and a button-down shirt he wore for work, and he'd added a tie that he'd custom ordered with Lying Cat in different poses on it. There was a spare blazer in the car that he'd put on at the restaurant. He hadn't cut his hair or shaved, and for the first time since he'd left home, he was going to see his parents and feel like the man he was away from them.

"You more than do, as always," he said. "Come here, I want to take a selfie. Remember this night."

She beamed at him and strode over as he lifted his arm, fitting snugly next to him, tipping her head back to catch his eye. When their eyes met there was a flash of heat through his entire body. Lust mixed with affection and caring. He lowered his head and gave her a consuming kiss before pulling his phone out and opening the camera app.

They both smiled as they took several serious selfies, then they took a few silly photos before he dropped his arm. "So Nan first. How's she doing?"

"It's just a visit. No one has called me out for anything serious, blessed be," she said as they got into his car. She had synced her phone to his car's radio. "I'm playing my season of the witch playlist, okay?"

"Sure," he said, starting the engine.

The first song on it was "Dancing in the Moonlight" by

Toploader. He knew the song because she'd played it for him at his house after the last D&D session. And then she pulled him out into his backyard to dance in the moonlight with her. It had been magical and sensual, a living dream.

He parked at the care home as the song "Disturbia" finished playing. Singing along with Liberty in the car was a special experience, especially moments like when one of them got the lyrics wrong.

The playlist was a lot like Liberty herself: eclectic and quirky. But all of the songs fit her. She took a small yellow thing out of her bag as they got out of the car and approached the home.

He was curious, soon recognizing it as one of the spell dolls she made in her shop. According to Liberty, those dolls were meant to promote healing and comfort, often during grief and hard times. He hugged her with one arm, knowing that his fierce witch, who never let anyone see her vulnerabilities so blatantly, was using all her knowledge to give her Nan strength. Liberty had told him the spells were to bolster the purchaser as much as the person or people they wanted to bewitch.

"I just want Nan to feel comfortable," she said.

"I'm sure this will help," he assured her. It might not be something he believed in for himself, but he'd been around Liberty long enough to know that she was attuned to something that he wasn't. He was sure whatever incantation she'd used when she'd made the doll would bring what Liberty intended to her Nan.

When they arrived at the door to her Nan's room, he hesitated. "I'll wait out here."

She gave him a slightly sad smile. "Thanks."

Liberty went inside while he stood in the hallway, leaning against the wall. Tonight she seemed like that bold, brash woman she'd always been…and a bit more. Which stirred old fears and worries that she wouldn't find him attractive. But one glance down at Lying Cat and he couldn't hide from the truth that this all stemmed from seeing his family tonight. They brought out the worst side of him and he didn't want that energy with the Liberty who was at his side tonight.

She deserved a man who accepted his entire self instead of hiding from who he truly was. Slowly, through this relationship with her, he'd started to lean into being authentic and now he wasn't sure he could go back to the man he'd been before.

He couldn't use Liberty as a barometer to decide if he liked himself or felt comfortable in his skin. That wasn't fair.

He pulled out his phone and looked down at one of their recent selfies. He had live photo on, so while he'd been looking at the phone trying to get the camera set up, he saw Liberty's expression changing, evaluating him while he got the right angle.

Her face was softer… He'd never noticed her looking at him that way. It was only for a split second before the photo froze with both of their smiles. But in that moment, he'd seen something that his heart wanted to recognize as something. Caring? Friendship? Affection?

Could she love him?

Did this mean he loved her?

His gut said yes. His brain said yes. His heart, which he'd carefully encased in steel to keep it safe, wasn't as sure. He wanted Liberty. He liked her more than any woman he'd ever been with, but he still wasn't sure what that meant for the two of them once her journey of self-discovery was over.

What it meant for the future. Their future.

He didn't want to admit it, but he was like his father, who had fallen in love with his mom the first time he'd seen her. It was hard to think of his über competitive father as a man in love, but he'd caught glimpses of it in his parents more than once. They might not be the most understanding parents as far as he was concerned, but he never doubted that they loved each other.

Love. Do I…?

He hadn't want to let anyone in. The only people he'd loved were his family, and that love wasn't always a great feeling. With them, love always meant competing with each other and that wasn't something that had ever made him feel content or happy.

Liberty did make him content. Happy. More than both of those things.

The door opened and she poked her head out. "Nan wants to see you."

He shoved the messy thoughts out of his head and followed her into the room. Nan was sitting up, looking small on the bed, but the smile on her face was genuine and there was mischief in her eyes. He was pretty sure he was getting a glimpse of what Liberty would be like when she was her Nan's age.

"Hello, handsome. So you finally asked her out?" Nan laughed as she teased him.

"I thought she'd make the first move—"

"I did. Nan, you know I wasn't waiting," Liberty joked.

"I do, my girl. Have fun tonight," Nan said.

They chatted with her for a few more minutes. When they got outside he noticed that twilight had settled around them. A strong breeze blew as he opened Liberty's car door, her hair brushing his cheek.

But the real question was…how did she feel? Because if he knew anything about the Wakefield women, it was that they were perfectly fine without a man in their lives.

He saw the love and fear in her eyes as they left. There was no denying that she had a lot going on in her life.

So where did that leave him? Did he take a risk?

It was too late. He'd already taken the risk and let her in. He wanted to protect and avenge her, soothe her hurts and fears and show her that he was the man she needed by her side.

He'd never go back to the guy he'd been before, letting her flirt and tease him and then dance away. No matter the outcome, he had gone all in on his witch.

Nineteen

Merle's hands were sweating and as they approached the restaurant. He was tempted to just leave. There was no reason to do this.

"Stop."

"What?" he asked, glancing down at Liberty. The noise of the other diners inside the restaurant, their muted conversations a sea of sound in front of them, didn't make this any easier. It was a busy day which wasn't helping either. There were too many people. Sweat dripped down his back.

"I can literally feel you overthinking this. Or trying to come up with a strategy. Whatever happens isn't going to play out the way you think it will."

"You don't know my parents."

"I know you," she said, a playful glint in her eyes. He felt a rush of electricity as she discreetly gave his ass a squeeze for emphasis.

As the words left her mouth, he couldn't help smiling. Liberty made him feel like he didn't have to be ripped or conventional to turn her on. There was something to be said for feeling like he was enough for her. He held her hand and they walked into the sports bar—Coach always wanted to keep up on whatever game was playing and always had a match he didn't want to miss. They were forty-five minutes early so they decided to get a drink.

Merle ordered a beer and Liberty opted for hard cider.

"Merle?"

He turned to see his middle brother, Manford, making his way toward them. Alone. Normally he had his fiancée, Ashley, with him.

"Hey," he said.

"Dude, love the hair. When did that happen?"

"It's been this way for a while. I just wear a baseball cap on the family calls so Mom and Dad don't freak out. This is Liberty. Liberty, this is my brother Manford."

"Nice to meet you," Manford said, holding his hand out for a handshake.

"You too," she said. "Are you the one we're celebrating tonight?"

"Uh, no. That would be Marcus. I'm the one who…" His eyes scanned the restaurant nervously. "Hell. I might be letting Dad down tonight, but I don't want to steal Marc's thunder."

"What?" Merle exclaimed. Manford was Dad's chip off the old block. He was a natural at baseball and even when he stopped playing, he stuck with the team as a coach. "I doubt that."

"Ash and I broke off our engagement and I have no idea what I'm going to do next. I might even quit my job," Manford said.

"And here I thought my hair was going to be the big talking point," Merle said. "What's going on with you?"

"I'm just...tired. Dad is always telling me how proud he is of you and how you did your own thing and it's worked for you," Manford said. "My life just feels like it's in flux, you know?"

Merle shook his head, stunned. "Dude, I feel you. Just so you know, he never says that to me. Dad spends most of his time talking about you and your coaching job. He really was impressed by what you did with the team last year."

"He was?"

"Yeah. I mean, I don't know why he doesn't tell us these things," Merle said with a shrug as he finished his beer in a long swallow.

Merle didn't get it. His parents were always bragging about Manford. Like he was the son that personified everything they thought was successful. It was disorientating to hear that Man didn't really love his life. That he didn't know how proud their parents were of his successes.

"You two should ask him," Liberty said.

Merle shook his head at the same time as his brother. "Uh, definitely not. Coach isn't the touchy-feely type."

"Yeah, wait until you meet him," Manford added. "That's nice to hear that they're proud of me. But even if they are, I'm not sure about going back to coaching."

Something more was going on with his brother. Though they weren't close, Merle knew that Man had always wanted to be a coach and seemed to love his job. "Why not? What does Ashley think? Is that why you broke up?"

Man signaled the bartender for another round and then

leaned back in the bar stool. Pursing his lips, he shook his head in a slow way, then just shrugged. "She's moving to California next month for a new job. She didn't even discuss the job offer with me before she took it," Manford said.

Merle didn't know what to say. Ashley and Man had been together since their freshman year of college. They had always seemed so suited for each other. Like a perfect fit. Hearing from the brother he thought had everything and had his life together that it was all actually shit and falling apart was a shock. "I'm sorry, Man."

"I am too. Turns out I was spending so much time at work, she thought... It doesn't matter."

"Yes, it does. What'd she say?"

"That she didn't think I'd care since I was never home," Man said.

Merle hurt for his brother who looked devastated and lost. The way he and his brothers had been raised didn't make it easy for them to accept failure. Training and hard work got results on the diamond but not always in life.

"That sucks," Liberty said. "Did you tell her you do love her? That you don't want it to end?"

The waiter dropped off his brother's beer and Man immediately took a long sip. Merle was pretty sure that his brother hadn't said jack shit about his feelings like this to anyone, not even Ashley. That wasn't the Rutland way.

"Uh, no."

"Then I don't feel sorry for you. If you want her, you should tell her. Women don't want to feel like they are second in your life to everything else."

"It's too late. When I pointed out that this was a shock, she told me that I never talk to her about the important stuff. We had a fight and we're officially—" he emphasized the words "—taking a break."

Merle looked at his brother, questioning everything about his own life. Manford had always been a mini-Dad. His earliest memories were of Man running faster, pitching harder, everything in the name of pleasing their father. Apparently he took some of the not-so-great traits too.

"You've always been the most like Dad, to a fault. Maybe she wants you to fight for her."

"I don't know about Ashley or Dad. Like you, I'm just good at sports. I don't love them obsessively. Playing and coaching sports is just always something that's easy for me.

"I fell into dating Ash and things were going good. I just coasted along, probably because it's easier than facing the hard stuff. I know she wanted more from me, but I'm a fucking mess right now."

"In what way?"

Man put his head in his hand and then downed his beer in one gulp. "I'm not a mini-Dad. I'm turning into him. Ash, the coaching job… It's like I'm following his path…not my own. It took Ash leaving to make me realize it. I can keep taking the easy route or maybe it's time for me to step up."

The same thing had happened to Merle because of Liberty. Not that he was going to say that to his brother with her sitting right next to him.

Then Marcus and his parents arrived and they made their way into the dining room, the ghosts of their conversation still lingering. Merle had always thought he was the most observant of his brothers, the one who saw the truth of their family, but he'd been oblivious to Man's struggles.

Liberty could see why Merle had been nervous about this dinner. His parents were everything that was healthy and fit. His mom looked probably ten years younger than she was and his dad reminded her of every PE teacher she'd ever seen. They were pleasant but stiff.

They were intense, almost intimidating. But Liberty had never been what anyone considered normal, and neither had her mom, so she had a lifetime of being herself and not giving a fuck what anyone thought, no matter how strange they might believe her to be.

Merle, on the other hand, looked sweet and comforting sitting next to her. Manford was also obviously nervous, ordering beer after beer.

After everyone had placed their drink orders, silence took the whole table captive and Merle attempted to switch gears. "Mom and Dad, this is Liberty. Liberty, meet my parents."

"Liberty. That's an interesting name. You work with Poppy, right?" Mrs. Rutland asked her.

"I do. We're all partners in WiCKed Sisters," she said.

"Heard that's going well for the three of you," Mr. Rutland said, offering her his hand.

She wasn't a hand-shaker by nature so, like with Manford, it ended up with her fingers brushing his in a chaotic jumble. He shook his head and pulled his hand back before moving on to Merle and getting the handshake he'd been after.

"Good to see you, son," Merle's dad said to him.

His mom gave him a hug and stood back, touching his hair

where it curled against his collar. "Your hair is really...different." Her eyes darted, taking everything about Merle's outfit in. "Do you like this that way?"

"I do," he said.

Her mouth tightened for a moment and then she gave him a strained smile. "I guess I do too."

"Manford, where is Ashley?"

"She's taken a job on the West Coast and we are taking a break," Manford told her. The words came out on one long breath. "Also I'm thinking of quitting coaching."

"That's a lot to take on board," Mrs. Rutland said.

"I know, but I figured I'd get it out of the way now so we can celebrate Marcus." Manford clapped his hand on their youngest brother's shoulder. "We are so proud of you."

"Thanks, dude," Marcus said, bro hugging him. "You okay?"

"Yeah, I'm fine."

They all settled around the table, Liberty silently watching the dynamic of the family. Merle's brothers looked like she knew he would have if she hadn't made him leave his hair alone and let his beard stubble grow out. They were clean-cut, good-looking men who were clearly athletic, just as their parents were. The conversation while they were waiting to order centered around sports and scores and games. Liberty turned to Mrs. Rutland after their drinks had been served and she'd taken a healthy swallow of her dry martini.

"You should come to the Halloween party we're hosting at WiCKed Sisters. I know Poppy would love to see you," Liberty said. She'd always gotten the impression that Poppy's family didn't understand the store's mission. Maybe they were put off by the witchcraft elements.

"Thank you for the invitation. I'll check our calendar. I think my tennis club is having something that weekend," she replied. Mrs. Rutland deftly avoided eye contact, scanning the menu.

Okay then.

"What is it you do, exactly? Are you the book one or the witch one?" Mrs. Rutland asked after a beat.

Because Merle and Poppy were so close, Liberty had expected his parents to know more about Poppy's life and their shared workplace. Merle was close to Poppy's mom. But apparently Merle's parents were different.

"I'm the witch. I do different types of spells and charms for customers and tarot readings. That sort of thing. My mom and Nan are witches too," she said, injecting the pride she felt into her voice.

She felt Merle's hand on her thigh. Did he want her to not talk about being a witch? She'd never hidden who she was and didn't intend to start now.

"Oh, that's…interesting," Mrs. Rutland said.

"Coach, I'm glad that you talked to Stanfield today. I know the two of you are friends, but that's all that conversation can be. I'm thirty and will make my own job decisions," Manford said in a loud voice, capturing everyone's attention.

"We can discuss it later. Tonight is about celebrating Marcus," Mr. Rutland said.

Merle sat back in his chair and let out a long, low sigh, his eyebrows furrowed in frustration. This wasn't the kind of dinner she'd been expecting, but it explained so much about Merle and why he felt so insecure about his parents and their opinions on his life.

"Marcus, when do you start your new gig?" Liberty asked after a tense three-minute stare down between Manford and his dad. The restaurant still buzzed around them but couldn't break the tension. It seemed that everyone else was content to let them have their pissing match.

"I actually started last week. They sent me a bunch of tapes to watch for training."

She had no idea what that meant, but Merle leaned forward. Apparently it meant something to him.

"Are they still sending tape? Or is it digital now?" Merle asked.

Marcus answered, and soon they were talking about players and formations and other sporty stuff that she didn't really understand. Merle squeezed her hand under the table as he talked away while his parents silently ate their entrées. She was relieved that things had settled down, but the meal felt like it lasted a lifetime.

When they cleared away the dinner dishes, the waiter offered them dessert. Mrs. Rutland said she wasn't interested and Liberty quickly realized none of them were going to order it. She felt a quick sense of disappointment—it was her favorite part of the meal, even if this was the dinner from hell. Probably thanks to another family rule.

"I'll look at the dessert menu," Merle said, getting a few surprised looks from his family.

Liberty grinned. "Me too."

They ordered dessert while his brothers and parents just had decaf coffee, no milk or sugar. Merle and Liberty made light conversation and laughed with each other. She obviously wasn't going to impress his parents, but at least she could have fun with Merle despite it all.

Merle told his brother Manford to check in with him in the next few days before they said good-bye. Manford hugged Merle tight and nodded.

When they were in the car, she waited until they'd left the parking lot to check in.

"Thanks for that."

He arched one eyebrow at her.

"Dessert."

"I figured you'd curse me if I didn't do something."

"You know that's not how I operate," she said.

"Yeah, you'd much rather cast one of your spells on me."

She shook her head. "I don't have to cast any spells on you, do I?"

Samhain was weaving its magic around her life and making her find that comfort she always had from the changing of seasons. One thing that it was making very evident was that she wanted Merle in her life for more than one season.

She really admired the way he held his own with his family and stood up for his brothers, sometimes diverting the heat to himself and directing the conversation around them.

"I think you were nervous for nothing," Liberty said.

"That's because Man had so much shit going on," Merle said. "That was not a normal dinner for the Rutlands."

He had never seen his father so...lost. But Coach was never at a loss.

Tonight was a shift. He hadn't even joined in the discussion about Marcus's new job, sitting silently for the rest of the meal.

"Yeah? Well your dad seemed pissed but he didn't say anything."

"He definitely was. But Man is an adult and Coach really shouldn't have gone behind his back to talk to his boss."

"It's crazy that he did it. Is that why you picked a career and a life so far from them?" she asked.

"Maybe subconsciously. I just wanted to be far enough away that I could do my own thing. And Aunt Jean and Uncle Richard had a vacation rental in Birch Lake that I could live in during the off-season."

"I didn't realize that was why you picked Birch Lake."

"Yeah. My work was remote even then. I could have stayed in Bangor but didn't want to."

"I'm glad."

Something warm and fuzzy settled in his stomach. After the tense dinner, he started to relax with Liberty. "You are?"

"You know I am," she said.

"I don't know that for sure," he said, signaling to turn off the interstate and onto the county road that led to Birch Lake. "I'm winging it with you."

"You don't wing anything," she pointed out, putting her hand on his thigh. "From the moment I sat down across from you at the Bootless Soldier, you knew what you wanted from me."

"You wanted it too," he pointed out. She came to him because she'd felt she had nowhere else to go. And he liked that—having something that no one else could offer her.

"Definitely. I'd been dropping breadcrumbs forever," she said.

"But you didn't really want me to pick them up," he said.

"I'm not so sure about that. I guess I'll have to thank John Jones for forcing my hand," she said.

Merle lifted her hand from his leg and kissed the back of it. "Me too. Speaking of John Jones…"

"Yes?"

"The internet search came back successful earlier today. I found yours. Where he lives."

The car became silent for a moment, just the sound of the machine cruising along the highway.

"You did?"

"I did."

"Oh, okay."

She placed one hand on the door of the car and looked out and up at the sky. He wasn't sure what was going through her head. He had thought getting the location of her biological father was what she wanted. But rather than looking excited or relieved, Liberty seemed uncertain.

He knew Liberty needed nature around her during hard times, so he turned off before they got to town and drove up the small, two-laned road toward Hanging Hill. He stopped in the dirt parking lot at the bottom.

She looked around the parking lot. "How did you know I needed to be here?"

"You're not subtle," he said. "I can read you."

"Can you really?" Liberty clasped her hands. "I'm not sure I like that," she admitted.

"It's not a bad thing. You can read me too. Tonight you were doing it with no effort," he pointed out. Dinner had made it very clear that he and Liberty could be a very good team.

He'd always thought of himself as a loner, a solo player. On a team there was a chance of letting others down, but on his own, that didn't matter. But with her...he never wanted to let her down. He wanted to improve himself until they were unbeatable.

"Yeah? I'm not sure. I thought... I need to go up to the top and see the moon."

"Hold up, I'll grab the blanket from the trunk. We can sit up there as long as you need."

She got out of the car and waited while he got the blanket. He used the flashlight on his phone to find it, because it was almost the new moon and the sky was dark. "I talked to Mom. You already know that. But she didn't want to give me any more information. I just don't know if I should keep pursuing this."

"This is about you," he said, slowing down as they reached the top of the hill. There was a small stone circle with the remains of a long-ago fire in it. Liberty moved away from him, spreading her arms wide as she tipped her head back and looked up at the sky. She was saying something under her breath, but he couldn't hear the words.

God, she was beautiful. Out here in the clearing on this hill, with the night sky big and open above them, he felt like he couldn't hold her. That she was a creature that belonged to the universe and would never really belong to him.

She turned around and he immediately saw the confusion and the sheen of unspent tears in her blue-gray eyes. He opened his arms and she ran the short distance between them, throwing herself into his arms. He hugged her tight.

This was what being part of a team meant. It wasn't about

winning or about being the best. It was about holding each other and supporting each other.

At least that's what it was with Liberty. He'd never let anything hurt her. Not her father, not her mom and not even herself. She might hesitate to get the answers for herself. This time Merle would have to be stronger than Liberty.

Twenty

Liberty had been so vague in her invitation, which had been hand-delivered by Lucy, who she had recently hired to help her out at WiCKed Sisters. Lucy handed it to Merle when he'd started his shift in the tea shop.

It was October thirty-first and the ladies who ran WiCKed Sisters had gone all out, delivering all of the Halloween feels. The entire staff were dressed in black robes that had the WiCKed Sisters logo embroidered on the top left.

He was pretty sure that Liberty was in charge of the playlist, or maybe she was just recycling her own because he recognized all of the songs that were playing. The shop smelled of pumpkin and spice, apples and cinnamon, books, tea and the special autumn oil blend that Liberty had put in the infusers around her area.

The tea shop was busier than ever, especially since Amber Rapp gave the shop another shout-out on her socials, reminding her followers about her favorite witches. They were slammed. Poppy was reading tea leaves for every customer, Liberty was doing back-to-back tarot readings and Sera had been putting intentions in the special grimoires and journals she'd made for the event nonstop since opening.

So the fact that Lucy had brought the invite to him now sparked his interest.

He recognized the scrolled handwriting.

Hanging Hill, 10 p.m. Bring your wishes for the new year and anything you want to leave behind.

That was it.

He watched Lucy with interest as he finished making two chais. She handed an invite to Wes as well, who was helping Sera with the bookstore.

So, it wouldn't just be Liberty and him.

Which was probably a good thing given that, over the last few days since they'd had dinner with his parents, Merle had shared that he had found the actual John Jones. After their visit to Hanging Hill, she'd left without giving him a kiss. She'd been avoiding him ever since.

She'd been busy in the run-up to Halloween, and last night she'd had some All Hallows' Eve thing with her mom, Nan, Poppy and Sera. Her female coven. So he didn't think it was all intentional avoidance, but at the same time, he felt her hesitating.

After the dinner with his parents, he'd walked away free from the past and the worries he'd always carried about being himself. About letting the world see the man he truly was. Things with his family hadn't changed, but his confidence had, and it made all the difference.

He wanted that for Liberty. The ability to trust who she

was wholeheartedly and unapologetically, even if her father remained a mystery. There was no way they could move forward until the both of them were free of the past. And until she confronted her dad—or at least made peace with not confronting him—they were stuck in the same spot.

Merle hadn't minded it before. But now that he had begun to face his fears, he was itching to get some sort of permanency to the relationship he had with her. A confirmation that they'd gone far past being friends with benefits.

He'd fallen in love with her, after all.

Which was why he was watching her read tarot instead of paying attention to the teas he was making in Poppy's shop.

"Dude, hurry up with those drinks," Lasseter said.

He focused on working in the kitchen with Poppy while Lasseter, a recent hire, was out front tonight because they were slammed.

"Sorry. Lost in thought."

"It looked like you were lost in Liberty. I get it—she's sort of extra magical tonight, but the customers are getting impatient," Lasseter said.

Merle nodded and delivered the drinks to the waiting customers before forcing himself to work on the next orders.

There *was* something extra special about Liberty tonight. Her eyes had seemed bluer than ever when she'd come in. She'd applied black eyeliner and her hair had a slight curl at the end. The figure-hugging black dress she had on under her robe was getting him hot as hell. It accentuated her curves and the low neckline revealed her ample cleavage.

They could stay like this for…well, forever. Friends and lovers who supported and brought out the best in each other.

He couldn't think of a time when he hadn't wanted her, and wanted her to see him. Really see him. And while he'd been hiding from everyone, only letting himself be free in the privacy of his home, that had been okay.

But not anymore. He wanted her to see that she figured out the chaos in her life because he had been by her side. His soul had been hungry to be her hero.

For the final hour that the shop was open, he worked with a new energy as he acknowledged to himself that regret had no place in his life anymore. He was done hesitating and trying to second guess what Liberty wanted from him.

Until he stepped up and told her how he felt, how could expect her to do the same?

The last of the customers left as he finished cleaning up the tea shop with Lasseter. Poppy came over and hugged him. "Thanks. Are you accepting the invitation to Hanging Hill?"

"Definitely."

"I'm glad," she said. "I think this will do you good. Liberty mentioned you took her to meet your parents."

"I did. It was really eye-opening," he said.

"Yeah? Good. I like you two together," Poppy said.

She went to grab her things. He looked around for Liberty but she'd already left.

When Liberty got to the top of Hanging Hill, her mom had the bonfire going in the center of the stone circle. Even though they were ignoring the unspoken topic of John Jones, Samhain was important and they always prepared for the night together.

This year was different, of course, without Nan. Earlier in

the day, Liberty and her mom came up and got everything ready for the ritual tonight. She'd set pumpkins around the clearing while her mother created the frame of the bonfire.

"Everyone on their way?" Mom asked.

"Yes. Mom, before we start tonight, I need to know we're okay," Liberty said.

"Why wouldn't we be, baby girl?"

"Mom, don't ignore the truth. I'm talking about how Merle found my…sperm donor."

Her mom looked down at her fingers, which were twisted together. Her mom wasn't ready for this discussion, but for the Wakefield women, the new year always started on November first. Liberty didn't want to bring this uncertainty into the new year, not when time together was precious.

She hadn't felt any satisfaction when Merle told her he'd found her father. Not that she'd been expecting to, but her father had sparked this larger journey for her. The more she sat in the knowledge that she could contact him, the less urgency she felt around it.

Her mind had been puzzling over that. Trying to figure out why she wasn't as motivated to meet him. And the answer hadn't come to her.

"What are you going to do?"

Her mom's voice was low, so quiet that Liberty had to struggle to hear it over the crackle of the fire.

"I don't know. I'm not sure that this was even about him anymore," she said to her mom.

"What else would it be about?"

"Making a huge problem for myself so I didn't have to think about Nan," she admitted. Her voice broke as the words came out. And tears were in the backs of her eyes. She couldn't stop them.

"Oh, baby girl." Her mom pulled her into a hug. She felt her mom's tears drip down her face. "That's definitely part of it. I've been running away too, because that's what I do. Working out of town so I wouldn't have to see her deteriorating."

Liberty had always believed she was strong in the ways that her mom wasn't. That the two of them were built to protect each other. "I think I knew if I brought up his name it would put a wedge between us."

"And then we would fight and Nan would try to make peace, like when you were little?"

Liberty shrugged as she stepped back from her mom. "I guess. Maybe she wanted that too. She did tell me his name. Maybe it wasn't her mind fog. Maybe it was a moment of clarity where she wanted me to know before it was too late."

"Perhaps. So where do we go from here, baby girl?" her mom asked, picking up her pointed silk hat from the ground and placing it on her head.

"I think I need time with everything. John Jones isn't the answer to what's going on with me," she said. "He did give me someone to be angry at."

"Is that all you needed?"

"I'm not sure. But I do know I can't keep blaming you for not talking about him. He hurt you, and it was his choice to leave me. No one else's. Sorry, Mama."

"It's fine. I wish we'd talked about this sooner. But the goddess must have realized we couldn't go into the new year with this unresolved."

"I think so too," Liberty said.

As her tears dried and the twilight settled around them, people started to arrive. Liberty had invited Poppy, Sera, Wes and Merle. Her mom had invited Cressida and Pam, her good friends. Once everyone was settled around the bonfire, it was time to begin.

Liberty wanted to concentrate on letting go of the past and the fears of the unknown. She knew it would be hard, and having her mother and the family she'd found and made for herself up here on Hanging Hill gave her a surge of strength. She stepped forward to lead the circle with her mom. As they all joined hands, she felt the energy flowing through her.

The wind stirred, blowing through her hair, teasing her. She felt lighter than she had since before she'd learned her father's name. Lighter than she had since before she'd set herself a task that had never truly been one she'd wanted.

She opened her eyes, and the first thing she saw was Merle standing across the bonfire. Their gazes met. The goddess was showing her a path toward what she should be focused on for the new year.

She had never focused on a man, on a romantic relationship, but as her life was changing and she was starting to leave behind some of the more childish things that she'd been afraid to let go of…

Maybe it was time.

Liberty was buzzing after midnight, and when she asked Merle to stay with her after everyone left, he couldn't say no. She led him to a ring of trees along the edge of the top of the hill.

Standing there amongst the trees with the dappled moonlight falling around her, he couldn't take his eyes off of her. She was radiant out here like this. He felt a jolt as his cock hardened. There was more to this woman than met the eye. He reached out to touch her hair, letting the soft strands fall through his fingers.

She looked up at him, those blue-gray eyes big and wide, standing in the clearing with the faint smell of fire in the air. The crisp after-midnight chill around them should make him cold, but he didn't feel anything except the heat that came rushing through him any time he was near Liberty. There was a flush on her skin, as if she was feeling it too.

"There is something ethereal about you in the moonlight. I can't take my eyes off of you," he said.

"Thank you," she said in a husky voice.

Merle brushed his finger over her high cheekbone and couldn't resist traveling down her face, rubbing his thumb over her lower lip. Her eyes and mouth widened with surprise. He bent over and brushed his mouth over hers. It was languid and sweet, and he closed his eyes despite himself. He didn't want to miss a second of this night with her. Now that he'd admitted to himself that he loved her.

"You have a very tempting mouth. Tonight, every word you uttered felt like it was just for me," he said.

"Maybe they were."

"Maybe? Seemed to me that you were begging me to kiss you," he teased.

"Perhaps I was," she admitted.

Her mouth under his was soft, warm and delicious. He took his time kissing her, placing featherlight pecks until her lips parted. The warm exhalation of her breath against his skin sent shivers through his body.

Her taste was addicting. He wanted more of her. So much more than just her kisses. He slid his hands in her long red hair. It tangled around his fingers and he tugged lightly, pulling her head back as he deepened the kiss.

He couldn't resist touching her, moving his hands over her shoulders, his fingers tracing a delicate pattern down to the globes of her breasts. He caressed her, lower and lower, until the very tip of his finger dipped beneath the material of her top and brushed over the edge of her nipple.

Exquisite shivers racked her body as his finger continued to move slowly over her. He found the zipper at the left side of her top and slowly lowered it. Once it was fully down and the material fell away from her to the ground, he took her wrists in his hands and stepped back.

His gaze started at the top of her head and moved down to her slightly cinched waist. Outside, with her naked, with the smell of the bonfire still in the air, everything felt right. Like this was the place he should be making love to Liberty. Now that he knew how much she meant to him.

He circled his hands around her waist and drew her to him, lifting her. "Wrap your legs around me."

She complied, the backs of her heels digging into his ass, and immediately he felt even harder than he'd been before. She was warm and wet against him. He shifted until he was leaning back against one of the trees and then carefully lowered her to the ground.

"You've enchanted me, witch." The words came out in a rough growl.

"Should we roll the dice to see how effective my enchant-
ment is?" she joked, her tongue running over his ear.

Damn. He didn't want to laugh when he was about to enter
her body. But she was seeing Merle Rutland, world-class nerd,
and embracing that side of him. That made him fall a little
more in love with her.

"We don't need the dice to tell me anything. You've got
me," he said. As the words escaped him, he knew how true
they were. He hadn't planned on letting her know that yet.

With her skirt pushed up, he nudged her legs apart with
his thighs until he was between them, the ridge of his cock—
still encased in his jeans—rubbing against her clit until she
was moaning his name.

He palmed her through the panties until she squirmed
under him, and then he leaned lower to breathe in the scent of
her sex. He caught the edge of her underwear with his teeth
and drew them down her legs as she raised her hips for him.
Once they were off, he tucked her panties into his back pocket
and pulled down his jeans and underwear, freeing his cock.

"You are magic tonight," he said.

His voice was low and husky even to his own ears. She
reached up and gripped the base of his cock, making his blood
roar in his veins.

"It's you," she said in a raspy voice. "You are the one who's
making…"

"I am making you what?" he asked, thrusting into her grip.
"I'm not going to be happy until you come harder than you
ever have before."

He lowered his head again to rub his chin over her mound
in a back and forth motion that engorged her clit and made

her wet. He parted her with the thumb and forefinger of his left hand and then brushed his tongue over her clit. Her hands were in his hair, holding him against her as she thrust her hips up into his face.

He scraped his teeth over her clit and she pulled him back, panting. "Get inside me, Merle. I want to come with you."

"Are you sure?" he asked against her body.

"Yesss!"

He shifted, rubbing his body against her until the tip of his cock was against her pussy. She linked her right hand with his left and he shoved his right hand under her hips, angling her so that he could get deeper.

She gripped his shoulders as he slowly entered her. He thrust into her again and again until she screamed his name and he felt her come, clenching him tighter. He couldn't hold back anymore. He felt his orgasm roll through him like an earthquake, and he continued his movements until he was empty.

When they both were spent, he rolled them over until he was on his back, holding her on top of him like a blanket.

He had never felt peace in his own body the way he did at this moment. This was the gift that Liberty gave him. He loved this woman and wanted her to feel the same way that he did.

Twenty-One

Samhain night had given her all the feels. Liberty basked in the joy of a successful holiday and didn't let herself think about the stuff that was fucked up right now. So that meant no thinking about John Jones. Instead she was focused on the harvest celebration that WiCKed Sisters was sponsoring in the park off the main street, at the top of the hill just beyond the Bootless Soldier Tavern.

The staff they'd hired for the shop were running it today while she, Poppy and Sera set up little booths where they were offering hands-on workshops for their crafts. They were also selling special T-shirts that promoted the Charm, Curse or Confluence game that they developed and sold in the shop.

"Want a hand? Poppy's got her booth handled," Merle said.

She hadn't seen him since Samhain. They'd been texting a bit, but he'd mentioned he was busy with a big work project. She'd never been clingy—hell, she'd never really had a relationship like this one—so she'd been surprised that she missed him so much.

"Were you looking for someone to handle?" she asked, because she'd missed him, and because he looked really good wearing his faded jeans and Roll To Hit hoodie.

"I was looking for you," he said, coming closer to her until there wasn't even an inch of space between them.

He put his hands on her hips and leaned down, the warmth of his breath brushing over her mouth a moment before his lips touched hers.

Merle was a good kisser. There was no doubt about that. The way he let his lips rest on hers for a moment before he parted them seduced her every time. As if he needed to savor every moment. He was a details man and never rushed anything.

She put her hands on his waist and went up on tiptoe to deepen the kiss. It was a few moments later when he lifted his head. "So, you're good?"

She laughed. "No, I'm hot and horny. But there's no time for that right now. I have to get these crystals organized and I need to put out the tarot card cloths."

"I'll take care of the first later. For now, do you want me to unpack the cloths? That's right in my skill set."

"Everything's in your skill set," she said. Merle was efficient at everything he did. He never hesitated to volunteer to help with any job, no matter how small, and she really appreciated that. And him.

"Ha. Glad you think so," he said, smacking her butt before he went to work on unboxing the cloths.

Watching him just made her want to drag him into the wooded area at the end of the park and do something very elemental with him. So she forced herself to turn away and went back to the crystals.

Someone cleared their throat, and she looked up to see her mom standing there.

"Morning, baby girl," Mom said as she came closer. "I brought some apples and some different herbs from the sunroom. Do you want my help mixing them when the festival starts?"

Liberty looked at her mom. She was still a little mad at her for their talk the other night, despite what they worked through on Samhain. Her mom was probably here because she wanted to move on. If Liberty could just let go of being petty and stop holding on to her hurt…well, that would be the adult thing to do, right?

But she wasn't ready to yet. She had promised her answers but had been avoiding her since Samhain. What good would pushing do? Liberty acknowledged that she'd shut down if anyone backed her into a corner, and she was definitely her mother's daughter.

Except her mom looked sad and tired, and even with her weary smile it was clear she really wanted to be here with Liberty. So Liberty sighed and said, with all the angst-y bitterness of her former fourteen-year-old self, "Sure, if you want to."

Her mom moved behind the tables and started to set up the booth. Merle glanced over at them. He lifted both eyebrows and shifted his head toward her mom. Liberty just gave him the finger.

She knew she should talk to her mom.

She knew that it was her mom's prerogative to tell her about the past.

She also knew that she was being a brat.

So why wasn't she letting it go? It wasn't as if she was going to stay mad at her mom forever. She wasn't. She just wanted her mom to know…

She put the last of the crystals on the table and joined her mom. She threw one arm around her in a hug. Her mom squeezed her back, and Liberty put her head on her mom's shoulder, feeling the weight of their strain settle over her.

"I'm not being a bitch just to be one. I'm hurt that you won't tell me whatever it is you're hiding about my dad."

"I know. I'm sorry. I just can't figure out the right way to tell you what you've asked for."

"Was it easier figuring this out when I was sixteen?" Liberty asked.

"Yes and no."

"Mom."

"Sorry, Lib. It's just… I knew what the sperm donor said in his letter, so that would have driven what you asked me."

"Is there something you don't want me to know? Is it that bad?" Liberty asked.

"Yes. So much. My life before you were born was a hot mess. I'm not going to pretend that it wasn't. I don't want to remember being that person, and I certainly don't want you to know about her. She made bad choices and mistakes."

Liberty hugged her mom closer for a second. No matter how conflicted she was about John Jones, the last thing she wanted was to hurt her mom. But her mom also owed her the truth. Liberty was an adult.

"We all make mistakes," Liberty reminded her.

"Thanks, Lib. Let's talk after the festival," Mom said.

Liberty glanced over at Merle and he just lifted both eyebrows again and tipped his head to the side, as if to say "See? That worked." She went back to setting everything up without acknowledging his told-you-so moment.

She wasn't sure how she felt that he'd made her do the right thing. Liberty was used to indulging in her tempers until she finally was ready to let things go. Merle made her want to be a better person. Disappointing him did something to her, made her feel something she couldn't name.

But no matter. She wasn't going to give it any more thought.

Work had kept Merle busy, but he'd also dug deeper into John Jones. He'd even gone so far as to compose a draft e-mail to the man since Liberty wasn't sure about contacting him directly. He'd planned on talking to her about it today, but seeing her and her mom, he hesitated. If they'd just been straight up friends-with-no-benefits or if he'd just been doing her a favor, then he might have simply texted her the info and left it at that. But they weren't. Merle wanted to work through it with her in case she needed him.

He'd seen her the other night, hurt and quiet over her Nan and coming to terms with her illness. That wasn't the Liberty he knew, so unsure of herself.

But when they went apple picking and she defended him—forcing him to face his own fears—and then on Samhain, full of her witchy-womanly power, he saw that she was coming back to herself, and he'd missed that version of her.

Watching her being bratty with her mom made him want to laugh and hug her. Liberty wasn't subtle. When she was pissed at you, she let you know.

Hopefully she wouldn't feel that way about him.

He was aware that she might not appreciate him sitting on the details of her father this long. But…he thought it would be better for her if she fixed things with her mom first. Her mom more than likely had the same information he had uncovered. It felt wrong to avoid asking Liberty about it again, but it also felt wrong to take away the chance for Liberty's mom to be honest with her first.

After Liberty and her mom set up the tarot booth, he'd gone back to working in Poppy's area for the festival. His cousin was demonstrating how to read tea leaves while he served hot cider and apple muffins. Apples, like Liberty told him, played a big role in Samhain. Poppy had explained it all in detail as she made the muffin batter, but Merle had drifted off as he debated what to do about Liberty.

"Whew, that last group had so many questions. And those little kids dressed in witches' robes were so cute," Poppy said as she came over and threaded her arm through his.

"Yeah."

She indicated to Liberty with a tilt of her head. "How's that going?"

He and Poppy were close, and he loved her more than anyone in his family. She understood him and she knew Liberty really well.

"Not sure," he said. "I like her. Maybe too much for what she's expecting from me."

"I'm sure that's not true. Why do you feel that way?"

He shrugged. Not really comfortable telling Poppy about Liberty's struggles. Liberty told her friends a lot, but it was clear that this latest development with her mom was something she needed to sit on. "Just do."

"Just do. You sound like your dad. And you never sound like him. If you don't want to talk about her, it's okay," Poppy said.

"I do and I don't. I'm just confused."

Poppy smiled at him. "Join the club. Relationships are hard."

"Like Alistair? What did he say about the wedding?"

"Nothing. He's doing some kind of a beer brewing now and is part of my tea society."

"How's that?"

Poppy twisted her fingers together and then shook her head. "Strange. He's like the guy who I first met at uni. Funny and interesting."

"And?"

"I can't trust that. He was totally putting on a show the first time," she said. "I don't want to be dumb enough to fall for the same play twice."

Being involved with Liberty had made him realize how complicated liking someone could be. There was no two ways about it—falling for Liberty had him dancing to her tune.

"Has he changed?"

"I don't know. When he's like this, he's so charming and sweet. It's hard to resist," Poppy said.

Merle had liked Alistair when he first started dating Poppy. The man had been so in love with his cousin, or so it seemed, that of course there wasn't anything to dislike. But that had changed after they'd been married and Alistair revealed he'd married Poppy for the tea recipes handed down to her from her grandmother.

Honestly, Merle didn't like the dude at all anymore. But he loved Poppy and wanted her happy.

"Yeah, well, whatever happens, I'm here," Merle said.

"Do you think he's changed?"

"No clue, but you have," Merle said. Realizing as he uttered the words that he had changed with Liberty too. Maybe it was time to start asking for more instead of just being available when she needed him.

"I have changed," Poppy admitted. "He doesn't know it."

"Maybe it's time you do. Maybe it's time for you to be happy in the relationship, whatever that looks like, instead of just making him happy."

Poppy dropped her head and he saw her blinking a lot so he knew she was trying not to cry. "Or ignore me. What do I know? I'm not even sure how to make this relationship with Liberty last."

Poppy shook her head. "You know what you're talking about. I know you're right about me too. And if you want Liberty, then you'll find a way to make her yours."

Liberty finished demonstrating how to do a five-card spread. Meanwhile her mom was busy mixing some potions; they were a surprising hit.

There was something so familiar about this; it reminded Liberty of her childhood. Of all the times when she'd gone to craft shows on the weekends with her mom and helped out in the booth. It made her miss Nan, who would be reading palms or doing tarot cards while Mom sold her potions.

Liberty felt a wave of sadness. It wasn't lost on her that they had already moved past Samhain, the night when the veil was thinnest between this world and the After. It was a season of endings.

Nan wasn't going to be with them for that much longer.

In her head, she could hear all the sappy stuff that people said. Sure, she'd have the memories of Nan and all that Nan had taught her. But she wasn't ready to let go of her grandmother. She never would be. She wished her Nan wouldn't leave this world.

A child's wish, when she was a woman and knew better. But she didn't care if it was childish to wish that her grandmother would live forever.

The uncontrollable cocktail of emotions hit her all at once and roiled around inside of her, like that one time she'd mixed jack, wine and sambuca. Except this mixture was more potent with grief and anger and fear and love and all of the other messy emotions she hated to deal with. She preferred them in quick bursts—out and gone. That wasn't happening this time.

She signaled to her mom that she needed a break. Liberty headed away from her and the booth and the festival that she'd been so excited about just a few hours earlier. She didn't stop until she was in the copse of trees, finding a big sturdy tree with a huge trunk and sinking down next to it.

The pointed witch hat slid forward on her head and she didn't bother righting it. She drew her knees under the full skirt of her black dress, letting herself feel like a kid again. The woods were her refuge.

So, she let her guard down and started to cry.

Leaves rustled around her and she lifted her bleary eyes, feeling the hat slip the rest of the way off her head as she spied Merle's sneakers and the bottom of his legs in front of her.

"Stay or go?" His voice was a deep rumble. There was a note in it that made her stomach stop spinning.

"You can stay. But I'm not my best right now."

He sat next to her, his back against the tree, his hip pressed against hers. She wiped her eyes and lifted her head to rest it on the thick trunk of the tree. The woods around her smelled earthy and rich like her favorite candle, and there was the slight trace of Merle's aftershave in the mix.

He put his hand on his thigh, palm up, and she reached over, twining her fingers with his. He held her hand for a long while without saying anything. The thoughts and emotions that had been so overwhelming were still there, but he was anchoring her, and she let him.

She let her guard down and took the comfort and strength he was offering her in his grip.

"Want to talk about it?"

"No."

"Okay."

"Sorry. I just finally let myself admit Nan's not getting better," she said.

He squeezed his fingers around hers. "I'm sorry."

"Thank you."

She tipped her head to the side until it rested on his shoulder and thought about all the things Nan had taught her about Samhain and about death. It wasn't as if she didn't know that Nan's spirit would live on after her physical body was gone. Nan had prepared them, but that didn't make it any easier.

"So...about your dad. John Jones," he said.

She lifted her head and turned to face him.

"What?"

"I think you should contact him."

Honestly, the way her emotions were at this moment she

wasn't sure if it was a good idea anymore. Her mom was going to talk to her this afternoon, so there potentially wouldn't be a need for the info that Merle had gotten for her. She felt a thread of frustration that Merle was pushing this now, after seeing how conflicted she was. "That's not for you to say."

"I think it is—at least to share my opinion. I'm your boyfriend. What happens to you matters to me."

Her *boyfriend*.

She had been thinking of them as a couple, but this was the first time he'd said it. "What does that mean, Merle?"

"The boyfriend bit?"

"No, nerd. The 'what happens to me matters to you' part," she said.

She had never seen him so serious before. There was something on his face that she couldn't read, and she wasn't entirely sure she wanted to know what he was thinking.

"I think you should resolve this with your mom. If you don't, this is always going to be between you. And you started this search for your biological father... I know he means something to you."

He had a point and she'd pretty much reached that conclusion on her own. But she hated that he knew it too. It made her feel weak, having someone know her almost as well as she knew herself. She just wasn't happy doing what anyone told her, even if it was for her own good. "That's not for you to say. Even if we are dating."

"I know that, witch. When your emotions take over, you don't always think first. I don't want to see you make a mistake."

Twenty-Two

What the actual fuck? He hadn't mean to be so real, but he needed to be honest before it ate away at him. Liberty had every right to set the pace of her own self-discovery, but they'd been on this journey together. She came to him when things were a mess and he'd always be there for her, but it was as if she didn't consult his opinion or respect his feelings.

He was going to end up in the same situation that he'd been in with his parents and the different compartments of his life. Forced to play a role in her life instead of being independent with her.

It was time she heard that too.

"Don't hold back, nerd. Say what's on your mind," she grumbled, though there wasn't any real heat in her words.

But she held herself stiffly like…maybe he'd hurt her, though he knew he hadn't. She was tougher than that. She liked poking and prodding everyone else around her but he never poked back. Now it was time for that.

She seemed sad and confused. Pushing her now might not be the right move, but it was the only path that he saw. If he didn't show her he wanted to be by her side for everything, then how could she know that he was there? "Don't be witchy about it. You asked for my help and you've poured your soul out to me. I am engaged in this with you. I don't like standing on the outside…just waiting. That's exactly what I do with my folks… You know I can't do that with you."

She put her head back against the tree and closed her eyes.

"When did you start to see me so well?" she asked.

It felt like he always had. He'd denied it to himself for a long time, but from the first moment she'd glided into Poppy's apartment, he'd been mesmerized by her. Her red hair flowing out around her shoulders as she talked and gestured. Her lethal curves. The magic she exuded.

He hadn't understood a word she'd said, but he knew he'd never be the same. Then she turned that blue-gray gaze on him, her eyes pinning him in place. Her gaze had slid down his body and he'd felt a stir of desire.

"The moment you looked at me in Poppy's apartment," he said. "Do you remember what you said to me?"

"'Like what you see, nerd?'"

He laughed because she'd used the same intonation as she had that day. It had been teasing and daring. Like she knew that he'd been checking her out the whole time but wouldn't do anything about it.

"I do, witch."

"That's not what you said," she pointed out.

"No?"

She shook her head, then crossed her legs and reached out

to toy with his hair, pushing it behind his ear. The love he had for her almost overwhelmed him in that moment.

"Nope. You blushed and then looked at Poppy and said 'I'll see you later' and left," she said. "Why did you do that?"

He shrugged.

"Not saying? Are your lips sealed?" she asked, moving her hand over his lips, running her finger around his mouth.

There was more than a shiver of lust now. It was full-on blood pumping harder through his body; he shifted as his erection grew and reached down to adjust it.

"Are you going to try to pry my secrets out of them?" he asked.

He liked this side of her. But they were both using the heat between them to keep from talking about the real stuff.

"Why would I reveal my intentions?" she asked.

"Oh, you want to get me to talk, witch," he said, touching her lips with his finger. He loved the little Cupid's bow on her top lip, how full and sensual her bottom lip was. Touching her just made him harder.

He wasn't sure how much longer his mind was going to be in control. There was a haze that always came over him when he was touching Liberty. Something that made it impossible for him to do anything but think of turning her on, performing his own version of witchcraft.

His heart started beating to the rhythm of a song that he only heard when the two of them were this close.

He wanted her.

He wanted her more than he wanted his next breath.

He wanted her forever.

This afternoon was the start of a new point in his relationship with her. Forever. It scared him but not as much as the thought of letting Liberty slip away.

She shifted around, her hands going under her skirt, and she shimmied around until she took her panties off and stuffed them into the front pocket of his jeans. "This is what I wanted to do when I first saw you."

She straddled him, reaching for his zipper and lowering it. He pulled his erection out and then she was on top of him. But as he felt the moist heat of her center against his shaft, she brought her head down until their foreheads touched.

Their eyes met.

"Why do you do this to me?"

When he heard his voice, he realized he'd spoken out loud.

"Don't you like it?"

"More than you know," he said, his voice was getting huskier as she kept moving her hips slowly against him. He put his hands on her waist, tipping his head until he could rub his lips against hers. She sucked his bottom lip into her mouth and he groaned. He wanted to take his time making love to her.

Liberty was different. She had been from the beginning but this time...*he* was different. He was ready to be her man.

"Liberty? Liberty!"

Merle reached between their bodies to tuck his erection back into his jeans as Liberty got to her feet and rounded the tree to find her mom. She sounded frantic.

"Mom, what's up?"

"The care home just called. Mom's... Nan is... They need us," Lourdes said.

Merle came up next to her and put his hand on the small of her back. "Can you drive yourself or do you want me to?"

"Thanks, son, I can drive us. But your booth... Greer offered to watch it so I could find you," Mom said. Greer worked with Liberty at WiCKed Sisters and with Wes at his new bookbinding and antique bookshop two doors down. They'd been a nice addition to the WiCKed Sisters family, and Liberty thanked the goddess for having help in a time like this.

Her blood was still rushing from the almost sex with Merle, and now her heart was pounding as the fear she thought she'd gotten under control coursed through her body like a banshee crying out a warning of death. Tears burned her eyes and she shook her head, dashing them off her face with her hand.

"I'll take care of your booth, Liberty," Merle said. "Leave everything to me."

She gave her thanks to him over her shoulder as he lifted his hand and wiped another tear from her eye. She nodded, following her mom. When they got back to the festival, Sera and Poppy were waiting.

"I'm driving," Poppy said. "Merle, will you work with Greer to take care of all the booths?"

"No problem. Already on it."

Sera and Poppy surrounded her and her mom. Lourdes wasn't talking and kept rubbing her lapis lazuli bracelet, which was her talisman. According to her, it had healing properties and was worn by all the Wakefield witches to help them harness their physic abilities. The bracelet had been a gift from Nan when her mom had turned sixteen. Liberty had her own lapis lazuli bracelet that Nan had gifted her but, as fate would have it, she hadn't worn it today.

Around them people were laughing and talking, enjoying the energy of the festival. Which just made her feel odd and out of sorts. She wanted to throw her head back and scream at the universe.

Poppy put her arm around Lourdes and was talking quietly as they jogged to the lot behind WiCKed Sisters where Poppy's Land Rover was parked. Sera looped her arm through Liberty's.

"I don't know what to say. Do you want to talk?"

"No. I want to scream or… Should we do a healing spell, Mama? I can grab some crystals from the shop. I made some healing water for Nan on the last full moon," Liberty said.

Her mom stopped and faced her. Liberty had never seen her mom like this. Her aura was dark and clouded. This was something else. Like Lourdes was lost. Liberty knew how hard this was for herself, and her mom was feeling it just as much—probably more. She let go of Sera and went over to Lourdes, pulling her into her arms.

Her mom held her so tightly. Liberty felt the warmth of her mom's tears. "Let's get everything we have. I've been working on a special hand lotion with some healing and clarity herbs in them. Get your crystals… I'm not sure what state she'll be in."

"Is it like the last time?"

"They said she was agitated at first and then collapsed. The doctors are with her now," Lourdes said. Her voice cracked while she was talking and went into that low, husky tone. She only heard that tone from her mom once before, when Grandpa had died.

"Okay. I'll be fast," Liberty said.

"I'll help you," Sera said.

The women all went into Liberty's back room and gathered everything they needed before driving to the care home. When they got there, Liberty hesitated to get out of the Land Rover even though her mom was already in the lobby. She didn't want to go in there and see her Nan at her worst.

What if this time the collapse meant that everything that had remained of the woman she loved was gone?

She wasn't ready for that.

Poppy went with Lourdes while Sera waited with Liberty. Sera stood there with her hands in the pockets of a tweed jacket that looked like it might have been Wes's. She'd rolled the cuffs up to her elbows and had it on over a pair of leather leggings and a pussy bow blouse. It felt fitting that her friend looked so put together while Liberty was falling apart.

"Whenever I saw a new car in the driveway of one of my foster homes, I knew that meant the social worker was inside. Sometimes they were just checking in on us, but if it was too close to the last visit, I knew someone was leaving. I'd sort of hide outside, knowing that if I don't talk to them… I wouldn't have to leave. But the truth was, the decision had already been made," Sera said. "Even if I didn't go into that house, my time there was changing."

Liberty just looked over at her friend and realized that Sera got it. She knew why Liberty was sitting in the parking lot of the damned care home instead of going inside. But Liberty wasn't sure she could get out of the car, even with her friend's help.

"I'm not saying I know what this is like. I didn't have a grandmother, but you do have me by your side. Whatever has happened, you won't have to face it alone."

With those words, the strength that she'd always taken for granted came back to her. Liberty got out of the car and closed the door behind her. She hugged Sera and they held hands as they walked into the care home. Liberty took strength from her family, knowing that her mom and Poppy were waiting. Whatever came next, at least she knew she wasn't alone.

Merle moved between the different booths for the WiCKed Sisters, first making sure everything was good with Poppy's tea shop and the baker and server she had assisting. He felt comfortable letting them run things in her absence. Greer texted Wes as a call for backup, and they were both working Sera's booth, so Merle went back to Liberty's. He was busier than expected and, though he wouldn't have mixed his friend groups in the past, he texted Darren who had come up for the day and asked if he could come down.

Darren showed up ten minutes later.

"What can I do?" Darren asked.

Merle put Darren to work taking payments while he answered questions and put orders together for the customers. Being busy helped keep his mind off of Liberty. He was worried for her. A part of him wished she'd asked him to go with her. He also understood why she didn't. Her strength came from those feminine bonds that she had. They were her deepest roots, and they gave her strength in a way romance couldn't.

But that didn't stop him from wishing he could be the one she turned to.

He shook that off and concentrated instead on something that he'd read in *Titania's Book of White Magic*. He'd picked it up after he'd slept with Liberty the first time. The book said everything in the world was connected, so Merle sent his strength, caring and support to Liberty by taking extra care of her customers. He fed that energy into the universe and hoped that she'd feel it.

When the festival ended at two, they all worked to box everything up and get it back to the store. The store closed at four on Saturdays and the staff that the women had hired were working until then. Greer's boyfriend was waiting for them because the two of them were heading out to a Headless Horsemen Halloween party. After they left, Merle invited Wes and Darren to join him at the Bootless Soldier.

He wanted to go to the care home, but he wasn't sure that Liberty would want that from him. Plus he wanted to go back to WiCKed Sisters at closing time later and make sure everything was in good shape.

Both men said yes, and a short time later they were seated in the busy tavern with beers in front of them. Darren and Wes had met last winter when Wes had joined their D&D game for a few weeks.

"You should come back and play with us," Darren was saying.

"I'll think about it. Now that the shop is opened, I could maybe do it after Christmas," Wes said.

"How's your shop doing?" Merle asked.

"Not too bad. Most of my business is online, so having a storefront here is just for the tourists really. Sera and I are talking about using the space in my shop to do some in-person bookbinding workshops. She gets a lot of requests from the people who buy her journals, asking if they can learn how to make them. So we might be adding that next year," Wes said, taking a sip of his beer.

Wes had grown up in Bangor but spent his summers in Birch Lake with his grandfather, Ford. Merle had seen him a few times when they'd been kids, but they hadn't really hung out. Wes and his brother were always playing video games or exploring their family property. Merle's dad kept his kids sharp even on their summer vacations here. So Merle was at the baseball diamond every day hitting, pitching and running bases and plays.

He remembered those long, hot summer days for a minute. He'd never thought about standing up to his dad and saying no. He'd just gotten up at six and followed him down to the park, spending all day practicing a sport that he hadn't really wanted to play.

Merle's entire life had been about following his father's plan instead of his own until that fight. It felt good to close that chapter of his life and enjoy the fruits of his labor with friends like Darren and Wes.

Merle's phone pinged and he glanced over to see a message in his family WhatsApp group. His parents wanted to have dinner the night before his brother's first game. No news from Liberty though, which only made him more nervous.

"Any news?" Wes asked as Merle lifted his phone.

"Nothing from Liberty," he said.

"Everything okay?" Darren pressed.

"Yeah." As okay as it could be, knowing the woman he loved might be losing someone dear to her.

"Heard your brother got a coaching job in the MLB," Darren said.

"Yeah, with the minor league Sox team," Merle said.

"That's cool. I remember your family was super into sports. Are they still like that?" Wes asked.

Even though they'd hung out a few times, he and Wes had never really had a chance to get to know each other. Probably because Wes was totally into Sera from the moment he moved to town, and Merle had been helping out with the shop and flirting with Liberty around the same time.

"Yeah, totally. My dad is a high school baseball coach and my mom is the tennis pro at her club," he said. "I'm sort of the only nonathlete."

"By choice," Darren said. "Dude is pretty good at all sports."

"True?"

He shrugged. He was good for Darren, but just okay for the Rutlands. It felt good to have his friend see his skills as valuable even if he was still learning to do the same.

Ping.

Liberty texted.

They were taking her Nan to the hospital. He messaged back saying he'd meet her there. "Wes, will you go down to WiCKed Sisters at four and make sure everything's locked up? They're moving Nan to the hospital."

"Yeah. Go," Wes said.

Twenty-Three

Liberty wasn't entirely sure how things had changed so quickly in the span of a few minutes, but then that was the way her life had been going this year. Success beyond her wildest dreams with WiCKed Sisters after the Amber Rapp mention. Despair and grief as Nan's condition worsened and required her to live in this very care home. Anger at finally learning the name of the one man who had summarily rejected her before she'd been more than an embryo.

And Merle...

She'd started to let herself fall for him. There was no pretending otherwise.

Over the last six weeks, as she'd readied her life for a change and Samhain, he'd been the only person she'd wanted by her side. Well, the only new person. She cherished having Sera and Poppy—her kindred spirits—with her as she tried to navigate everything that had been changing in her life.

But even with Poppy and Sera here with her, she wasn't

sure how to handle this change. They were at the hospital. Nan had fallen in the care home and broken her hip, and she was also confused, asking for her own mother.

Lourdes went to talk to the doctors. Sera sat next to Liberty, holding her hand. Poppy had gone to get them all some tea to drink.

"This hospital has some of the finest doctors," Sera said.

Liberty appreciated that her friend hadn't tried to give her any false reassurances. But right now she had no idea what to do. She had texted Merle that they were here, at a shared community hospital about thirty minutes from Birch Lake.

"Thanks." She didn't know what else to say to Sera. Liberty was mad, but not at her friend. Even as she tried to identify where it stemmed from, she knew that there wasn't anything rational she could point to beyond the unfairness of the world.

She wasn't sure she'd ever be able to get the image of Nan out of her head. The way she looked when they'd gotten to the care home. They'd managed to beat the ambulance there, so they saw her in such a fragile state.

It made her hands shake to think of Nan that way. Sera just tightened her fingers around Liberty's.

"It's okay to cry," Sera said.

"I'd rather punch something," Liberty admitted.

"That's okay too. Do you want to go outside and kick a tree or something?"

Liberty almost smiled because Sera knew her so well. "I would never kick a tree, but maybe this building."

"Go do it. She's going to be in there for a while. I'll stay here and come get you the minute she's out of surgery," Sera said. "You need to be outside and feel the wind around you. When Poppy gets back, do you want me to send her out?"

Sera was right. Sitting here in the hallway waiting for news wasn't doing anything but letting her think of worst-case scenarios. "No, I think I need to be alone. Thank you."

She hugged Sera, who hugged her back tightly and then kissed her cheek. "No problem."

Liberty wandered through the maze of hallways that were all colored exactly the same empty white, following the exit signs until she was outside. It was late afternoon in the first weekend in November. The sky was cloudy and gray. The air was cold and the ground was hard under her feet. She crossed the parking lot to the small, wooded area that was just beyond it. The wind was biting, wintery, not her beloved autumn wind that held the crisp chill but still had a hint of summer.

She tipped her head back and let the breeze stir her hair as soon as she was in the trees. She let out a long scream, yelling her frustration and fear to the trees. The wind seemed to echo her feelings, whipping around her and making the branches of the trees stretch and sway. They were bare of leaves, and the branches made a rickety sound when they brushed against each other.

She continued a little farther into the woods, looking at the trees until she found one with a large trunk that felt right to her. She went and sat next to the trunk, pulled her legs up to her body and put her head down on her knees.

The tears she'd been afraid to let fall in the hospital started and she didn't try to keep them in check. She just stayed where she was, letting out all the emotions that she never wanted anyone to see.

Nan wasn't going to be the same after this. Life wasn't going to be the same.

And as much as she'd welcomed the new year on Samhain in words and dancing, her mind and her heart hadn't been ready for this. She wasn't entirely sure she ever would have been, but this was too much.

Maybe that was why she'd let the search for John Jones stall. Why she'd pretty much decided not to contact the man that Merle had worked so hard to find. She hadn't needed John Jones to make her life different. It had been changing already without him.

It was too late now. He could never mean anything to her. He was a stranger. A name for a man she'd never needed. She'd used that search as a wedge between her and her mom because she'd known Nan wouldn't want to leave them while the two of them were fighting. But it didn't work. The wheel of life kept turning.

Liberty was only now recognizing that Nan had no control over when she would leave them. Her indomitable spirit was at the mercy of her failing body.

This was something she couldn't control. She hated it more than she would ever admit out loud. So she stayed underneath the tree until she had no tears left to shed.

Merle showed up as she was walking back into the hospital and everything inside of her relaxed. She felt safer with him by her side.

Two weeks later, Merle was still trying to figure out how to tell Liberty he loved her.

They'd been spending most nights at his place and she had

continued bringing more of her little touches to his house. It was starting to feel more like their place than like his. Those empty rooms in his home were becoming full of Liberty.

She was gearing up for Thanksgiving and then the Winter Solstice. He'd mentioned John Jones a few more times but she'd told him to stop asking. She wasn't ready. So he'd left the contact information on the nightstand she used at his place. He'd found the man for her, and if she wanted to get in touch, she could.

He finished a big project at work the night before and Poppy didn't really need him in the tea shop today, but he came in anyway. He missed Liberty since she'd stayed at her place the last few nights.

Poppy could always use the help so she put him to work as soon as he showed up. Liberty was doing a tarot reading and Sera and her assistant, Greer, were busy taking custom orders for journals for Christmas and the winter holidays.

"I'm not much of a tea drinker. Do you have any coffee back there?"

Merle glanced up at the customer that Poppy was taking an order from. The dude was definitely familiar. He was older, with thinning reddish blond hair. It was longish, about as long as Merle's, and curled at the back of his neck.

Where did he know him from?

"Cappuccino and a slice of the apple cake for the gentleman," Poppy said.

"Doesn't he look familiar?" Merle asked her as he went to the espresso machine and started to make the cappuccino. The WiCKed Sisters logo was printed on all the mugs and cups they used in the tea shop. He couldn't help rubbing his thumb over the witch in the center for good luck.

"No. I mean, I guess he looks like most old dudes. Do you think he's one of our moms' cousins?" Poppy asked. "Mom mentioned that someone was coming to stay in the cabin. I went up yesterday to get it ready."

"Nah, I don't think so. If he was our cousin he would have told you."

"Yeah, you're right."

Poppy turned back to the counter to take another order from someone who was taking their tea to go.

Merle continued studying the gentleman from the corner of his eye. The man wasn't his family, that was for sure. Was he from college? He sort of looked like a professor.

As soon as the thought popped into his head, he did a double take. Merle glanced over to where Liberty was still on her dais doing her tarot reading and then back to the man.

Fuck. He tried to catch Poppy's attention, but she was busy talking to Mrs. Jenkins who came in once a week to have her tea leaves read and to buy a special blend for her arthritis.

He needed to warm Liberty. Because unless he was wrong, that man was John Jones.

Liberty's biological father that she'd decided not to pursue. The man whose contact details were lying on Merle's nightstand.

Had she contacted him and just not told Merle? She *had* told him to butt out.

He glanced back over to Liberty. By the way she was gathering the cards, she was wrapping up the reading. He couldn't be sure, but it seemed like she had no idea her father was in the store.

"Merle, take the coffee and cake over before the customer hexes us," Poppy said.

"Sorry, cuz, just got distracted," he said.

"No problem. He just looks…uncomfortable. Like he's not sure he wants to stay."

Merle guessed the man probably was. "Did Liberty say anything about contacting anyone?"

"Like who?"

"Like John Jones."

"No. In fact I'm pretty sure she's not going to. She said it was a distraction from Nan and she doesn't need to know him. That was the last I heard of it."

"Oh."

"Oh? Merle, what does that mean?"

Now that he had confirmation that Liberty hadn't invited him here, he needed to warn her. "That's him. The guy over there is John Jones."

"Fuck. Did you invite him here?"

"Do I look stupid?"

"Not really," Poppy said. "Crap. Try to distract him and I'll go talk to Liberty."

"Sure."

He took the cappuccino and the cake over to John and set the tray on the table harder than he meant to. Merle wasn't really sure what to do about him. But he wanted to protect Liberty. Not that she needed his protection. She'd proven more than once that she was capable of taking care of herself, but this was going to throw her.

She wasn't prepared to meet her biological father and he

knew that being caught off guard was one thing she hated. Really hated.

"Hi there. What are you doing in Birch Lake?" Merle asked.

"I'm meeting an old friend," he said. His voice was neutral and polite. And really didn't invite further conversation.

But Poppy needed time to talk to Liberty. Merle stood so that he was blocking the other man's view of where Liberty was seated.

"Thanks for bringing the coffee. I'm fine for now."

He couldn't linger any longer without making things awkward, so he turned to go back behind the counter. As he did so, he glanced again toward Liberty's shop and saw the look on her face.

Anger, and a kind of rage he hadn't seen from her before swirled around her. And as she came forward, he realized it was directed at him.

Poppy's face told her something was up. She had no idea what was going on, but the last time Poppy looked so concerned it had been when she'd found out that Alistair saw their marriage as one of convenience and not a love match. Someone must have hurt Poppy, and badly. Liberty had been thinking about taking Merle into the back room and having him get naked on her meditation pillow after her shift, but now she was ready to defend her friend, by kicking someone's ass if necessary.

"What's up?"

"Uh, that old dude that Merle is serving is the jerk wad who told your mom to get an abortion," Poppy said.

Liberty heard a ringing in her ears and the room spun

slightly. She looked at the table as Merle moved away. It had never occurred to her that the expression on Poppy's face had been for her. "Fucking hell. How is that bastard in our store?"

"I don't know. Merle said—"

"He called him? I told him I wasn't going to get in contact."

"I don't think—"

But Liberty didn't hear anything else her friend was saying. Instead, she stormed over to the tea shop where Merle had finished making a drink for a customer. As soon as he put the tea down on the counter, she grabbed his wrist and dragged him toward the room behind Poppy's shop and then straight out the back door.

Merle wasn't resisting. He followed her. How was he going to defend this?

She hadn't felt this mad and betrayed and hurt. But she wasn't going to even let herself think about what being this hurt meant. Not now. Not yet.

"How could you?" she demanded as she spun around to face him. It was one of those gross November days that was cold and gray. It had been raining earlier, but since then it had turned to an early sleety snow.

"I didn't."

"Don't lie. That's never been something you've done before."

"Yeah, that's because I don't lie. I didn't contact him. You made it clear that you didn't want to speak to him."

Relief coursed through her. It would have been devastating to learn she'd been so wrong about him. She couldn't have handled a betrayal like this from the man she loved.

"I did. So how'd he find me? And what's he doing sitting in Poppy's tea shop?"

Liberty heard the quiver in her voice, felt the rage turning into fear and shoved it way down. Not now. She didn't have time to think or to process anything. She needed her guard up so she could defend herself. Against the man who didn't want her.

"He said he was waiting for a friend," Merle said. "I sent Poppy over to warn you. I didn't want him to ambush you."

"Okay," she said, flustered.

"I'm hurt you'd think I'd go behind your back. I keep telling myself that you are starting to see the real me, that you are starting to accept me into your life, but I'm just kidding myself, aren't I?"

"No."

"Just no?"

"Yeah. Sorry I'm still wigging out about fucking John Jones being in the shop and I don't know what to do," she admitted. "I'm sorry. I know you wouldn't have contacted him. I just reacted."

"That's what you do, isn't it?"

"Yeah. I can't… I don't know what to say to him," Liberty said. "But I do know what to say to you. I am truly sorry."

"I know you are, witch. But you have to stop thinking I'm going to turn on you or leave you behind."

"It's not just you."

"It seems like it is. You didn't suspect Poppy or Sera of calling him, did you?"

"No, of course not. They love me."

"They aren't the only ones," he said quietly, coming closer

to her. "But you can't see that. You won't be able to until you sort out whatever you feel about your father."

If Merle didn't contact her father, then who did?

Liberty knew she was missing something. If she could just see past the feeling of betrayal—that wasn't exactly what it was, but something like it—at the fact that her biological father was in Birch Lake. He wasn't familiar. He'd never been here before. At least not in her lifetime.

But that didn't matter. The breeze shifted, and the icy rain hit her face, and she realized that she wasn't really thinking about whatever was going on in the shop. She was watching Merle leave, after she disappointed him, after he confessed his feelings for her.

"Wait. What should I do?" she asked him. She'd been unsure from the beginning. Unsure until that moment she'd walked into the Bootless Soldier and asked Merle to help her. He'd been by her side, quietly supporting her and teasing her, giving her a safe space to be herself and grow into a stronger woman.

He didn't say anything, just stood there the way he had so many times in the past when she'd been flirting with him, trying to see if he liked her or not. She'd hurt him, and as she thought about how, she replayed their conversation.

They aren't the only ones.

That's what he'd said.

Someone else loved her.

"Merle?" she said as she walked, until the gap between them was barely an inch. Her heart was racing. For the first time she admitted to herself that she hadn't gone to Merle about her father for any other reason than she'd always liked him and trusted him.

There wasn't another man she wanted by her side and she knew that. She loved him. And he loved her too.

"Liberty."

She spun around, surprised to see her mom standing in the doorway. "I'm sorry to interrupt, but Merle didn't contact your dad. I did."

"Why?"

"You wanted to get to know him, and he has wanted to meet you since you were seven," Lourdes said. "It was time I stopped standing in the way. I already made that mistake once."

"What?"

Liberty felt like she was spinning out of control. Then she felt Merle's hand taking hers.

Twenty-Four

A different man would have left, and in the past Merle would have been that man. He'd always run when things got tough. Found a comfortable spot and escaped into his own world. One of myths and lore, battles and characters. But he wasn't going to leave Liberty alone right now.

He stood next to Liberty because he had seen her face. Heard what Lourdes had just said. That John Jones had wanted to meet Liberty since she was seven.

"Why wouldn't you tell me that?"

"Uh, Merle, would you mind giving us some privacy?" Lourdes asked.

"Of course," he said, starting to step away, but Liberty tightened her hand in his.

"I want him here," she said. "Mom, how could you?"

Lourdes was pale. He saw the signs of stress and maybe regret on her face; her eyes were the same blue-gray as Liberty's, but her face was rounder and, Merle had always thought, softer. Maybe because Lourdes had always seemed so motherly toward all of them.

"He didn't deserve you, baby girl. And I was mad. He walked away after he gave me that money. He disappeared and I didn't hear from him until one day he showed up at the house when you were at school.

"He said he wondered what I'd done—if I had the baby or aborted it. I was so angry at how nonchalant he was, I almost told him I'd had an abortion. But I couldn't deny your existence. You were my gift from the goddess. The karmic balance for the way that John had treated me."

Liberty's nails dug into the back of Merle's hand. "What happened when you told him about me?"

"He…he left. Then he came back two weeks later and told me he wanted to meet you. But by that time I'd talked to Nan and I wasn't sure he was ever coming back. She and I had decided to protect you by keeping him out of your life. And that's what I did."

"Then when I was sixteen?" Liberty asked. "What had changed?"

"You were older and I thought you could decide for yourself if you wanted to meet him. You said no, and I was happy enough for that. I honestly didn't think that John would try again after that."

"Did he?" Liberty asked.

Merle was surprised at how small her voice sounded. This wasn't his flaming goddess witch who took on everything and everyone. This was a wounded girl who'd been rejected before she'd been born.

"No. But once I knew you had learned his name and you

started asking questions, I realized that I hadn't really given you the chance to decide what you wanted. So I e-mailed him and told him you knew his name and might be interested in meeting him."

Liberty let go of his hand. "I don't know if I want to. It was one thing to imagine he'd never known about me but this… He knew but…"

Her voice trailed off; Merle hurt for her. He put his arm around her and pulled her into a hug, but Lourdes was there too. She wrapped her arms around both him and Liberty. "I'm sorry. I still don't know if it was just curiosity that made him ask to see you or if he wanted more. I'm sorry I was so mad and didn't talk to you about it."

"That's okay, Mama. I understand what you did," Liberty said.

Merle thought the two women might need a moment alone. "I'll wait inside."

Liberty nodded at him.

He went back into the tea shop. All of WiCKed Sisters had been closed up and it was empty except for John Jones who still sat at one table by himself. Sera and Poppy were staring daggers at him.

"Is she okay?" Sera said.

"Yes. Lourdes is with her," he said.

"I'm glad. I tried to tell her it wasn't you," Poppy said.

"We're cool."

But he knew that a part of him was still shaken and unsure of where he stood with Liberty, He'd pretty much told her that he loved her, but there wasn't time to check in about it, and she needed to figure things out with her dad first.

"I'm going up to the Bootless Soldier Tavern. Let her know when she's done here," he said.

Poppy nodded and hugged him.

He let himself out and hiked up the slight hill on Main Street until he got to the pub. It wasn't too busy as it was only four in the afternoon, so Merle found a table. And it was only as he sat down that he remembered it was the table he'd been at when Liberty came to him asking for that pivotal favor.

He ordered a beer from Lars and tried to distract himself by reading a new D&D ebook on monsters that he'd just bought, but for the first time, his fictional world wasn't an escape or a distraction. His mind was firmly rooted in Birch Lake— down Main Street and around the corner in WiCKed Sisters.

Liberty hadn't ever really been able to picture the man who fathered her. She looked a lot like her mom and Nan. So she'd assumed she got nothing from him. But he had reddish hair, so apparently that was what she inherited from him. Her mom was at her side and her friends stayed close by.

"John, this is my…our…daughter, Liberty."

He stood up and looked her over from head to toe. She stood a little bit taller and realized she was holding her breath. Damn. She wanted to say that his approval didn't matter to her, but that was a lie. In reality, she wanted him to look at her and regret that he didn't know her.

She looked around for Merle's calming energy but he was gone.

Suddenly whatever John Jones thought or liked about her didn't matter so much. Where was Merle? Was he still hurt? Did he assume she ignored his unintentional confession?

"Thank you for meeting me," John said.

"You kind of left me no choice," Liberty said, looking over at Poppy.

"I thought you said she wanted to meet me." John stared at her mom.

"I wanted to know more about you," Liberty said, stepping in front of her mom. "Once I knew your name, you were a person instead of, well, nothing."

"Ouch."

"Truth hurts." Liberty hadn't liked the way John spoke to her mom. This was probably the reason that Nan hadn't liked him.

"You remind me a lot of your mom."

"That's because she raised me," Liberty responded.

"Yes, and she did a good job," he said.

She didn't know what else to say. The questions she'd thought she'd have weren't there. She could see why this man hadn't been in her life. He hadn't loved her mom, and he hadn't wanted a child unless it was on his terms, so her mom had made the right choice to keep him out of her life. He would have only added pain to it.

"Thanks for coming," Liberty said.

He just nodded and then got up and put his coat on. "Good-bye."

Sera followed him to the main door of the shop and unlocked it so he could leave. Then locked up as soon as he was out.

"That was surreal. What a jerk," Liberty grumbled. "Are you okay?"

"That's the way he's always been. He makes me doubt myself, and I knew I couldn't be what he wanted me to be. I had to be stronger for you. I wanted you to have all the strength that I've always struggled to find," Lourdes explained.

"I have your strength, Mama," she said. "I'm sorry I started this."

"I'm not. I should have told you a long time ago, but I was afraid."

Liberty thought about how afraid she'd been to talk to her mom, and it seemed silly now. She promised herself she wouldn't let fear affect her that way again.

"I love you, Mom."

"I love you too."

She hugged her mom and then looked to her friends. "Where is Merle?"

"At the Bootless Soldier Tavern. I think he wasn't sure if you wanted him here or not."

Of course. She'd pretty much accused him of trying to manipulate her and then almost told him she loved him.

Liberty didn't hesitate; she knew what she needed to do. She raced out of the shop, hearing her mom and friends behind her closing up and following her. The November wind still whipped around her, making her hair fly around her face. It was cold, but this time the chill was at her back, pushing her up Main Street toward the Bootless Soldier Tavern and Merle.

She walked in and the noise seemed to stop as she skimmed the pub until she found him sitting at a table to the left. Their table. She headed straight for him and plopped down in the chair across from him.

He set his phone on the table, but his fingers were shaking.

Which was only fair, because she was nervous too. This was the scariest thing she'd ever done, but she had to do it.

"Earlier when you said that Poppy and Liberty weren't the only ones who loved me... I almost missed it," she said.

"Seemed like you did miss it."

She shook her head. "You are quiet, Merle Rutland, but I have always had a connection to you. I see through that image you want the world to think you are."

"You do," he said.

"Only fair since I'm pretty sure you see through me too."

He cocked his head to the side. "Do I?"

"You do, which is why I'm not sure how we both missed the fact that we were falling in love with each other," she said.

He picked up his beer instead of answering her. He took the longest swallow she'd ever seen him take. And just when she was about to demand he put the glass down and answer her, he stood up and came around to the other side of the table.

"I love you, Liberty Wakefield. You are the only person I know who could make a declaration of love feel like a dare."

She stood up too and put her arms around his neck and went up on tiptoe until they were eye to eye.

"I love you too. And it wasn't a dare. It was a challenge. To keep on dating me and see where this love takes us."

"There is nothing I want more than to be yours, witch," he said, lowering his head and kissing her long and deep.

That was all she wanted too. She'd spent her life afraid to trust men, keeping them at a distance. Until Merle. He'd always been so strong and solid with his sexy, nerdy self. Tempting her to see him. Truly see him as he saw her. And once she had, she couldn't resist falling in love with him.

Later that evening, while their friends and her mom were seated with them at the table and Merle was holding her close

to his side, he whispered in her ear. "I asked the moon for
you on Samhain."

"The goddess granted both of our wishes," she said.

★ ★ ★ ★ ★

Acknowledgments

This book was so much fun to write. I knew the minute that Liberty started chatting about Merle in the draft of *The Bookbinder's Guide to Love* that I wanted to write their story. So when I tentatively pitched it to John and they came back with an enthusiastic yes! I was beyond thrilled.

Thank you to Lucas for his Dungeons & Dragons knowledge and for introducing me to the game during COVID when we were locked down. I fell in love with it. The world building that Lucas did for our games was incredible. Creating my own character was a lot of fun. Normally when I do that it's for a story but this time I was living and playing in Lucas's world. So much fun. Any D&D mistakes are my own.

I'm grateful and lucky to get to talk to Courtney every day. She keeps me current and makes me laugh (even though she's not as funny as Lucas according to her aunts). Our conversations on the world, Love Island, and—of course—Star Wars always spark ideas for me.

I'm so blessed to have found writing at an early age and even more lucky to have a group of writing friends who are kindred spirits. Joss Wood, my writing partner who I sprint with every day, keeps me on track to deliver my books on time. To my Desire Forever friends, Karen Booth, Joanne Rock and Reese Ryan, our online chat group has become like the break room in an office building where I can always find my best work buddies.

Merle and Liberty's conflicts all stem from family and I wouldn't be who I am today without mine. My mom and grandma had such an influence on the woman I became and I'm thankful for the traditions I learned from them and the love they always gave me. My parents also encouraged me to participate in sports even though I wasn't and still am not very athletic. All those years swimming helped to make me into a writer so I am grateful that Mom insisted I go to practice and swim even when I "forgot" my swimsuit.

Thanks to my husband, Rob, for being my partner in life and listening to me talk about the story and then worry about the story and then get excited about an idea and run to write it down before I forget it!

Lastly, thank you for picking up my books and reading them.

I hope you won't mind but I never got to thank the people who helped me on the journey of writing *The Bookbinder's Guide to Love*. That book was one incredible journey for me from the moment I heard that Harlequin was launching a new line. The remit for it was to do something different, which was something my muse was ready for. I couldn't have done it without the support of my fabulous agent Sandy Harding and my awesome editor John Jacobson. Thank you both so much.

Special thanks to Nancy Thompson and Eve Gaddy for saying yes when I sent them the first chapter and asked them to read it and give me feedback. It's always scary to try something new and knowing that two writers who I respect and trust had my back made it easier.

Thanks to my kids, Courtney and Lucas, who have, from the beginning of my writing career, been the reason I want to succeed and do better. I have always wanted them to know that any dream you have is possible if you put in the hard work, which I learned from the example that my parents gave me.

My life was challenging when I was writing this book as most of our lives are. I got through it with daily writing sprints with Joss Wood, an incredible writer and an even better friend.